THE HANSENS

THE HANSENS

MAC TERZA

The Hansens
© 2024 Mac Terza

ISBN-13:
979-8-218-36029-0

Throwaway Press
Woodstock, Georgia

DEDICATION

This book is dedicated to my best friend, Eddie, who I hope is riding Harley's in heaven. He wanted me to be a comedian, yet I ended up doing something completely different. I am grateful to him for believing in me even if I chose to write poetry and stories instead of tell jokes. Eddie always aimed to excel in everything he did. I thank him eternally for showing me to not be as I already am, but be who I should be. I owe you one.

Also, for Sharan, and Courtney. They are some of my favorite women in my life, one so much so I fell head over heels for at one point in time and named a character in my novel after her. I figured if I could capture a fragment of her brilliance in my work, I would sell more books than ever. Yet reality is often no extraordinary fairy-tale. I am the first to say that sometimes when we make mistakes, the stains always remain, no matter how hard you try to wash them away. We may have gone our separate ways, but I still love them both all the same.

Sharan is my extravagant friend who loves K-pop and tells me "You got this, dude!" Sharan is a one in a million friendship, she's equal parts smart as she is funny and kind. Most people are all sorts of weird when created, Sharan is one of the few who seems to have been created in equity. Courtney is my more reserved friend, who makes me think of "stargazing when you've set your eyes on the sunset." She's the beauty behind the beautiful itself. Both of these women remind me that princesses really do walk among us. Thank you both for pushing me to be greater and for reminding me that it is not a punishment to be reminded of your errors.

And for Nicole, who stuck by my side with diligence through all the tough times writing this novel put me through. She is one of the most wonderful lovers and funniest people I ever met. I hope one day she will run towards this talent instead of from it, because the world deserves to laugh as hard as I have when I'm with her. Just like Courtney, Nicole has also faded into the proverbial sunset. But I've learned that it's part of the process of becoming a good lover. To love someone and lose them is much more profound than to have never loved them at all. I have tried my best to find solace inside of my artwork. I hope I reflected enough of the good energy these women brought to me. There's no sense in telling this story without it. Thank you, Nicole, for being so genuine in a world that doesn't reward that virtue very often.

I have a long list of people to thank, including my mother who was always my biggest supporter, even if I was too young to understand the complexities of her love. However, for this book's dedication I chose the ones that motivated me in regards to this particular story. I hope in my other novels, I can take the time to thank the others. To my best friends, you were not just good. You were the greatest. Till death do us part, even then, I expect much longer.

TABLE OF CONTENTS

ACKNOWLEDGMENTS

To Amber, we did not work together for very long but your advice about my book was astounding, never forgot it even to this day, thank you for being my first official editor. Means more than the world.

To Chloie, who did end up becoming my editor, has been nothing short of a joy to work with. We have a much deeper connection than just Author-Editor. I can call us friends. We just clicked like two magnets attracting to another. I couldn't have asked for a more intelligent, insightful, and intuitive editor, her love for her craft is the same I hold for my own. Hers perhaps is greater as she speaks with such enthusiasm! Its infectious. Most of the times I call her I'm not particularly in the best mood as this journey has been long, hard, and arduous. It continues to be so, and I wouldn't want it any other way. But when I call, she is always a source of positivity. She's no shy critic either, I still live by the first page of remarks on my first draft of The Hansens that she wrote for me after reading it. She's genuinely a great editor, but more importantly, a great person. I pray we can work on many more books together! I never would have imagined working with an editor anytime soon in my life, I am most appreciative that I got to work with someone who challenged me to bring out the best in my work. I'm in your debt for that.

To Peter, there aren't enough words in my vocabulary to express how grateful I am that you chose to take on my story! Working with you as my publisher has been a hell of a ride! You've been patient with me when I really needed it. You treat me like one of your own, always happy to call or shoot me a text when I need to talk about authoring. I am new to this journey, if I am in a dark cave then Publify Press has been my flashlight. His team has done wonders for me and have made me feel extremely included in his publishing culture. Especially his assistant Mimie, she's awesome. It feels like fate to have stumbled upon his metaphorical doorstep. I have emailed dozens plus some editors, literary agents, and publishers trying to find one that would invest in what I had to say. To this day, Peter has been the only person to believe in me enough to give me a chance. I hope like with Chloie, Peter will publish more of my books. I am excited to see what this journey ahead unfolds. If it is anything like my first book, then I will be more prepared this time. Thank you for everything Peter, I try to keep the business aside from the personal life. But I grew up without a father, and missed out on a lot of moments. For a strong role model like yourself to come in my life and provide a spotlight of opportunity for me is pleasing to say the least. I appreciate all that you have done, just know that, Guru.

To Maria and Garrick, who has always been there for me to read my story when it seems like no one else gives much of a damn. You both consistently shine through as fans of my work. I would be nowhere without your guy's guidance and time taken to read through my work. Always spilling ideas out to me, so much so I have humbly taken them for my own. With permission of course. It's awesome to know that even though I wrote the book by myself, that the story was created by so many influences. So many conversations and moments of recollection with my friends. Especially these two. I hope you both will read all my stories, as you have diligently with this one

And to all the people who have given me advice, read my story, to the folks on the app Stage24, and anyone else related to helping me in some way shape or form. I have never forgotten it. I promise if you come up to me in the street and mention what you did, I'll remember it. I promise.

"Never underestimate your opponent, nor the capacity of the evil they may possess."

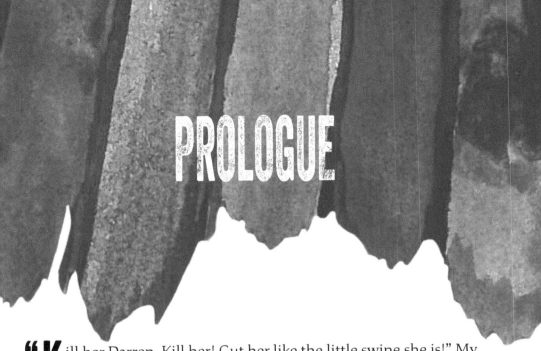

PROLOGUE

"**K**ill her Darren, Kill her! Gut her like the little swine she is!" My father screamed at my brother through the empty space in the staircase banister, while squealing like a wild warthog. He antagonized this woman's fight for survival like a leopard walking around a wounded gazelle. Darren gazed at the floor, angry that this woman resisted his wishes to bludgeon her black and blue with his baseball bat. The thought of pursuing this already doomed woman seemed to irritate him. His face... his weathered gaze... they spoke loudly. It said, "How dare she fight for her ability to continue living life." Darren firmly planted his feet down, prepared to smack this lost little lamb with his rust-encrusted baseball bat. A bat littered with Phillip screws skewed into the top, along with a handle made from someone's broken tombstone. While he dragged his bat on the floor, he left a path of forking scratches resembling what children would leave behind when scraping chalk on their parents' sidewalk. Darren tiptoed over what remained of a fractured floral vase he splintered across his victim's temple when the woman decided to run away. He stepped only on the glass fragments with little flowers painted on them. The woman pleaded, "What?! What do you people want from me?!?! Please don't hurt me and my husband! I have children....... downstairs!" As she ran around her banister as aimless as a headless chicken would, Darren swung his bat at her slightly cleft chin, snapping the upper portion of the bat clean off. Screws were stuck, better yet, *embedded* into her cheek. The once beautiful wife of the man being attacked upstairs now appeared ghoulish. She collapsed, then started bleeding from her mouth. I pushed my urge to scream deep into my internal thinking so no one would hear me. Especially my father. If I ever exhibited any emotion other than joy on these murder sprees, I would receive unimaginable beatings. I would look like this woman on the god damn floor! Darren had smacked her so hard, he splattered every sweat bead she had accumulated over the course of tonight straight off her shattered face.

She twitched on the floor abnormally; like a squirrel that was hit by a car while driving ninety miles per hour down the freeway. In the rear-view mirror, one may only see a furry sphere spinning in circles, ramming its face into the pavement needlessly. My brother never relented. Not for anyone or for anything. Each and every prey on his plate was given the same consideration and complete effort as the one before. I assumed the sheer impact from his bat bashing into the woman's skull severed her brain's hemispheres into two separate halves like splitting open a globe. The woman was dribbling crimson-colored droplets out of her ear canal onto the granite tile floor she was writhing on. Blood began pooling solemnly between the clay-colored cracks bordering the floor. The thunderstorm outside roared alongside flashing streaks of lightning, but in this case, the rain was unable to wash away the stains. Darren stood over the carcass that remained of the woman he had just hit a home-run on. He didn't allow himself to feel anything other than stoic as a Spartan, he would tell me at dinner when I brought up this sentiment that "emotions are for the poorly educated, do not waste your time with them." As this woman gasped for the inkling of being remaining inside her, she sputtered with blood and broken teeth seeping out of her mouth, "You…belong in H-ell." Darren resisted the urge to stomp her face into her brain, I could tell by the way he twitched his foot when she spoke. Darren knelt down with impassiveness and replied "Weep about it some more, why don't you? Hate to break it to you but…. there is no Hell. And if there is, then I will see you there. Sound fun, honey-bun?" She melted like the Wicked Witch of the West at the prospect that even her afterlife wasn't ensured with complete freedom from his torment.

After slipping away into her forever slumber, drowning in a whirl-pool of her own bodily fluids; the house's chaos continued to ensue like the thrashing thunder outside continued crackling in the clouds above. Darren displayed no sign of amusement while I ran towards the basement door. He called out saying "Hey! Don't run...why don't you join us for once, Thomas?" "Why don't you die for once, Darren," I replied. He shrugged past me, completely unnerved by my slurs, the surreal engagement of his primal predatorial instincts kept him on a highway to hell. There were no detours towards his destination. Darren took his mask off for a moment and inhaled deeply, pon-dering above his freshly slain prey like a lion did above a ripped-apart gazelle. He licked his grinning lips before slicing a souvenir off of her mangled mouth, then placed it into his left jean pocket; storing her splattered smile for future attachment onto his mask. Even plugging my nose up could not rescue me from its so sickly stench. I did not understand his obsession with collecting such horrendous souvenirs, however, he sure was efficient when he wore his 'creation'.

I tried to slip away into the basement since my brother was pre-occupied with applying someone's skin to his mask. I desperately needed to clear my head, yet, my mother appeared from the veil of insanity taking place. Her face was dripping blood. The paint on her face, or as she would call it her "makeup," was splotched all over. It appeared as if Dolly Parton had made love to Pennywise the Clown! I was dumbfounded on what to say; I figured the children down-stairs were off limits. My family did not bother kids. I can't attest much to their character, yet harming babies is something I can with low levels of pride say my family has never displayed an interest in within their "art of murder." I asked my mother the oh-so-horrible question "M-Mom, did, did, you kill them?!" "Oh honey...I did. But don't look so sad sweetie pie...They were definitely older than you, I would never harm anyone younger than my baby boy. I was sooo gentle with them, I promise. No need to worry about them now my love, they're rotting with the maggots now." She rubbed my cheeks, wiping the tears off while staining blood on my face. Whenever I felt my mother's touch, she seemingly sprinkled pixie dust onto me. My captivation for my mother was hitherto no matter how insid-ious she may be. Sigmund Freud would say I suffer from a slight

Oedipus complex. Yet, I would tell him meet my family and see for himself who he's dealing with. Nonetheless of my opinion... a child will always want their mother no matter how torturous loving them may be.

My mother led me back up the two steps I traveled down, enticing me to watch my father butcher the husband of this household. Her soulless, porcelain-esque makeup bled down her cheeks, swirling from her own hand prints scathing across it. Like raking a slope into a flat surface, where the hills roll no more. The world in this current moment was a total cataclysm, a roaring torrent of scorching-hot emotion. I felt I was rolling into the gates of Hades on a chariot made of molten tungsten. I did not know what made my parents pick this particular house. Then again, I am lost to find a reason to pick any in the first place. I scream endlessly into the infinity; yet no one can hear me, nor is anyone even listening. My brother, Darren, took his mask off for a moment. Not for any noble reason, only to gaze upon the person he turned into a carcass one last time with his own eyes, without the rose-tinted glasses his mask provided. I assume it's much easier to slay someone you have no intimate connection with rather than someone you're quite fond of. As it is to bare a mask rather than show your face, I can imagine the difficulty of gazing straight through someone as your about to filet them rather than hide behind a layer of leather. Or in Darren's case, a layer of decaying human flesh and skin of animals he's slain. What an abomination that monstrous mask was, and how more hideous the monster who wore the damn thing was.

The house trembled, shaking from its very base. The bass of the thunder outside corrupted the night sky, lightning strikes provided light for the pitch-black vibrancy inside the living room. My father wrestled with the woman's husband up and down the flight of stairs leading to the living room. Once he realized his wife had died, the man fought with all of his might. This surprised everyone, including me; no one considered that a victim could have murderous capabilities. The husband snagged a picture frame off the wall, one with him and his wife when they visited Turks and Caicos, then smashed it onto my father's face. His frenetic rage alarmed my mother, who wondered if they finally found someone who had the capacity to fight back. Yet, amid all of the peril, my father peered emptily into the husband's psyche. Blood and fractured glass formed a line on his forehead to the bridge of his nose, appearing as if it was a pizza sliced in half not into eighth's. Crimson hands were painted on the picture frame, not of my father's prints however. His inertia was jump-started by the husband's intense energy, which was ironic because my family had caused his initial energy spike to begin with. No matter how valiantly this man wanted revenge for his dead wife, he could not dance with a man who has spent years making murder an art form. My father dragged his half-conscious body into the bathroom and repaid the glass-stained face he received in equity. Not by allowing him to live, but by allowing him to die. My father grabbed the back of his neck then hurled him into their sliding shower door. The shower shattered, like firecrackers crackling under the sun on the Fourth of July. The poor man could not muster the strength to get up; he had been bested. My father picked him up like one of his children then shoved his face onto the sole remaining shard of glass standing in their shower frame. The sound of my father turning around towards my direction while stepping on shards of shattered glass sent shivers down my spine. My father was omnipotence incarnate. Our eye contact was brief, nowhere near intimate. My mother's makeup-covered face flushed with fanaticism, she proceeded to smear the husband's blood onto her face. She licked the little droplets falling off the edge of her blushing cheeks. She has a particular love for the taste of it, since murder just wasn't enough for her lust of blood to be satisfied.

After almost vomiting inside my clasped hands, I ran downstairs into the basement towards our getaway vehicle. *Ten minutes, they're cutting it close tonight.* Each step I descended down creaked miserably, my anxiety was hissing and spitting venom a mile a minute. I counted to five, inhaled, and exhaled the feeling of Hell quelling in my chest. I've learned if I dwell in the dungeon too long, then I might become lost there. Their basement was as dark and ominous as the upstairs part of the house. I dared not enter the children's room, in fear of my mother avoiding telling me the truth about how old they were. Yet, the gaming console covered in Call of Duty stickers I saw seemed to indicate they were a bit older in age. What kind of mother could do that to someone else's child, let alone their own? I observed my surroundings a bit more before going out to my father's black Cadillac Escalade. I noticed a small picture dated sixteen years ago taken with a janky Polaroid camera. A picture of the husband and wife, holding their second son as they sat upon the Smoky Mountain range. On the back of the Polaroid someone wrote in sharpie "Best Day Ever! Thank You Marlene For Giving Me The Greatest Gift Of All: Being The Father Of Two Children With The Most Wonderful Woman In Existence!" It took every fiber tying my being together to not shriek in complete agony. I put the Polaroid in my pocket, as I did with all the mementos I took when brought along these murder sprees. Even if my family would forget about the families they've slain, I would never. They haunt my dreams and appear in my nightmares as side character's. *How many families will I allow to be ruined by not intervening?*

The getaway car was kept running by my other brother, Miles, who received the gift of seniority over me. His days of forced participation were long gone. Ever since I came around, the lenience was transferred to him. He was no longer the "odd son out." I was. Darren took to murder as a monk took to philosophy. There was no inherent forcing. Like gravity pushing upon our planet, it just seemed to happen. My brother and I however were on the opposite end of the spectrum. Which ironically, caused us endlessly more suffering than our brother Darren. Who realistically, is the epitome of evil in the eyes of a pair of loving and caring parents. As soon as I entered the car, Miles damn near leaped to the ceiling as if a ball of spikes was shoved under his seat. "Holy hell bro, can you knock next time?! I'm on the edge of my boat over here, don't scare me like that! Did-did everything go smoothly?" My brother asked, fidgeting his fingers as he usually did when stressed. "Smoothly? That's a bit condescending, isn't it? Our family just murdered two children along with their parents! Can't you at least share some sensitivity with me? How do you live like this?" I said. He replied "I don't, I haven't been alive since I realized I was in this situation. I have distanced myself from their actions, I am not responsible for their behavior any more than God is." I took a moment to respond back, weighing my thoughts and options. I said "Does it make sense to watch senseless violence day in and out?!" Miles took a deep breath, then said, "Does it make any more sense to try and stop something that is a part of us? Something deeply ingrained into our system? Perhaps God himself is afraid of his own creation; he aspired for civility yet received nothing resembling it. Why else is he too afraid to show his face?! Our family was not created from the hands of a loving father, rather, by a force beyond reasoning." I hated hearing my brother speak in such bleak terms. I told him, "You're morbidly divided by your own mind, science will not bail you out this time. If there's no god then what stops us from entering total annihilation?" Miles concluded our discussion by saying "Our nature, we conceive it as evil when in retrospect, that evil has infiltrated itself into us. Confusing our causality for morality." I snapped back "If you have all this knowledge why can't you stop them?! Can't science bring their diseased minds back to life?" Miles proceeded to put the killing blow on our conversation. He said "It doesn't work like that! Why can't a preacher bring down God to meet with them? Some things are beyond our control even when we have the tools and capabilities to change them." My brother's words sunk into my fallen heart. The fallacy of reality was blinding, my intuition told me that this wouldn't last forever. Yet, my ego made me feel it would. I remember years ago when I wondered if we were finally hanging up the gloves after my father was almost caught red-handed (literally), then years before that when my mother snapped at her co-worker who soon became disgruntled. The times have taught me to never stand in the rain and pray that one day the sun's rays will take its place.

I admired the house and her seemingly frowning face. The rain washing away the debris and leaves helped display this affection of sadness. She was marvelously astute, with walls made of cardinal-colored brick. The rain became increasingly louder and ruder trying to intrude through our car's windshield as I pondered upon the house. The clouds above began rolling thunder while leaving behind a trail of rain drizzle. For a moment, I admired water reflecting along the top of her teal-colored shutters. In the path of my life's madness, I often missed the beauty of the things existing around me. Like this storm draining rain while flashing occasional lightning bolts among a black backdrop. Momentary light emitted from the turbulent electricity shed the sight of this rain painting the color sad under her window shutters. Water delightfully dripped down the sides of her stellar windowpanes. Within these walls, past her broken foundation, screams of ongoing pain occurring in the living room expelled outside towards our car. Even though the screams ceased minutes ago, these were the echoing sounds of similar sobbing and screaming like her hanging shudders expressed. The sound of screaming came closer, yet not of wailing, but of ferocity. Her open window frames displayed a slight glimpse pertaining to where the origins of this house's sadness could have possibly come from. Miles however, did not seem to mind the house, nor its residents. He has placed too much distance between him and our parent's actions. His levels of cognitive dissonance surpassed those with split personality disorder! But that was just my observation, it carried no weight unless tested then proven.

After the five-minute silence between me and my brother, our family came trampling out of the weeping house's mouth. Darren walked calmly, as usual, not particularly concerned with getting caught. He spends little energy worried about possible outcomes, rather than real results. My mother and father appeared flustered, probably from taking longer than usual. My brother had a bad habit of collecting souvenirs for his skin-bound mask. God, that thing smelled horrendous. It belonged in a trash heap, yet it rested eagerly on his cheeks. My parents appeared bewildered, which was usual considering these people just "looked" crazy. You know, those people you see at your local superstore with tremendous "enter the dragon" energy exerting through their rapidly blinking eyelids. The ones you can hardly gaze in the eyes at for too long before feeling icky, guilty, empty, or a combination of the three. "Drive, Miles, drive! We have overstayed our welcome!" My father barked. The eruption of violence had now condensed into slices of silence. I did not even consider breathing until my father sliced the elongated silence. We learned our lesson from countless dinner-interrupting beatings that we should shut the hell up when our father abruptly stopped talking. It grew so silent you could hear a mousetrap snapping miles away if you wanted. Miles kept driving as my father instructed, certain of what would happen if he didn't. Darren contently read *Christine* by Stephen King (which seemed virtuous, it was indeed up until learning he stole that from my room while I was at school! Right after returning my copy of the Divine Comedy. That thief treated me like a walking library with endless books for him to read. As if above my door-frame displayed the words "please do come in, take what you wish is yours. Wear your bloodied, muddy shoes and walk on my floor, why don't you?!").

My father finally snapped through the silence, "That was—incredible! Oh, kiss me honey!" They were utterly disgusting, even when displaying affection which was a rare phenomenon. My mother, Regina, pressed her blood covered lips onto his, smiling maniacally through the process, as if the blood she drank from was coated in caffeine. Darren, however, acted like his consumption was covered in codeine. He gazed blankly at Christine's pages, assuming perhaps they would turn themselves if he concentrated hard enough. I turned away as quickly as I could. Miles was unfortunate enough to look in the rear-view mirror. I observed through his knee-jerk reaction that the vomit in his thoughts nearly exerted itself into the real world. Why blood was less detrimental to my psyche than watching my parents make out five feet from me was something Sigmund Freud should look into from the confines of the afterlife.

My father pushed away from my mother for a moment to nudge Darren on the shoulder, like he had just brought home another flawless report card. "My son! That home run you hit on that woman's face was... exceptional" My father said, with a slight smile. "Another successful night of letting loose, don't you think?" Darren nodded, continuing to stare at himself through the mirage of his knife. Deep down, knowing Darren felt like a fairy-tale to me. Like Achilles dawning his legendary armor when Troy needed to fall, my brother turned into a different person when he put his mask on. As if all of the internal hatred he has compartmentalized in his lifetime found an outlet. As if he experienced true transcendence, morphing into a marauder who has mastered turning murder into an articulate art form.

It was like trying to navigate out of a labyrinth to get out of the neighborhood. Yet, we eventually hit the main road. My brother was slouched in the backseat like a buzzard perched up in a canopy, waiting for a deer to die. My mother used to tell me, "You can tell when someone is not right by if they have no light inside their eyes." Darren was a walking exhibit of this. His eyes pondered upon the pages with a desensitized gaze, like a computer comprehending information. It was not the gaze of a human enjoying the artwork of someone who has worked so tirelessly to cultivate it. When I looked back at my parents, my mother's makeup had made the great leap forward onto my father's face. My father playfully punched Darren's shoulder one more time before scolding me with the most scornful stare. His stare tingled the dead ends of my hair. He said "Tommy, once again, you disappointed me. One of these days, I WILL give Darren the go-ahead to sever your head! You hear me?!" My mother interjected, "Don't listen to him Tommy, you did great today. Michael, honey he is your son you nee-" "He needs to obey what the hell I tell him to do! I brought him into this world, and I'd be damned if I couldn't take him out too! I get it, the odds of both my twin boys being like me is slim, but you Tommy, you CHOSE to be a failure. I know exactly why, it's because your damn mom kept me from smacking the skin off your ass-" "That is enough! Michael! There is no need for this... we are a family. We are in this together." "...Hmph. How long do you think you can keep him from me, Regina? I will skin him alive while he watches! How dare he make a mockery of our family legacy." "You antagonize him every free second you have, Michael. It is no wonder why he doesn't listen to you." "You don't know anything, Regina. Discipline is what that kid needs, not compassion... He doesn't listen because I haven't hit him hard enough."

I avoided turning around for a while, and Miles patted my shoulder like my father did to Darren. But when I did manage to turn back around, my face was flushed with disdain. I saw a sedan-sized shadow ominously following us, which wouldn't have caused any alarms except for me seeing the distinct bull-bar accompanying all cop cars. *Oh no.* Was this my possible vindication or salvation, or was this another horror story packaged into a more glorious wrapping paper? The bonfire red and baby blue lights swirled in a harmonic symphony, the sight of which trapped me within a whirlwind of paralysis. My father jolted forward, now aware the lights behind him were those of the police. He began wiping his face, then my mother's, with a torn Metallica t-shirt. Hiding the evidence seemed futile, we were in a vehicle filled with it. It's like running away from robbing a bank while holding bags with giant green money signs on them.

My father told Miles, "Drive slow and pull over carefully. Do not give this cop any reason to search this car. If you say one word about what we do, I will butcher you and the cop on the spot! I mean it." Miles was not handling this information well. I could sense him crying from within his insides. He was already a terribly anxious person, and putting him under this kind of intense situation only triggered it even more. I remained still, while whispering to my brother "Stay calm, you got this. You're my big bro, remember?" He took my words of encouragement, stiffening his back to match my father's overconfident posture. The rain outside was whimsical; it was light as a feather. The softness of the water droplets falling onto the car created an atmosphere of remarkable weather. It differed from when we entered that family's home.

The officer tapped on the driver side window softly, as lightly as the rain tapping onto the car's windshield. Miles rolled the window down slightly, trying his hardest to avoid eye contact, and the drizzling rain dribbled through the open window. The officer asked, "Hey bud, you know why I pulled you over?"

"Actually, no, sir, I do not. I was going the speed limit, was I not?"

"Yes, sir, it is nothing concerning your driving. You have a tail light out. Couldn't tell if your turn signal was on or not. On a night like this it's best to be safe than sorry. Get it fixed as soon as you can, young man. Next time it's a ticket." Miles felt the sweat beading around his eyes, he replied "Oh...okay. I had no idea. Thank you. I will get it fixed right away."

"Good deal. Say, what are you doing out here so late at night? These windows are surprisingly tinted. Are you sure these are regulations?"

"I believe so, sir; they came with the car. And we just wanted something to eat sir. Me and my brother work all day, so we normally hang out at night. We were just on our way home." "Is that your brother? You don't look so good, kid. You guys been drinking? I'm getting an uneasy feeling about this; why don't you two step out of the vehicle, and we'll see if the sobriety test lets you get going."

"I'm not sure we need to do that officer. I promise we're okay. We just want to get home now."

"I wasn't asking you a question. The law is not built on promises, my friend; it's about ensuring the written words it instills are enforced. No matter the predicament or circumstance. So, just step out for me, boys. We will make this procedure nice and easy."

As soon as the cop reached his hand inside to unbuckle Miles seat-belt, Darren stabbed it with lightning quick speed. He didn't even have time to react before being blasted back by my father's loaded Remington shotgun. The officer dropped to the road, twitching like chicken who'd been hit crossing the road. My father screamed "DRIVE, MILES, DRIVE!!" I withheld my indiscretion to scream, "WHAT IN THE HELL WAS THAT?! DAD?! You just shot a cop!! He wasn't going to do anything. Holy hell!" I yelled at my dad, clenching the corners of my seat with disbelief injecting into my endocrine system. My father yelled back "We would've been caught if he wasn't shot, you dumb shit! Think before you speak, child." Paranoid Schizophrenia reeked from in-between the gaps of his gritted teeth, his soul was rotten to the core like a three-week-old apple, infecting the very mouth his breath dwelled in. The words he emitted surged with spit dripping behind his throat as he spoke. That man just SOUNDED like his screws were loose whenever he voiced his feelings. His mind was sewage draining from a dirty pipe, into a prosperous river filled with leaping salmon. My father was gospel for the damned and wretched. Darren had his knife in hand and was back to reading his book before noticing what he did was probably the opposite of intelligent. It was his *instinct* to be free, unconsciously harming anything that tried to pry him of that freedom. Miles held his head with his left hand, churning in agony from having a gun loaded off right next to his ear! My father barked "Dammit Miles, drive like your life is on the line! What the hell are you doing?!" I interjected "He probably lost his equilibrium, you jackass! You shot a gun right next to your son's face! are you okay Miles?" "No, I'm not okay! Owwwwwow, my ear is bleeding. I can't drive, Tommy you take over." Flustered as Poseidon without his trident, my father leaned over to hold the steering wheel while we swapped seats. I couldn't believe this was happening, after all we had gone through that night this was by far the worst part. The forest appeared wide and vibrant like an exotic jungle. I tried to keep my eyes on the road. These trees kept me at ease. It was easy to wander off and get lost in them.

This parabola sent my father into a ball of rage. He feels anger damn near every day, yet he felt angst for the first time in forever. He barked "This was your fault, Thomas!! You sickly shit. Now we have to change locations again! As soon as we get home, have your bags packed before the sun rises! If it touches the horizon before you're in the car, have fun finding us!" My mother intervened, always aiming at my father's offense towards me when in good conscience. However, the other woman was rather quite content with my suffering. My mother said, "Do not speak to your son like that! He is your child!" Darren did not refrain from explaining his decision making, rather using his opportunity to speak to insult the dead and gone officer. "That little piglet had it coming. He put his hand on my brother, so I used a deterrent." I couldn't help but laugh about the whole ordeal. I responded by saying "a deterrent? Really? You chopped his goddamn hand off, I don't think that's considered deterring someone." "Was he not indeed deterred?" "You are quite the Draconian-Mongolian aren't you? Genghis Khan would've been proud to have you on his cavalry if he had the opportunity to recruit you," I replied with as much sarcasm in my tone as possible. "You know, Thomas, I like you better when you are too scared to speak. It would really save my brain from the aching it is currently experiencing sitting here listening to you talk," Darren said. "Well, if it helps, I <u>never</u> like you and I despise your ongoing decision to ride our father's dick into submission. You wanna be daddy's big, strong boy so bad don't ya?" I said back. "Do you want to be dead by dawn? I will carve out your little heart then leave your body rotting on a flag pole" Darren said, swinging his switchblade open with intense swiftness. "Hey, hey, hey now. Be careful. Don't poke anyone's eye out with that thing," my mother said while glancing upon Darren's coconut-colored eyes. "Then tell your son to watch his tone when speaking to me, and he shall continue living," he said abruptly, not much concerned with what my response would entail as he put his attention back onto Christine. I uttered from the bellows of my breath "You're a sheep dressed in wolves clothing. You're about as useless as a nameless king, better yet, as the king of nothing. You have the same importance as someone who rules an empty kingdom looming with tumbleweeds instead of people. Childish freak."

Miles looked over to me with concern. Sometimes my anger writhes and bubbles to the surface. I gripped the steering wheel tighter than I already was, and flashed Miles a wincing smile. The smile spoke volumes louder than how I was actually feeling. I cut off the smile by giving him a good wink, making him think I was just being terminally sarcastic. I turned around to check on my mother, the only one whose safety I gave a fraction of a damn for, to find her causally playing with a bouquet of human fingers! She smiled, crinkling each one to her satisfaction while humming "do you love me, do you love me not?" I turned away, with a strong flavor of distaste flushing through my gums. *What is with them and their souvenirs? Where do they even keep these things?* Miles seemed to notice as well, giving me the stink eye for trying to hide a smile. I couldn't help it, nor understood why. The initial surge of anger subsided, followed by a sudden burst of internal laughter. My mother was playing with someone's fingers as if they were Lincoln Logs, it was hard not to find that slightly funny.

As I drove into the dark domain, unaware of rested ahead, I finally opened my eyes at this indignation. Seeing how desensitized from the situation I had become was undoubtedly horrifying. It was astutely beautiful, like losing a loved one. Like what Edgar Allen Poe said in his *Philosophy of Composition*: "When it most closely allies itself to beauty, the death then of a beautiful woman is unquestionably the most poetical topic in the world, and equally it is beyond doubt that the lips best suited for such topic are those of a bereaved lover." Within these whirlpools of thoughts, I never knew how much like them I had become. I knew from the moment I drove home that I'd have to leave another house, another state, another vault of memories behind. All for the opportunity of my family pursuing the most elusive murder spree known to mankind. As we drove by the final few houses before arriving at my house, I considered all the nice, middle-class houses ahead. There was a family eating together at the dinner table in one of the houses. I wondered when the last time I actually ate a real dinner was. Like one of my nightly binges of 'Friend's', I wanted to be right at that dinner table talking to people I love. I put myself in their homes for a moment, wondering what life would be like if just one indifference was present. If I had been born in another family, anyone instead of this one. I could only escape temporarily, yet within my final moments of daydreaming, I prayed that all those who didn't have to life this life appreciated what they had. I wanted to find the strength to one day runaway and start my own family. Pursue my own destiny. Hopefully one day, I gain the gall to go write about these things. The world deserves to know what evil lingers right under them. Most people are too young and dumb like myself to understand that ignorance is bliss. And that innocence is ignorance disguised in a cloak full of cheap tricks to dissuade discovering it's real intention. Writing became a way to fill my thousands-of-shattered-shards heart with miraculous vitality. My soul is given a podium stand when I record my thoughts, I am able to third person spectate over my body and feel this human's heart be ripped apart from the teeth of hungry hyenas while he is wearing a necklace of searing steak. Being able to feel my very heart drained over a page so I can valiantly express this pain became a grain in a field of wondrous white wheat. I await patiently for the day I am able tell this story. Since explaining the origin is too complicated for me, I wouldn't know where to begin. My fourteen years of life does not prepare me to tell the story for the lifetime my parents were together before having me. Yet, until then, here I am, traveling with the most insatiable family on the planet: The Hansens.

CHAPTER 1

Four Years Later

The sunshine hides under the cloud-ridden horizon, a skyline littered with cotton-colored clouds took away the sun's radiant display. I much preferred the shade anyways, anything that imposes blinding light is not to be trusted. I counted the clock above my teacher's desk until it ticked its way to three. "Getttt me out of this classroom," I muttered. My senior year should be spent anywhere else but here, trapped in a classroom surrounded by other idiots filled to the brim with teenage angst. I go to sleep every night wondering if I will wake up the next morning, while these pubescent, sex-crazed gremlins are obsessed with things like the latest fashion trends. I whispered to my best friend, Andre, who was sitting at leg-hair length away from me, "Are we still smoking before we go to work?" "You know it, I got three doobies stashed in my center console," he replied. I smiled, excited to spend as much time away from home as possible. As I fantasized about my time free from thinking about my family, the bell rang with belligerent repetition. I excused myself sooner than the other kids; they always took too long socializing with the other inadequate individuals inhabiting this classroom. However, Andre was the exception. I'd always wait for him.

We became best friends when I first moved to Helen, Georgia. Not many people are accommodating to the new folk, yet Andre was. Andre and I walked over to his Red '67 Shelby Mustang, which was a manual. His mother owned the twin, the Blue automatic that sat idle inside their refurbished garage. She was beautiful, yet usually covered in a luscious, grass-green tarp that was rarely removed. Andre reached into his car's overhead slot and slid on his vintage Abercrombie glasses, before fishing into his center console to retrieve the three pre-rolls he rolled beforehand. It was a glorious sight to behold. I had never smoked dope before until becoming friends with Andre. He completely changed my worldview on weed, and drugs in general. I was led to believe only the weak fled from their fleeting reality, however, I quickly learned that some drugs actually enhanced life's vibrancy, not the opposite. Some mind-altering substances do not steal from the beauty of life, they amplify it. Especially those substances grown from God's ground, how could a gracious creator create something able to happen naturally without any human interaction or intervention? Even if no god at all was responsible for this divine revelation, nature itself should be appreciated for this grandiose creation.

"So, tell me, you gonna marry that chick you're with or what? Cause if you do, I deserve bonus points for setting you up with her. I hope I don't lose you, though. She is quite beautiful after all." Andre said smoothly while lighting the other end of his cigarillo. "That's such a random thing to bring up Andre, you're funny. You really are the Mercutio to my Romeo," I replied. "Don't dodge my question little Cupid, you act like we weren't friends before I introduced the two of you. Why are you so persistent against commitment? You know, as both of your friends, it's not my place to say what should happen. Yet, as your brother in every facet except blood, I gotta know why you're acting this way? It seems wildly irrational." I lit up the other cigarillo then exhumed my thoughts through the clouds of smoke that funneled out of my mouth. I replied "Andre, I, I really don't like when people get too close. I feel like if they really understood who I was, then they'd run away from me. I'm not keeping her at arm's reach because I don't love her, it's because I do." "How do you think allowing her to get too close will frighten her, isn't that what you want with someone when you're in love? What are you hiding from her Thomas? What, what are you hiding from me......? 'Cause in my eyes you're a phenomenal person, you're the type of friend that has no end. All needs are met when I'm around you, that's why I don't understand why you are acting this way?" Andre took his time to toke on the cigarillo. "Just don't let her down man, you need to be able to hear the sound of the storm when it comes. You can only apologize so many times before she uncovers how deeply disappointed she feels because of you."

It feels like the Titanic crashing into a sheet of ice when someone tells you something about yourself that you just know was a 'hammer on a nail' response. His pinpoint accuracy rivaled Hawk-Eye from the Avengers. Andre had this weird ability to see right through me. No matter how hard I tried to hide my inside thoughts with jovial comments or sarcastic remarks, he bashed past my walls I thought were built so strong. The very walls that were guarding my inner-most heart and my vault of sorrows. I smoked a little more, feeling the tune of Bob Marley exhume through my mind. I asked Andre, "I am afraid of what you'll see, can you promise to not think dif-ferently of me because of the things you see?" " I'm not the one you should be worried about, because I am accommodating to all ends. It is who I am. However, your lovely lady might find some-thing too dark and disparaging, too displeasing to continue dealing with. What are you hiding?" He asked. "Let's just listen to music for a moment okay? We will discuss this later, I'm not going to abandon your friend, okay. I happen to care about her deeply. I just need to find a way to release myself from this fear of showing her who I truly am." "This has been a problem longer than just today. The longer we put this off, the only more intolerable it will become. Tommy, you have to know no matter what, you are already worthy enough to be loved. Nothing you can show your partner will be too daunting if their the right one. I mean goddamn Tommy, did you kill someone? Why are you so reluctant to share these insecurities, we all have them!" Andre posed a good argument. "How do you have them, Mr. Valedictorian? You are loved everywhere you go. How did I even end up with Courtney? Why wouldn't the golden boy get the golden girl?" I asked in response. "Is this what it's all about? Damn it, Tommy, I don't even like white women! I'm sorry, but they're just not my type. You know when you go to Ben and Jerry's, then you pick a flavor you most want, I just don't want freaking vanilla okay! She's my friend, Tommy, I don't think about her in that way. Do you not feel worthy of having her? Cause if so, then you should realign your chakra correctly. I'm a Valedictorian, so what? Take away the title, and I'm just smart! It doesn't matter. You're intelligent, creative, funny, almost all the things my peers are not. I see you clearly, Tommy. I'm not the one who deserves your woman. You know why? Because you're right here! Why was she single when you randomly appeared? Wasn't cause I was just sitting in my car wondering which restaurant I could possibly take her out to. Courtney has never made an advance towards me, as I to her. Kings respect Queens. What causes you to think you don't deserve her, and for preposterously thinking I for some reason do?" I took a breath before responding. "I-I really don't know, I'm sorry to put that on you, my parents.... Can I show you something tomorrow? This is going to be hard but I want to let you in on who I really am. You're a great friend. Thank you for setting me straight. You do deserve that woman however. I am just fortunate enough to court her." "Of course, Tommy. Have you ever considered that I don't equate happiness to having a woman? It's really to me an indifference. If it provides me pleasure then bring her, bearing the most beautiful appearance and features too divine for the human spirit to handle. However, unless that woman appears, it makes no difference to sit and wish it. Does the joy of life lose its abundance when one loses love? Does the water around us lose its value? Do the colors that form in the sky dwindle in shine and vibrancy because you are not in love with someone? That is quite a presumptuous way of thinking, romanticism has killed entire generations. I think I am most happy when I am alone. It is my solace. I appreciate life whether I am with someone or among my own solitude. Just like you, if I were to lose you it wouldn't make life less beautiful. It would just mean the opportunity of it being more beautiful because you are here is not there anymore." Andre was always deep when he talked. I responded, "How do you think of things so enlightened? Is it really how you think or is it the weed talking? I am so burdened by my indecision. I want love but not at the expense of showing my true colors. It's a dumb conundrum," I confessed. "I want you to love my friend too, Tommy, but you are also my friend. So, I seek to understand why you feel you aren't enough. Show me what you must tomorrow and hopefully it will illuminate your situation a little better. Maybe it will open some doors not approachable at the moment. Let's change the topic. Have you heard any more news on the triple homicide that happened near Mulberry Lane? It's quite scary to think around the same time you came around, these sporadic incidents started occurring. Like a lightning strike attracted to a metal pole I suppose. I predict that there's more than one killer. There's no way that over four years these people have been in multiple locations at the same time. I've done some research, and it's quite alarming how many unsolved murders have been happening in Georgia. Then, like a gust of wind, swept upon our little Helen. What do you think about the whole situation? They really come and go as they please, huh?" I felt my whole body pixelate then put itself back in place. I hated talking about this topic. It hit too close to home. "Uhh I don't know, Andre, I can't wait for someone to catch them. It's alarming that none of the Clint Eastwood-type police are around anymore." As someone suffering from 'shut-up, sit-down-and-be-sad-syndrome', I grew increasingly disturbed the more Andre talked about "these killers." Failing to recognize that I knew these people profoundly... yet after tomorrow, that barrier between us would be there no longer. For the first time in forever, I would let someone inside my home to show them something far too awful for public decency. I plan to show him the extent of terror hiding behind my family, the one that trails behind my life in a linear line like a rainbow road.

Being the gypsy that he was, he shut up. I don't know if he felt my negative waves or just trusted his intuition, yet he always treads lightly on that subject. Maybe he took it as I was too empathetic to enjoy discussing other people's deaths, yet when rubber meets the road, I was harboring immense selfishness. For four years now, I've kept my distance on this topic with Andre, yet with the reality that school was about to end, I believed I should finally share my peace. What if perhaps I never saw Andre again after the summer ends? I would like him to know how I felt about the situation, truthfully.

Especially with the situation between me and Courtney growing more powerful by the second. I could not continue to love either of them if I remained this dishonest. We continued to smoke in peace, ignoring the situation as we usually do. I chose this time instead to rear my head back to the ugly conversation. "Andre, I love you. And I love your friend. I would never do anything to hurt either of you. So let me justify my actions tomorrow, I will start with you. I don't know how I will show Courtney this information. Yet I will find a way. I appreciate you bringing this to my attention. Things with her lately have been rough. I have so much pent-up frustration and I can't express it, cause if I do, then you both are pulled in too! I've hid this thing from you and her because it's beyond me. If I let you in then you're included too, and I don't want that!"

Andre flicked his cigarillo ash out the window, concerned with my lack of eye contact. "Tommy, look at me. I've been your friend for four years now. You *always* have panic in your eyes. What are you so eager to run away from? I've tried my best to give you distance with your situation, but I cannot continue being friends with someone who will not let me in. Especially when you're hurting my friend man, all she wants is some time and attention, why can't you give that to her?!" I coughed as I responded, "Because, I'm afraid of what will happen if I let her in! Okay! I can't have this conversation right now, not before we go to work. But tomorrow, I promise we will have this conversation. I will make everything abundantly clear as to why I have to put you both at arm's length." "Some people don't run from danger, they run towards it. They welcome it. Tommy, I love you, but for you to hide something so clearly important for so long shows me a lot about your character. I get you're a protective person, but don't consider Courtney and I incompetent creatures who can't understand what a man's going through. My father left me when I was three years old, I've never known how to be a boy, a man, or be anyone other than myself. As you already know, you're little innocent doe has a stepfather. Not a real one. Maybe if you gave enough of a fuck to ask why, you'd know that our lives aren't glittering gold either. I can't predict the information you're about to tell me but Tommy, wandering in the darkness only hurts the person who's lost there. No one can suffer with you, they can feel you, sympathize or empathize, however no one can take away your pain. You can though. So just know no matter what you tell me, I will be here for you. I am sorry to give you the third degree but when my friends feelings are hurt I cannot budge. Even for my best friend. She's someone's daughter, she deserves to know why you haven't been calling back. No woman should feel like their bothering they're boyfriend for attention. Never. And as a man, I can't refrain from saying that's fucked up. Hurt people hurt other people, Tommy, don't let your hurt continue to hurt others. Especially those people diligent, persistent and willing enough to love you."

I nodded, pulling my hoodie over my face so that the softness of my tears would not be seen. He was right. I've spent my whole life trying to hide my identity when in reality I've only hurt the people who tried to love me. *Tomorrow would be different*, I told myself. One day I will wake up and realize this was all a dream. I did my best to believe that, yet reality had a tendency to pierce through your veil of serenity whenever the opportunity presented itself. I'm glad I had a good friend, my only one at that, he was the best of the bunch. A silver dollar among an armada of pennies. I closed my eyes for a moment before arriving at work, thinking of the pyramids in Giza and how beautifully each piece of stone put there was. One day, I hope I am just like them. A mortal who molds the deformed portions of his soul into something beautiful, brick by brick. The pizza diner Andre and I worked at was dainty. It appeared like it belonged in an age several decades ago, yet somehow, someway, resisted the withering rain father time tends to exhume. Like a cockroach after an atomic fallout. The neon sign was far from its original quality, some of the bulbs didn't even appear on when lit. Instead of Darnell's Diner, it read Darn Die. Quite the message you'd like to read before entering your neighborhood pizza place. I was quite surprised to pick such a place to work at, yet Andre talked me into it. He said the human interaction would get me 'out of my shell.' I didn't believe I needed any more time with people than necessary, but the job paid surprisingly well, so I accepted it. I liked Darnell a lot too. 'He has quite the personality' is the nice way of putting it. Saying he's as straight forward as shooting an arrow, a gargantuan-sized man who loves humor, booze and Cuban Cigars is the 'rubber meets the road' approach.

Before I opened the chestnut-colored doors, Andre pulled me aside and said, "Hey bro, I hope you know I love you. Sometimes I just feel like I gotta straighten you out. You are salutatorian after all. Your genius is a notch below mine, keep that in mind when I give you advice. I do not say it out of arrogance, however, I say it in attempts to provide you a latter to climb up to the tree of knowledge I'm upon. I wasn't always smart, I became so. Let's get this shift over with, I'm excited to see what you have to show me tomorrow. It's like finally arriving at your favorite show's finale episode, I get to in due time know why you have been so at arm's reach with me and Courtney. She deserves to know too." I smiled and hugged him with genuine affection. He really was my best friend. *I would not be excited to know this particular information. I would be the opposite.*

As soon as we entered the diner, Darnell came barreling towards us with a bottle of malt liquor in his hand. This more often than not indicated that sales were running low. I don't know why he tries to solve his problems with alcohol, the business isn't gonna fix itself with a little booze in his system. Yet, he will be damned to not try... every time. "Tommy-Boy! Andrepalooza, how you two doin'? I didn't know you guys worked tonight? We're uh, we're waiting on some deliveries as we speak. Ehh, why don't you both sit for a few, eat a pie with the big Capoochee, mkay?" Darnell's thick Cuban accent resonated long after the alcohol got into him. His whole family lived in Cuba, until they moved to Georgia when he was around our age. That accent wouldn't go away, even if he beat it in the brains with a baseball bat. All he knew of his youth was life in Cuba, and in my opinion, that fact drastically molded the man standing before me. I said to Darnell "Sounds good boss... say did Courtney ever come in and order a pizza?" "Let me stop you right there kid, cause I think I know where this ends up. Tommy you gotta stop asking about if that damn girl has come in, be a man and answer your own questions. I get it champ, love is difficult. Do you see a wife on my wall of pictures? Hmph, didn't think so. I've come across all types of women, even across different continents, yet, never a single one who's willing to stay. You have a wonderful woman who wants nothing but your time and attention, a real man would reciprocate that. Since you clearly need to be shaken, she did in fact come in today. Now eat up, this pie's gonna get cold. Stop being a freaking maluka, you can only be sorry so many times before that special someone loses love for you. Get a grip comrade." My response was stuttered, but well put together in my head. "Wait.. she really did come by-....you know what, I will take your advice. Andre reamed me before we arrived here so I see the message is prevalent enough for me to take it." Andre's eyebrows wavered, his eyes grew weary. He did not want to dive back into the paused argument, but my comment seemed to brush him the wrong way. He replied "I didn't 'ream' you, I simply reminded you that you are acting with little child with an even tinier brain. That girl you're messing with is one of my favorite friends. Imagine if I fucked your sister, then you'd understand where I'm coming from." I didn't appreciate Andre's hostility, even if he was right once again. I said "For the record, your "sister" came onto me. I didn't pull her into my realm, she entered into it willingly. Dante did say 'abandon all hope ye who enter here' didn't he?" Darnell chuckled at my attempts for humor, Andre however did not. He seemed increasingly irritated by me constantly shifting the conversation away from its main point. Andre sternly looked at me, scolding me with his eyes as a father of a runaway child did. He replied "Yeah... you know Tommy, sometimes I wish I could punch that perfectly-put-together face of yours. Maybe if it were rearranged, you would appreciate your place on this planet more. Sometimes I wonder what my friend even sees in you, sometimes I do too. Is there anything I can do right now, Darnell, I'm not really in the mood to sit and eat with a borderline jackass right now. Maybe later." He gave me the third degree, pointing his feet away from me. As if his toes were arrows leading to where this conversation was headed: the other direction. Darnell licked his greasy fingertips and then said "Don't take things so difficultly Andre, I'm sure Tommy was just joking. You know some people cope in their own ways. Some make humor of the situation, while others binge eat then buy nonsense until their wallet's and stomach's start screaming at them. Yet if you must, the pizza boards do need to be scrubbed. I would much appreciate it being done by someone other than me," Darnell chuckled in response. Andre rose to his feet and replied back

"I will get right on it Darnell, and I wish I could agree. Yet Tommy will keep doing what makes him happy. He doesn't ever think about other people's feelings as much as he hopes to believe. He's my best friend, but a real asshole when it comes to handling situations with people. Always has been. I don't know what it is about him that is so difficult to address. He's as stubborn as a mule who screwed an ox, then produced a little hybrid. Tommy is that little terrible thing birthed by them times a thousand."

Andre walked off, more irritated than he was in the car. I pondered at the pizza bar, recollecting the first time Courtney and I hung out outside of school. I thought she was just exceptionally gorgeous, I still do. Like one of those models you see online that you think is quite possibly an artificial creation, or an artist rendition of what 'the Muse' looks like in real life. I knew who she was, since Andre had talked to her several times during the day while they walked in the hallways. I was as abrupt as I am now about Andre's inclination to refuse dating her. It was like asking a thirsty person why they were not in search for water. She seemed like the archetype of beauty, like everyone's spectrum of what beauty could be should end on her. Given who my family is and what I've experienced with them, I am not the best in dealing with people. Especially those emitting a stronger magnetism than I did, her vibrancy antagonized the darkness that walks with me like a dog on a leash. Her initial, and persistent beauty resonated a crusade in my soul to seek her warmth even just for a single fleeting moment. Within that whirlwind of a moment, it was a world of wonder. A total difference in the inclination that I had to live this way. Andre opened those corridors for me, yet Courtney provided me a doorstop to keep them ajar. I reminisced on everything that lead up to where I was now, wondering if I did everything I could correctly. Yet I grew to be increasingly more dumbfounded as to how things had grown so far beyond my grasp. I pushed her away to save her from the inevitable chaos that follows me, yet, I have only seemed to cause her more misery than I would continuing to keep her close. Is this truly the consequence of coming from a family whose desire for bloodshed exceeds that of compassion or companionship? I didn't think I knew until these past few months of feuding with the two people I love most. As I pondered on that empty chair where I spoke my first corny joke to her, I wished she was there. There for me to never speak those words so I could leave her be to her own solace. I felt immeasurable guilt within this recollection for bringing her into my situation, the way I chose to solve the problem seemed to only further deepen the wedge between me and my queen.

Darnell smacked on his slices of pizza, then said "Will you quit daydreaming you mook! Lord have mercy son, you look like one of them damn ducks asking for bread every frickin' time I take my daughter out to the pond near William Boulevard! Eat the pizza, what the hell is the matter with you Tommy? Listen, you little shit, you can't be acting like this on your deliveries. Tell you what, eat the pizza. I'll tell you what you're doing wrong... everything! Tommy, you can't just ignore your girlfriend. Are you crazy?! Do you think she's not attractive enough to get up and dump your dumb ass? Tommy, I've seen that girl walk in here about ten thousand times now. That might be the hottest person alive I'm not quite sure-." I put my pizza slice down, visibly disturbed by what Darnell had said. I interjected by saying "Ew! Gross, Darnell you're like a century years old. You were there when Rome was founded, goddamn Greece was casting statues of you before Courtney was even born. Let me not divert the conversation with humor again, I know.... I know. I'm doing some-thing dumb and absurd, but things have gotten really crazy lately. My family isn't like other families Darnell... they're... they're an abomi-nation!" "Good joke, kid. Back in my day I would have already tagged your queen by now, don't forget that. Tommy, everyone has family issues to some degree. Some parents are too overbearing, some touch too much, some brothers punch too much, some don't call you down for dinner when it's done. Shit, if you're really unlucky, you get a set of parents who beat your ass for no apparent reason other than them holding an empty bottle of vodka-." "Okay Darnell... Damn. That last one hit too deep. Sheesh. But my family.... They are an entirely dif-ferent entity. They're literally-..." Andre bombarded our conversation like hurling a ball of flames aimed at a serene meadow. He barked at me "Tommy! We need someone delivering pizzas, can your guys' conversation wait thirty minutes until you get back? Then you can continue to talk about how much of a dumb-ass you're acting like."

Darnell lifted his eyebrow, conceded whether to be snappy at Andre's attitude or proud of his stellar work ethic. He chose the latter since it was the least taxing on his well-being. "You should be more like your friend, Tommy. You know he's right. Is that what's got you so hot, huh? Hmph. You can have many friends in all different hues and shades, yet you only get one true best friend, if he gives you advice then take it. You're a good kid Tommy; get your head out of the gutter, the game is still on! You got this champ! Now go sell me some pizza! I can't have you moping around here like some daffodil who hasn't seen spring or the summer breeze in years, okay? Okay." Darnell grumbled while finishing his bottle of alcohol. I did not appreciate being ganged up on. But how do you differ when you know deep within your innards that what someone is saying to you is true, even when it pierces right through you like Alexander the Great's spearhead into an Achaemenid soldier's chest? Among the devastation my battered ego left behind, I was appreciative to have two real people in my life give me well-needed advice, even if a part of me didn't want to hear it. My family is not the kind to give advice. Their advice usually followed with either beatings or forcing me to sleep in the garage. Because, as my father puts it, "Only winners sleep in my home! In here, There. Are. No. Losers! Losers belong in the garage, where the dogs belong!" I tried to wave Andre goodbye but he looked back at me blankly. I really went too far with my dissociation I suppose, which I thought was impossible. I guess to expect a man to walk on a tightrope for twenty minutes is an errand, but for two hundred years is a whole other endeavor. Bertram Russell was definitely onto something there. Even without being a murderer, I still hurt people. But tomorrow that will all change. I will for the first time let someone see for themselves what monsters my family have been, and have become.

The pizza van was rustic, something you'd expect out of a Teenage Mutant Ninja Turtle comic book. I technically wasn't even allowed to drive it since my parents had never taken me to get my license, nor had ever given me a vehicle to drive. Miles and Darren were the privileged prissy's who received vehicles on their sixteenth birthday. I was the black sheep so to speak. Once I got inside the van I set the pizzas aside, then put on the podcast Andre and I were supposed to listen to before we were rudely interrupted by a spurring argument. That man really could spit venom; I've never seen him so adamant about something before. To see him care about his friend so passionately showed me I'm not as grown-up as I want to be. The drive was only about nine minutes away, but from what I did take about the podcast was that Rome had fallen because of famine and disease rather than any actual sacking. However, Rome was pillaged twice, once by The Visigoth's lead by a man named Alaric, and another by a Step-Nomadic tribe called the Hun's led by a mighty man named Attila. He was a great unifier of the step-nomadic-tribes. I took a great interest in history, especially of the Roman's and Ancient Greece. I liked to believe the founding fathers didn't do enough research on history for basing our country's philosophy on a fallen empire. Yet, as Mark Twain once said, "History doesn't repeat itself, but it often rhymes."

I got out of the van, not entirely sure if I was at the right address since the mailbox numbers were mostly eroded. It didn't help that the streetlights in this city were powered on goddamn solar panels or something, because they just don't work right at night. I sensed evil lingering, it flashed across my mind like a lightning strike in the depths of night. I had a bad feeling about approaching the door for some unexplainable reason. I just felt immense terror with each step forward I took. I sat by the van for a few minutes, letting the lightheadedness fade on its own accord. Once I regained some strength, I walked towards the door. The trees were whistling with the wind, like a jazz symphony with no instruments, only harmonics. The somberness of this setting filled my fingertips with a tingling sensation. It was dreadful, I knocked on their door with persistence. I couldn't help but notice the window was flung open. The breeze blew through swiftly, making the curtains shoot out as if being electrocuted. It seemed odd to have a window open at this hour. But nonetheless, it took an eternity for me to realize that no one was answering. I don't know why I did this, maybe I already knew what was coming, but I decided to peer through the open window. My only reason being that I was curious. Curiosity was my highlight, and the noose I hung myself on. Like a seesaw, it went both ways.

My thought process was that if someone ordered a pizza, then they would definitely want it when it arrived. It's not common for someone to order a pizza and not pick it up. Especially if they already paid for it. I did not like being inside some stranger's home. The possibility of someone charging out from the darkness with a loaded pistol with assumption that I'm a burglar was playing in my mind. But, something continued to draw me in, I wasn't sure what it was. I peeked through the open window to see the TV was on semi-full volume, blasting the Adult Swim channel. I recognized what was playing immediately, it was 'Opal' by Jack Stauber. A brief, yet brilliant animation made to highlight childhood neglect. Considering the mini-show was only eleven minutes long, there was always a sense of fate when I woke up to watch Opal. I wondered why it was playing so early though, I assumed perhaps since Halloween was around the corner a few months away they were showcasing their scary stuff. I was tempted to sit outside and watch it, until I heard the most horrific scream. A scream perfectly synced with Opal screaming out of her skin when realizing her inner paradise was only just a daydream. I did not know what to do; I was caught in decision paralysis. So, I took a deep breath and trotted forward. I crept up the windowpane with hesitation in my fingertips, I did not want to encounter the monster that caused that god awful scream. Who knows what it would do to me!

The staircase banister railing screeched within my quivering hands. I did not display confidence in the slightest regard, but at least I was proud to admit it rather than convince myself I was Superman when I felt like Clark Kent. I noticed some of the paintings were turned over to the right a smidge, as if someone was peering at it from all angles to understand it's intricate lines and framework. There was only one person I knew of on planet Earth who carefully examined anything that crossed their path. I did not want to say his name, because I felt he was already here. To utter his name was like Harry Potter calling upon Lord Voldemort, it would only give him more abhorrence. I remained hopeful that whoever was suffering was so by their own hands, not of the ones I suspected was here. Maybe then, there would be a chance I could save them. If it was the latter, then it was already too late. The shag carpet clung to my torn-apart tennis shoes, causing static electricity to enter into the slits where my socks were showing. I could hardly resist the temptation to turn my dirty shoes around and head out of this house faster than if it were on fire. Yet, before I could pivot, I heard a horrendous hacking noise. Like someone smashing a grapefruit with a crowbar. Followed by the sound of Vivaldi's 'Four Season's' playing off of someone's smartphone. *Why me?* I wondered as I proceeded to put my hand on the doorknob to turn it.

I busted into the room disregarding my intuition to leave. I saw my brother slashing at the head of an already dead man, down to the base of his neck, leaving behind a ripe stump. I screamed, yet no noise exited my lips. Lightning strikes, but thunder shrieks. I felt my bone marrow grow colder by the second. Darren was the last person I wanted to encounter right now. Ever, really. I'd rather Hannibal Lector himself be standing before me while eating someone's liver on a dinner plate than the terrible tormentor himself. It struck me as odd however that he paid no mind to me being here. Like I was inconveniencing him, and not the other way around. That's usually how things played out in his mind in my observations.

Darren said "Thomas, would you like to help me slice his face off? I need his skin to repair my mask, some bitch grabbed at it when I stabbed her stupid ass in between the eyes." "Why are you here, Darren! Did you follow me or something?" I asked him. "Thomas, that is nonsense. I merely saw your pizza vehicle as I was passing by and thought it would be pleasing for me to drop by while you were working." "Darren, you're holding a dead person's head in your hands, what the hell is the matter with you?! God! You're insatiable! Turn that music off! I thought you all stopped this shit already! You know? After our father almost got you all caught for the ninth time?" Darren retorted, "You all? You stupid brat, you are just as much a part of this as anyone in this family. Just because you don't murder, doesn't mean you weren't born a Hansen. You hurt people too. Why's that little poodle of yours seem so droopy lately? Can't you be man enough to be honest with her, that's a fond quality to possess if you ever want to make a woman happy." My fingers crinkled in my palms. I wanted to punch his face as hard as an anime character supercharging their supreme finishing blow would. Enough to send him far into the Andromeda, where he is forbidden to harm another individual again.

Waves of blood spray coated this man's white window curtains, which in hindsight, was a bad decor choice in a room you're being murdered in. I was catatonic in that moment, many memories came flooding by on the river of thoughts they rowed on. The fear of my family starting up their traveling murdering circus again froze me into stiff coldness like a stone statue. Moving forward felt non-negotiable. I was already anxious enough these past few weeks with thoughts that they had returned, it was a feeling. A feeling that they never quit to begin with. It only crashed, died, then revitalized like the tide. But for my suspicions to be confirmed is a whole other ordeal. I just stared blankly at my brother, who returned my gaze with an even blanker expression. "This.... is who we are Thomas, why do you run from that? Does a lion try to be a sheep? Does a walrus stretch its neck out and act as if it's a giraffe? No, nature follows a strict structure. As do I. I don't need to kill to survive Thomas... I just want to. Like this gentleman here, he did not hurt me or cause me any harm. However, here he is. Dead as a doorstop. So, take with that as you must, but just know, you can't stop us. You and Miles can try to "fix" us, but there's no point. There's nothing broken inside me to be put back together. We want this. You two are what's in our path of achieving ultimate virtue. Stay the hell out of my way, Thomas. I will murder your girlfriend then wear her face as you watch and weep. You are safe because I allow you to be. Don't overstep your boundaries. One more thing, you're gonna have to accept who we are someday. Pushing people away who benefit you only brings your devastation, not theirs. Their withered flowers will recover, yet you will never escape your storm unless you learn to stand in its rain." My blankness turned to an expression of confusion. I said "Who are you to give me any kind of advice, you're an abomination. You create a wasteland everywhere you go and call it salvation. Yeah... maybe only for you! You're as selfish as a man with a million mirrors pointed on him at all times! What could you possibly care about my well-being when you are still killing people! If you cared in any regard about me, you would put that knife down and never hurt another person again." Darren responded carefully, "Life isn't black and white: it's

16

often hidden within the grey areas that the most important parts take place. I despise you, you are a total idiot and waste of human potential. There's a one trillion chance for the opportunity of experiencing existence and the universe decided to spew your stupid shithead self into the world. Yet you're my brother, my flesh and blood. Someone who among all odds, I never would want to harm. That doesn't mean I will not, however. And for you to say that, implies you have no finite understanding of happiness. If you loved me in any capacity you would be a part of our family, even if that meant to murder. Yet you don't. So don't ask for something you yourself would never return." "You have a twisted philosophy, Darren, the only true virtue in life is happiness. You are the mad scientist dissecting that down to its bare atom. You still fail to understand that your 'happiness' equates to the suffering of every single person who encounters you. I shouldn't expect much from someone born from two parents who care more about murder than their own children's well-being," I retorted. "I'm not blind, Thomas, the cost for my happiness is taking other's away from them. That is the price you pay when you want to achieve great things. Don't forget you come from the same parents as I did, you're an insatiable idiot, but we share the same blood." I was still standing in the doorway, with panic and anger rising in my beating chest. I said "Don't remind me anymore than necessary... living with this knowledge is almost as hard as watching you guys commit crime. You're a dark and despicable person Darren. You really don't care about anyone but yourself. That's evident, but why continue to follow me? I thought your saga of making my life a living hell was long over. Do you really have nothing better to do than to kill people while torturing me in the process?" Darren threw his last verbal jab at me. "It's an entirely different thing, you would never understand. Murder is not some hobby or pastime like watching the Yankee's play the Met's, it is a true art form. One that requires indulgence, individualism, and respect for the craft at hand. There have only been in retrospect 'an airplane full' of killers who subsequently became extremely notorious. Most killers are indescribably dumb, whether because most killings are emotion driven or substance induced, I don't know. But killing in cold blood requires so much more than just passionless murder. I thoroughly enjoy each and every person I kill because this... this is what I've spent my lifetime trying to perfect: the art... of murder."

I took a step back, done with the conversation long before it even began. Yet my brother had a compelling nature to his demeanor. Like the hordes of Nazi's listening to Hitler speak about such horrendous things, such atrocities, it is a wonder god did not strike him down from the very podium he spoke on. Even when Darren spoke grimly, I was intrigued. *"Separate the music from the man,"* I remembered. I did not have a response to follow with. We went too far in our conversation, I didn't even realize it until ten minutes after. His spellbinding ability to speak enraged me, yet also endeared me on a microscopic level. Darren was truly too intelligent for the broken body and conscience he possessed. After gaining enough comfortable distance in between him and I, he contently picked up his blade to finish the job he came here to complete. "Thomas, I only torment you because I love you. I need you to understand that if you ever try to take away this magic that I have, my wrath will cast you down from the deepest depths of the underworld. I know you're going to tell someone about what we do someday, maybe you already have, all I will say is you better choose wisely. Because if anyone gets too close, they got to go. I don't care who it is. You should already know this. We don't take prisoners, they are next to useless to us. Now go, I have a job to finish." Darren fished in the man's wallet for some tip money. "Here's twenty dollars for your troubles, consider it, generosity. Leave me to be, little lamb, I have a face to severe, and I can't do that if you're just standing there like a damn deer in headlights. So, scurry along, and understand that the Hansens are back from the shadows they've been casted in. For good." It wasn't his shrillness or his disregard for human life that concerns me most, it is the total 'matter of fact' way he speaks. As if this is the way things are supposed to be, as if he is holding hands with the Sisters of Fate; failing to see that him and my family are the outliers. Not the other way around.

I wanted to cry while walking down those carpet steps, yet the thunderous voice of my father yelling at me when I was seven years old rang in my head. I cried when my brother Miles was forced to sleep in the garage after refusing to take part in their schemes rang in my ears. My tears glistened in my eyes, yet refused to drop onto my face. My father's voiced bellowed within my abyss, "Don't you dare cry, wipe your eyes! I don't EVER want to see you cry. Only losers cry! Losers don't sleep in a house full of winners, they belong out in the garage like a damn dog!" From that moment on, I did not cry much. That bellowing voice always knows when to show itself from the shadows of my sunken abyss. I heard Darren hack away at the man's lifeless limbs as I slowly slid down the staircase, utterly numb to my surroundings. It had been so long since I have seen someone murder, or be murdered for that matter, it nearly hurt worse than the very first time. I wanted to be with Courtney this very instant, watching Naruto or Fairytale or whatever outlandish anime she could think of. I loved spending time with her, but after noticing my family's obsession brewing back to the surface, I have not been able to gracefully brace the blow-back inflicted onto me. If anything were to happen to her, I'd go mad like Romeo, or better yet, Hamlet. In my mind, keeping her as far away as possible was the only chance to keep her safe. It sucks to suffer through something that you only can explain to yourself, because to utter the words to someone would make you seem absurd. I left that house feeling like half a human. I didn't feel any semblance of emotion. I could not even bring myself to mourn for the fallen man anymore. I used to pray for them when they'd fallen to my family's antics, but now, it just seems useless. I knew one thing though, I needed to fix things with Courtney. She was the light peering into my dark cavern, pushing her away took that shine right out of my life. Instead of wandering in the darkness until my legs fell off, I wanted to step out of the shade it casted.

I ran into the pizza van, locking the doors behind me, then called Courtney. Hopefully, she would answer even though I have thirty-seven missed calls and one-hundred-eighteen unread texts from her. I was a shitty person for putting a princess back into her tower. But among all odds, even while not deserving a moment of her time, she replied... She said "T-Tommy? How nice of you to finally return my calls. Why-why have you been ignoring me? Did.... I do something wrong? I just don't understand what I did wrong Tommy..." I felt my heart crumble then rebuild itself back up from the rubble like Rome did. *You are an awful person, you do not even deserve to be called that, you're an awful animal.* "C-Courtney! I'm so happy to hear your voice. You didn't do anything wrong, I'm sorry. I-I can't explain to you why yet but I need to see you. I think I'm having another anxiety episode." "What the?! What the hell is going on with you Tommy? Are-are you seeing someone else? You don't have to lie to me if you are, I would just appreciate to know the truth." "Courtney, you are my sweet peach. Don't ever think that I would cheat on you! I may be in the hole for this one but I can assure you I'm not seeing or sleeping with anyone else. My god! You-you are the water to my withering garden. I would never do anything to hurt you. Ever." "Then why are you hurting me now, Tommy? You can't just pop in and out like this. Everything was fine until the night your family came in acting all funny while we were hanging out, what's up with you? What are you hiding from me? You're little boyfriend Andre, who's supposed to be my friend, is defending you over supporting me. You boys are mind blowing sometimes." "To be fair, my love, Andre has given me the third degree. He hardly will even talk to me unless I bring up smoking together. He really is my best friend huh?" "Yeah, duh. He loves you Tommy. I was a little taken back when we first started chatting, I did not want to intrude on a great friendship between you two or ruin mine with Andre. Yet I feel confident now that one of my favorite friend's and my lover can be connected. But I'm not happy with either of you right now, I've been crying myself to sleep this whole week. I've been needing you, Tommy. How can you push someone you say you love away? What kind of man does that?" I had no rebuttal. As my brother did, she left me dumbfounded. I thought by protecting her from who I am, I was performing justice. But I only hurt the person who wanted nothing from me but my time and energy. It made me very sad to say the least, my tears talked more than my mouth did. I couldn't believe how blind I had been. I have been so focused on my family that I was becoming a neglectful boy-friend. I could not just be around when times were good then dip out when the going got rough. Love required so much more than that. I was not accustomed to that fact. Partially, I felt Courtney's life would be better without me. Regardless of what she protested, I felt deep in my abyss that she belonged with someone not afflicted by their family's demons. By their own demons. But, instead of running away like the countless women I've tried investing time into before encountering Courtney, she stood her ground. She came to conquer. She came to storm the lands in search of what she wanted, and what she wanted, was me. A tidbit I still fail to believe, even when evidence and actions prove otherwise. Like Lil Wayne would say in a song I played while laying in my bed some days, when I'm withering away within the wind like little brittle leaves in the autumn breeze: "I never really figured out how to love."

After letting her vent her feelings to me, feeling piercing shards of glass enter my heart each time she stabbed me with her words, Courtney finally conceded. Courtney made one thing apparently clear: I could not continue being so inconsiderate. She gave me chills, like a Valkyrie scalding her men after failing in battle. Amid all of this, she apologized as well. She said "A man needs his space, so I understand in that regard, but damn can you practice communication?" I mumbled to myself "If I could, there would be no space in between us, you would become my life's epicenter." She stopped her rant to tell me to speak up because she couldn't hear what I said. So I rephrased my statement, "Listen Courtney, I will be real with you, I really want to see you. I know you're still mad at me and probably have a long list of things to tell me. I want to hear each and every complaint no matter how much it sucks. Can we compromise? Meet in the middle maybe? Could you come over tonight when I'm off work? We can sit and talk all night if you want, I just need to be with you, babe. It's been a hard week. It's been a hard life if we're on an honesty-binge here." "I'm sorry honey. I may be upset with you but I still love you, I figured you had another hard week. You get really distant when you're anxious. Tommy, I really think you should see someone for your anxiety. I don't want you to feel the rain more than the sun. I love you. And I can't just watch someone I love suffer like this. I-I don't want to feel so alone anymore. I will come over, but don't expect anything else. You're grounded until further notice. You may receive a kiss, and a touch on the dick for good behavior. Mkay?" I was stunned to say the least, I called her hoping to talk to her about my problems yet was quickly thwarted by hers. Which made mine seem more humane, if that was even possible. I always wondered how could someone harm her, she was so damn gorgeous. Then, I wondered how could she harm herself. She's so brilliantly charming.

But then that lead me to ponder on how could I become the man that harmed her. What steps led me into this direction. Like digging through the rubble of Rome trying to decide which decision made it crumble. I told her that we would talk when we saw each other, that I loved her, and that I would see her soon. Then proceeded to cry alone in Darnell's pizza van. I was disheartened by how much relenting terror I had inflicted onto someone too beautiful for this world to appreciate. And for the pile of lies stacked ten feet tall inside my mind. It was my first thought meeting her, *how is she even single?* It's like Snow White was walking among us and nobody even realized it. Perhaps I felt guilty for receiving such a wonderful queen, her worth and my own are about nine latter-rungs apart from each other. I am a product of a murder-fueled family who does not care for trivial matters, while Courtney came from such a loving household. Single parent and all, who in return cultivated an angel to full strength like Superman's 'parents' when he crash landed in Smallville. I cried until there was nothing left in my head, only an omnipresent sense of dread. I took a journey into that open void dwelling in my soul and returned back with clarity. I needed to protect this woman at all cost, she clearly was god-sent. But first, I needed to let her into my sadistic side of life. Inch by inch, of course. My greatest fear was letting her into my thoughts. *What if she thinks I'm just like them?* I began to dread the day I tell her any of this information. But until then, I could lose the best thing that's happened to me all because I am afraid of what she will see. I must put the skeletons in my closet on hangers so she can sort through them herself. She deserved that. I could no longer sweep demons underneath my sheets, and hope no one would notice their silky silhouette.

The next few hours of work were melancholy, nothing important happened except I almost dropped a pizza because I was thinking about how hungry I was. But other than wondering if I would encounter Darren again, nothing out of the ordinary happened. I told Andre I patched things up with Courtney and he was very pleased. He apologized for being so hard on me, and told me that "Sometimes I gotta be the father of the group. But I will always remember we are friend's first." I really did love the guy, no one gave me advice quite like him even if it was extensively rigid. I really needed a father figure even if he was around my age. Experience is everything. Besides that, the night at work ended somewhat comfortably given how it started. Our ride home was swift and silent. Andre seemed relatively ready to be done with the day. I asked him if he was okay, he replied, "Yeah, I'm all good Tommy. Just worried about you two man. Don't pull no Romeo and Juliet shit on me, I can't deal with another night of comforting your girlfriend while she's crying over you-" I cut him off, "I don't want to hear it again. We've argued enough for one day..." We pulled up at my house, and I held my hand out to do our 'dap-up,' he looked at me with visible emptiness inside his eyes. Then he stuck his hand out so we could perform our signature shake. Even if he was still annoyed with my demeanor, he still loved me enough to not leave me hanging. He truly was a 'friend to the bitter end' kind of person.

    I tried my best to slip inside unnoticed, but my father's bellowing voice caught me by surprise. He said "Thomas, you're out late again. We don't just come in whenever we like, now do we?" "I had to work, how do you expect me to come home any sooner?" "Leave him be Michael. Come sit for supper, love, I made some delicious chicken and dumplings!" My mother chimed in, always coming to my rescue to save me the sparring session with my father. "I'm okay mom, thank you, I'll take a quick bite, but I'm having Courtney over." "Why don't you have her over for supper one day? We would love to be able to speak to her for more than five minutes, dear. She does appear to be the one, now does she? Is she your gypsy, Tommy?" my mom asked me while setting the silver utensils onto our wooden dining room table. "I assume so, mom. I mean she's an angel. I am far below the standard of beauty yet she sits on top of the totem pole it's conducted on. I don't know what she sees in a guy like me even three years later. It seems like a fever dream. I'm afraid she will one day realize she's worth twenty times more than me then leave..." My mom cut in, "You are a gift from the gods Tommy, you are my son. I know you will do great things." She continued setting the table by herself as she usually did on every evening. My father didn't bother getting up to help; he treated my mother like his little servant. I wish I could strangle him in his sleep just for the treatment of my mother alone. Not to mention the hell he has put each of us and countless others through.

My father barked "That's nonsense, Regina. Thomas is like every other dumb boy with his dick stuck in between his legs. He doesn't know what a right hook is from a left hand, how could he ever defend his pretty little lady? And if you can't, how can you call yourself a man?" I responded, "Funny for you to say, considering you've punched my mother's face so many times she doesn't hardly smile anymore, are you even smart enough to recognize that? You stupid bastard, I wish Vietnam would've swallowed you up like it did the other 58,000 soldiers. At least they died fighting for something greater than themselves. You fight for no one. You're a shadow of a man! I can show you a right hand and left hook right now! Come and find out!" My father jolted to his feet, as if the chair he was sitting on was made of box springs. He pressed his forehead against my own, we took a Greco-Roman wrestling stance. As I grew older, I had become more determined to challenge my old man. He said, "Tough talk coming from someone whose never even killed a man, I could split your head in half like a cabbage, you little rat! I should've left you in the hospital so someone else could suffer the consequences for your existence." "I wish so too dad! Then I wouldn't have to be stuck in this miserable shithole with you! Out of all the families I was chosen to be born in, it was this god-forsaken one the universe found most fitting for me! What fucking irony! I am the salutatorian for my school even with your bullshit! In a normal world, I would be the golden child. But no.... no, I get to burn in hell every damn day because my family is fucking crazy!" I said, while refusing to back down. All of my unopened emotions were bubbling to the boiling, scorching hot surface. My father was getting better, until the PTSD became increasingly noticeable, to the point he was let go of his job again. His disdain for the economic system and the military for not compensating him fairly for risking his life abroad was palpable. He hated the authorities, the government, and any form of legality, really. This same government gave birth to the types of people my father despised. To the types of people my father relished putting on the other end of his spearhead. Once this revelation of insanity reached its peak, I suppose my father decided it was time to get back into the game. Ever since a few weeks ago, he's gone back to being a complete shithead. Not as if there was ever any Pax Romana for my father's treatment of his kids, yet it was a helluva lot better than what these tides brought in.

"Now, now, you two, settle down. No need to be violent inside my kitchen. Mike, your son has a point, you always pick on him. Leave him alone for once, you could learn a thing or two from him on how to treat a woman." My mother said, flashing me a wink while proceeding to wash her hands in the sink. "Eh, you don't know what you're talking about, Regina, you never do. I bully him because he's my son, and I don't want him to display any qualities that fill me with disdain. Yet he does, time and time again. Why can't you be more like your brother! He's the perfect mold of everything I want my son to be. He is a true killer! An Achilles walking among us in modern times! He will die as one of the greatest killers to ever exist. As his father, I am nothing short of proud. Your decision to go against our way of living disappoints me to my very core. You are my son! I want you to be better than this! People deserve to be slaughtered like little lambs. That's all they are, useless little creatures too feeble to even understand why they are here. Why do you think otherwise?" I said back "Because people deserve better. They shouldn't have to live in a world where people like you exist. You don't get to just go to war with society because it's left you in the street fucked unconscious! You change it! You see the world for what it can be instead of wither within what it is. Violence is never the answer to your own inner hatred for this planet. Try your best to keep your insatiable anguish to yourself while my girlfriend is over. She's one of those people who deserves so much better than the world she inhabits. It sucks she has to be scared of walking down every street and alley corner in fear someone like you will appear. You're not a man, you're an abandonment on what it means to be one," "You think you're so smart with your philosophical ideologies huh? Yeah I can read a book too, some people don't want intelligence. Some people just want to be happy, and for me, paying back the society that has shunned me is doing just that. And you better pray I never see your little girlfriend out on one of my raids, I would not hesitate to bash her face into the nearest wall or counter top. You are alive because I allow you to be, never forget that." "Thanks dad, that's some stellar advice. Is there anything else you'd like to add before I go try to patch things up with my woman?" "Hmph, why are you and the misses having issues? Set her straight! Is it Halloween or something? Take off your mask and be a man! Wha-wha is your dick not working like it used to? Jeez Tommy, if I were to lose a girl that looks like that then I'd probably shoot myself. Wouldn't you?" I took a breath before responding. "That's really reassuring dad thank you, no actually, I'm losing my god damn mind because every time I find something great in life, I'm reminded of your putrid presence! You guys are like an ant infestation, anything I try to do to make you go away doesn't work! I am trying to keep it together but ever since you guys started killing again, I can't even look at my own face anymore, let alone hers. God! You people are fucking insufferable, I can't stand being a part of this family. You're like the damn Roman's, you create a wasteland and call it peace. Fuck your peace. I'm going to make things right with my queen so I can leave and start my own family one-" *The doorbell rang.* "Speaking of which, there she is, man I love that girl. She even knows when I'm home from work, always giving me a little extra time to unwind from the day. Hmmmmm." My father scoffed, unabridged by my relenting verbal attacks. Back in the day he probably would've punched my face into my brain, but as an older, much more withered and withdrawn man, he stood less of a chance against his failing mental capacity. Besides, my father will never admit it, but he does love us. Perhaps under different umbrellas, but it was all under the same classification of what we call....Love.

I opened the door for Courtney, trying to redeem as many gentlemanly points as possible before being chewed out once more. Yet, she seemed impervious to our conversation before. She was glistening like Cinderella standing under a chandelier made from a million different shards of glass. I pulled her inside and tried to get her upstairs before my parents could care to call her down, but just like my entry was denied, hers was too. "Courtney!! My dear! Would you like to sit down and eat with us? The course is Chicken and Dumplings if you want some!" Courtney shot me a curious look. "Hello, Regina! I would love to but I ate before I came, thank you though! You're very kind, your food always smells delightful!" My mom was clearly disappointed. "Why thank you, sweet pea, one of these days Tommy will bring you over here to eat with us sometime! We would love to interact with you for more than five minutes at a time, I think Tommy's afraid we may scare you off." *Yeah no shit, because You. Kill. People!* "Of course not! If anything, Tommy has a higher chance of scaring me off than any of you. I'm just kidding baby, you all seem great. One of these days I will stay for dinner, okay?" *Dear god, no woman, what are you even saying? That's like staying over to eat egg salad with Bite-Sized Hannibal Lector, rip-off Dr. Doom and almost Alexander the Great's mother: Queen Olympias!* "Okay, that's enough you ladies, let me take my queen upstairs so she can tell me about her day," I said, taking Courtney's hand before she agreed to a three day vacation to the Baltic's with them or some shit. I absolutely adored Courtney, but absolutely hated that her relationship to my parents has grown increasingly strong. Their love for her was actually genuine, my father talks a big game about crossing her path in the night, yet has never smiled harder than when she walks in. Perhaps she's the daughter they always wanted, yet never had. Perhaps her ambivalent grace transcended through their primitive barriers. It certainly did mine. Yet, I felt terrible that one day I would have to perform the phantom of the opera and strip off their masks for her. How deeply intertwined somber and serene could be... in another life I suppose. Maybe my family and my lady would be the best of companions. Yet in this one, I could never let that actually happen.

The walk to my room is always a sight to behold, whether Miles is typing away at his thesis paper to understand psychosis and mental complexions specifically regarding violence of all types; or receiving a sneak peek into what a wild Darren would look like in his idle time was always a possibility. (It persisted of painting self-portraits or places, usually gardens surrounded by waterfalls, performing Shakespeare among himself as the audience, reading about history, and tinkering with his 'toys.'). As we walked by, it was such occasions. I sped Courtney through the hallway corridors, then turned around to scorn my brother for his arrogance of always leaving his damn door open. He blinked repeatedly, unaware that fiddling with a miniature, blood-stained recreation of the Roman's Gladius sword was abhorrent to non-killing visitors. I did not understand if he was damaged, or deranged, or a cocktail of similar elements. Considering who my parents were, I'd consider it was a concoction of all three.

My room was just like every other poster-littered teenager's room, the one exception may be the stack of books I've actually read. Not just shown my guest in hopes they think I'm a smart cookie. Mostly, because I don't bring by many guest. Those books aren't for show, they in fact, *are* the show in my world. Courtney often asks me about the books I read. Her attention span kept her from reading long novels, yet she was intensely fascinated with literature. Sometimes, I would read a chapter of one of the books on my makeshift bookshelf to her so she could sleep peacefully, then she'd return the favor for me the following evening. Like listening to a live-action audiobook told by your soulmate, it was one of my favorite parts of the day. Whenever she was in the mood, I would also read her my own writing. Mostly poetry, as I do not contain the concentration yet to keep on one topic for long enough to write a novel. Yet. Yet she loves my writing all the same. She was my biggest fan, my consultant, my editor and my manager. She believed in me almost demonstratively, with a total unapologetic attitude. Courtney never used the words 'if you could write,' or 'soon you'll be good enough to write,' or 'one day you can write.' She always talked to me as if I already was that person, as if I already was Stephen King or John Grisham. She was the lighthouse on the coast, casting light onto a cove which has never been shown that side of life before. This cove has only seen thunderstorms and pouring rain, it desperately needed something strong enough to penetrate through the impetuous darkness surrounding it at all times.

Courtney jumped on my bed and started flipping through Netflix, searching for the Anime queue she created last time she came over. Then, she looked at me solemnly, as if she had been struck in the eyes by lightning. "Tommy, I hope you know I'm still very upset with you. You're getting nothing except cuddling tonight, and you're the big spoon" I responded jokingly, and with hope still in my voice "Now that's too far..." "Zip it, Thomas, this isn't a negotiation. I wasn't making a suggestion; I am telling you it's happening. I don't like that you feel you can just ignore me then come back like everything's all good. You're so much better than this. Why are you acting like it's

okay to hurt me?" I responded, with borderline immense frustration. "Do you really think I feel it's okay to hurt you? Do you think
I wake up every day thinking to myself 'hmmm, how can I hurt the
love of my life more than I did yesterday?' Courtney, I love you but
goddamn, sometimes you're empathy can be next to nothing. I don't
want to dig into your past, this isn't a philosophical debate nor is it
my place to bring that stuff up but whoever hurt you enough to think
all people are intentionally hurtful is morbid. Even for my standards.
I am sorry I ignored you Courtney, I've been on the goddamn verge
of hanging myself on my goddamn door-frame with the chord to my
mom's Dyson Vacuum for a week straight! No one even seems to give
a shit! It's like I'm screaming yet no one is even listening or can even
hear me. I'm literally fissuring down the middle while still fighting
to keep myself bound together so I can be the best man possible for
you. If that's not love then what is?" Courtney stopped aimlessly
flipping through her saved section, having eyes that changed from
raging storms to serendipitous sunsets. I couldn't explain it, it was
like a mother seeing her child upset, and all she wanted to do was
make them feel better no matter the circumstances. I did not reveal
my feelings too often to her, I felt they would spiderweb into me
revealing who I really am. Who I really belong to and where I really
came from. But within this moment of agitated frustration, I disregarded my thoughts and I let that barrier go. For once under the blue
moon, I experienced transcendence into the wonderfully vibrant iris.

Courtney's face flushed red and her eyes swelled with tears ready
to release. I could tell she felt embarrassed to be angry at me, when
clearly, we both needed each-other. Her urge for self-harm and my
desire to want to take my life for this guilt I cannot escape is simultaneously a bond that fuses us together. One night when we were
eating dinner at Darnell's, we both made a promise to never harm
ourselves again. But... we both broke our pact. Well, we did not technically do so, but to almost break it is borderline abhorrent anyway
you frame it. It doesn't really matter if it was accomplished or not,
even engaging the thought process seemed just as terrible. I did not
know how to react; I never had profound conversations with my parents that transcended through the facades we put on. But Courtney,
who was raised with such a loving mother, knew what to do. She

hugged me, and refused to let go. Long enough for me to cry on her shoulder, something she had an intuition I was about to do. Like I said previously, she possessed spider-sense as if Peter Parker's Aunt May or Mary Jane got bit by the radioactive spider instead of him. I knew in that moment I picked the right person to share myself with, the woman strong enough to tear down my tall, heavily-fortified walls. A feat I considered impossible, yet I'm sure the city of Jericho thought so as well. I opened my bubbly eyes with blurry vision, my room seemed like waves rather than geometrical shapes. My posters looked more like splotches of paint tossed on my wall than any tangible forms of art, even my dressers looked like gargantuan globs of brown goo. Courtney wiped my tear-ridden eyes off with angelic gentleness. As if she never even touched me at all. She pulled my flustered cheeks close to her face, then kissed my larger-than-life forehead. Safely assuring me that she was the safe beach; I could land my raft on when I am out stuck on the thrashing sea for what seems like weeks, yet are merely minutes at most. Courtney pulled away from me, then said "Thank you for sharing with me, Tommy, I know that was difficult for you. I can see that I have much more to learn about you, I am sorry to have not considered your feelings. I forgive you, do you forgive me?" "What kind of question is that? You are my queen, you are always forgiven. I am sorry for not being there for you when you needed me, neither problem we have is more important than the other, both of our issues are valid. I promise to not leave you out in the dark. It will take some time to be able to open up like this more regularly, but... you make me feel safe. If I am to share this with anyone other than myself. It would be you, and Andre." "You just had to ruin the moment didn't you? You're funny Tommy," she replied sarcastically. "You can't still be mad at him babe, you know he's going to take my side, yet behind closed doors, he's got your back until the world stops spinning. I can attest to that." "You're right honey bun, it's not like I'm actually mad at him, I'm just upset at him if you understand what I mean." I sighed in response. "Trust me honey, I totally do. Up until an hour before closing at work, Andre hardly said one nice thing to me. I've come to learn the closer you grow with someone, the more prone you are to see them in their full array of colors. Like a peacock. Man are those pretty." "You're so stupid sometimes, Tommy, I love you. I don't want to lose you. It scares me when you just vanish out of the blue. It makes me feel that one of those times you leave, you won't ever return my calls or won't ever text me back again. That you wouldn't even remember me... I have never invested so much of myself and my time into someone, every guy I have been with before has not let me get this far with them. Just like you said about showing true colors, most people can't hide theirs forever. Some never even learn how to display them. It is very true the closer you grow, the more you see the full picture inside its picture frame. You are so different in ways I can't explain. I've had crushes on people before, but those were more, fanatical, in a way. But you.... I get to be with you. And actually have a persistent crush and longing to be your girlfriend. I've never felt this way about anyone before. Even now, three years later, which seems like nothing compared to fifty or something. Still, it's significant enough to wear off any lingering honeymoon feelings. Even when that has been long gone for a long time, it feels like it's never left. I just need you to know that. Since you were brave enough to be vulnerable with me, I need to do the same in return for you. I've learned you should never ask anything of anyone unless you're willing to also do it yourself. If you ever want to leave just tell me, and I will do the same. Which, I hate to be that person, but you're stuck with me unless you decide to leave."

I just looked at her and smiled, enjoying the present moment without any regard of if life continued forward or if I was afflicted by anymore bad memories. In this moment of true bliss, none of that mattered. If she was placed in any empire or ancient city-state then she would lead their kingdoms with immense grace. She was gentle even among her anguish. Any queen in Antiquity would have admired her greatly. We made great love, even when she said we wouldn't. It's funny how life works that way. You can be so stern with your words then watch them wilt then wither within the wind while you abandon them. I've told myself many times I'd run away and find a place to live, knowing all too well I have nowhere to go. Nonetheless, after we were done with our love-making, Courtney snuggled close to my arm. I assumed she was happy for now, I suppose. Although, I kept hearing creaking as we were... you know. So naturally I assumed it was me. Yet, with illicit tenderness climbing up the segments of my spine, I noticed my door was ajar about ninety degrees. Ajar enough to where I could see Darren standing five feet from the door-frame. He had his mask on, I could see it through the illumination of the vibrant lights casting outside his room. The new addition of that guy's face I watched be taken off while working earlier was sewn on. He stood as a silhouette within his own shadow. The stench of his mask was pungent. If Courtney wasn't pressing her nose against my chest she would have probably smelled it's wretchedness. I waved him away, mouthing, "What the hell are you doing!?" His response was to pull out his broken baseball bat, and mouth back "That's not a queen, that's a goddess, hit it right next time." Flashing me a signature wink before vanishing into the darkness engulfing our hallway corridors. I was mortified, I hated when he did that. One of these days he was going to startle Courtney. Yet, he walks alongside an omnipresent aura of foresight. Like the one Odin the all-father possessed. He seems to always know when she is asleep or preoccupied to come creep into my door frame with attempts to startle me. To him, I suppose he considered that humoring himself.

While I rustled to grab the remote from under Courtney, she awoke, ready to watch Naruto as if she had never fallen asleep. She said "I'm hungry, can we get something to eat pleaseee." I replied "Of course we can my angel, you know the only things open right now are Chinese and pizza, though. But they don't make 'em like we do down at Darnell's, we make them with 'Italian passion' as Darnell always says." "Didn't you tell me he was Cuban?" "Well yeah, but he loves Italian food. So he has a passion to make it I presume? I don't really know why that is, maybe his muse was once an Italian stallion. I have always found Roman woman quite pretty." "Oh really, well Caesar, you can order me an extra pizza since you're so pleased to share that with me." I smiled in response. "Oh you, your jealousy is quite cute. I've always been more fond of the Greek goddess anyhow." "Make that two, then," she responded. "Fine, we can make it even. Courtney who in history would you be attracted to?" "Can we stick to one subject please, I am hungry, what are we eating?" "The only pizza places open right now are the low end ones, you know, the 'fast food pizza places'.... you're lucky I love you. What do you want from Heath's Pizzeria? It's the only one I know of still open near here." Courtney smiled at me, saying with a tinge of tease, "You should know by now what I want dear." "Unfortunately, I do, I just always hope you will change it one of these days. Why do you insist on putting pineapple on a pizza, Hawaii isn't a flavor, it's a state. Don't ruin a pizza and call it Hawaiian, that place is too serendipitous for such condescension." "Tommy, you are ridiculous, pineapple on pizza is very delicious. It enriches the flavor of the cheese by providing an audacious sweetness to it." "Who even are you? Did you fall asleep to Gordon Ramsey again?" I asked. "Tommy, I know what I'm talking about, really, my mom taught me how to cook when I was a little girl. Did your mom not teach you?" There was a silence that had fallen upon us, I assumed she already knew the answer. She replied to the silence by saying "Oh... well that's okay, I know you hate pineapple anyways. It probably is just a flavor thing.... And hey, I am honored to one day cook for my man. Maybe along the way, I can teach you a thing or two." "You know, I would really like that. You're amazing Courtney. What is it that you don't know?" "Well for starters, I didn't know Cleopatra is closer to our time than she is to the Great Pyramids until recently. There's a lot I don't know, that's the beauty of life, to always wonder. Michelangelo said 'I am still learning' at age eighty-seven, which is quite incredible considering everything he's accomplished." I commented, "Your intelligence intimidates me sometimes, it makes me feel like perhaps I've met my match." "Isn't that the goal, to find someone who utterly compels you? You're the one who taught me about Atossa, the queen of the Achaemenid's. And about Genghis Khan's story from boy who wore rat skin clothing to almost conquering the entire eastern side of the globe. You're amazing too, Tommy, we as people are just flawed to not see ourselves as others do. Cause if we did, we would never feel like we didn't have something to offer." "You're very emotionally intelligent Courtney, your mother raised you right. Let me order you that pizza now my hungry princess." "I am not your princess, because that would imply you are my prince. You are my king; I am your queen. That's how it's supposed to be. But thank you, I want those little chocolate cakes too. The ones that come in their own little box, it's so cute!" "How did I get so lucky to end up with such a bundle of joy. I would buy you 900 boxes of chocolate cakes if it made you happy just for a moment, my love." She smiled, proceeding to kiss me before pressing play on Naruto. The episode where Madara takes on the Shinobi in the Great Ninja War. She loved that episode. She would watch it all the time, and explain to me how bad ass Madara was. She told me time and time again Madara would kick any anime villains' ass back to the manga they came from. Especially Sosuke Aizen, she was <u>adamant</u> about that. All the classroom banter about which one would win baffled her, no one considered how powerful Madara's truth seeking orbs really were. As if she was Prometheus wielding the original flame awaiting to bless it onto humanity. She didn't refrain from telling me ten thousand times though, that was part of the gig with women. Sometimes you get to stick your dick in them, sometimes you have to listen to monotonous conversations about how their friend really isn't her friend but really, she's her friend. No offense to women, the woman I am currently with is supremely brilliant. In all regards. But even she can bore me into submission with some of her conversation topics like I'm literally being gored to death by a wild boar. Luckily, this wasn't one of those conversations. Those conversations were rare for Courtney, like finding a four leaf clover out in a field of mostly three leaf ones. It just sometimes happened, I would not be surprised if Courtney was sugarcoating by saying she really enjoys hearing everything I have to say. Yet, I would be immensely if she really meant it. It would highlight how I am not as mature as I believe myself to be.

I heard the doorbell ring. "It's for me!!" I screamed, hoping my father wouldn't show up to the door with a shotgun pointed at the poor person unlucky enough to be sent to this house. My brother Miles came out of his 'dungeon' to see who was at the door. He was very timid, and didn't like unexpected guests, yet Courtney was always an exception. They bonded particularly well. If I've allowed anyone in this house the opportunity to get close to her, it's him. Even then, at a safe distance. You never know what to expect from a Hansen. "Tommy, whose at the door?" "Oh, sorry Miles, didn't mean to startle you out of your work. It's just the pizza guy." "No worries, I was more alarmed when Courtney walked in because I didn't hear her little innocent knocks. Anywho, would you like me to get that?"

"I would love that actually, but what's with the glasses dork? You only wear those when you work on-oh! Good job buddy. I will be helping you tomorrow, keep your schedule open." "Will do, little heathen. And hi Courtney, it's always a pleasure to see your beautiful smile. You're a lantern that Dante Alighieri wished he had when walking alone through the dark forest." "Can you stop making a move on my girl you goofball, can you please get the pizza? I will grant you a slice if you succeed. It's already paid for, you just need to sign it for me." "You can't bring a girl, a woman, who looks like that into this house and not expect me to flatter her. I'm sorry Tommy but damn, look at you! And look at her! The math doesn't add up! But I'll be right back." Miles ran to the door with swiftness under his feet. Courtney laughed, then said "I think you're quite handsome, especially those ocean eyes. They're magnificent to look at." Miles trotted back up the stairs with despair in his eyes, he said "goddamn, I've forgotten how bad I am at talking to people. Jeez, I'm some sort of stuttering freak! Anywho here's your food. I'm taking a piece of this chocolate cake by the way." "Don't tell me that, take that up to the hungry and bloodthirsty food gremlin sitting next to me. Courtney, can Miles take a piece of your cake?" Fire glossed over her dilated eyes, she definitely did not want to, but her compassion rose above her child-like inclination to not share with others. "Sure, Miles, here you go. Thank you for grabbing the food, it was very generous, I hope you enjoy your slice of my cake. Because my love will soon find out he may not receive one if I eat this thing in one whole. Sorry in advance, honeybun." I shrugged, content with letting her have it. As annoying as it sounds, even saying out loud, anything that made her happy made me just as happy. "Well you two have a good night, I'm going to get back to the books. Tommy, I hope to see you tomorrow in there with me. We have some updates to discuss." "Yes sir, brother, I will be there bright and early after I escort Courtney out the door. By the way, have you seen Darren?" "Hmm, I had my door closed so I'm not sure. He may be out and about. Alright I'm off to bed. Goodnight Tommy, Goodnight Courtney." "Goodnight Miles, I love you," I responded. He nodded, not usually comfortable with saying 'I love you' in return. Whenever I probed him about it he just said, "nothing in life is really ours, we just borrow it until it's gone. So to say I love someone or something that doesn't belong to me doesn't make much sense. I care about things, including you, but to love means you long for that thing when you lose it. I choose to avoid that burden."

Courtney stuffed her face full of food, then said "Your brother is an interesting person, I don't know which of the twins I like better though. Miles is a sweetheart, but there's something about your other brother that's oddly compelling. He has a way of swindling attention." I responded, "Yeah, because he's a full-blown narcissist. Darren is sort of interesting I guess, but his arrogance strikes down any chance of trying to understand him. Miles in my opinion is the closest thing I have to a real brother, he looks out for me, even if quietly among the introverted shadows he dwells in." "That's a good analysis, subjectively though, the more promiscuous of the two is Darren. He reeks of ambition mixed with ambivalence.....I wonder what fuels a guy like that!" *You don't even no want to know, darling.* As we uncomfortably continued chatting about my family, we both heard an extremely loud tire screech, more like a rubber meets the road moment, followed by what sounded like a bumper being punished by a curb. I kept my attention on the TV screen, eating pizza while watching anime with my hopefully future wife was worth more than checking out where the sound came from. I'm only human after all. Courtney however, being the angel she was born to be, asked me in the softest tone imaginable, "Tommy, wh-what was that? That sounded scaryyy, like a cat entering the dark then it itself becomes the darkness. Eeek! We should listen to more Fleetwood Mac by the way, just saying, you could use some culture." "You and your ADD, I think whoever just crashed their car will be fine. They will learn a lesson to not drive like a dipshit every-time they ride through a neighborhood." Courtney's eyebrows rose high enough to touch her hairline when she heard jumbled screaming coming from the direction of where the fender bender occurred. She didn't say a word, only continuing to eat her pizza with surmounting hopes that her big strong boyfriend would go check it out while she stayed comfortably in bed. The wife is always right, I suppose. "Courtney I hope you know I'm not going outside, whatever demagogue monster got them isn't going to get me. It's okay darling, I'm sure they're probably just irate that their new Chevrolet's bumper is now permanently connected to the curb." "You really have resistance to leaving this room, don't you? I bet I could make you leave quite easily...." Courtney said teasingly. "Oh yeah, how?" "Well it's too late now, whatever has gotten him has long devoured his carcass. All I will say is I would've done anything you wanted, but oh well." She giggled as I leapt on her and tickled her until submission. I could have died right there from the amount of joy I was feeling. It felt extremely unnatural. I received intense anxiety about the prospect of one day losing this joy. It seemed so irrational to not enjoy every second of this bliss in front of me, but my body reacted as if I was struck down by lightning. The anxiety was tranquilizing.

We played, then played some more. I was unsure if this intense paranoia would go away, I felt primal. Like some predator of the jungle was endangering me. I don't know why I sensed so much danger near us, I held Courtney tightly as we laid in bed. She was able to sleep peacefully as she had no guilty conscience of her actions on any day. She is the product of a parent who taught her acceptance, and to never relish in one's choices. I, on the other hand, struggled to see past that cliff-note that had befallen me when we were tickling each other. Why was the most joyous moments in my life always followed by extreme pitfalls into the dark and dreary abyssal fissure splitting the hemispheres of my brain. I played with Courtney's hair while she slept, telling myself it was my mission to give this girl anything she needed. Because she is one of the only few people to have ever seen true happiness expressed on my face. I prayed this feeling would never go away, and that the anxiety begrudgingly following it would. I looked out at my window, pondering on what my brother could be up to right now.

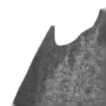

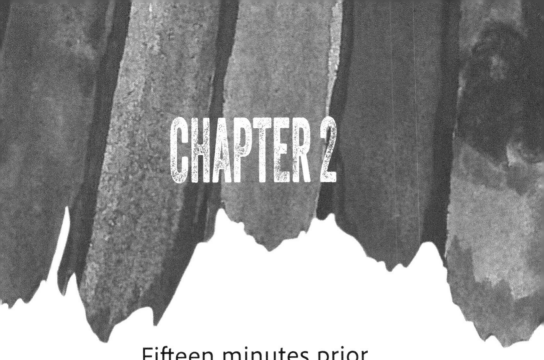

CHAPTER 2

Fifteen minutes prior

"What a stupid, privileged prick that man is, how could he not tip me. You live in a HOUSE jackass, you can't scrape together a few dollars, damn. I live in a small hovel with my whole family, and still manage to pay the tip. People are just growing more and more disrespectful by the second," James the delivery driver uttered, reversing his restored Corvette out of the Hansens driveway with shooting star speed. The trees seemed to wave him good riddance. His mind was focused on returning home to indulge in a twelve pack of Corona Lime while watching 'WWE meets Hollywood.' As he shifted into fifth gear, his tires squealed like pigs sent to the slaughterhouse. James lost control of his car and in return, swerved straight into the curb. A sole lamppost stood above the commotion, watching from above like a parent with their arms crossed into their chest, watching while their child sneaks their fingers in the cookie jar. James was livid, he exited his car kicking and screaming like that same child whose cookie was taken away from them. "Are you serio-shit! Shit shit! Of course this would happen to me, what the hell even happened?!" He investigated the front and rear tires, to his disbelief, a jagged piece of glass was wedged into his driver side tire. The trees waved even harder, an omnipotent presence stood about thirty meters from James's car, observing the commotion they had caused. During James' violent outburst, the presence crept closer. Only moving in a motion that required the most minimal movement.

It acted as a shadow cast from a fireplace, only moving when the fire allowed it to. Darren was inept in overtaking his prey, his shadowy figure was not noticed until James spun in circles from his outburst. It was then he noticed the looming doom pursing him. Darren stood there, unmoved by James' erratic display. He could have lost his kid in that car and it would all the same to Darren. He did not care for trivial matters, especially people exerting their insufferable emotions onto him. *Eeeek.* He wondered why people cry when they are about to die, why can they not just accept the fate the gods have bestowed upon them? "Who the fuck are you?! Did you do this to my car?? You son of a bitch, I'll run you over right now!" Darren considered the possibility of what if he was trying to help him, surely his slander would've been unwarranted. This notion gave him enough validation to label this murder under the category of 'justified' in his demented eyes. The hooded phantom remained motionless, this silhouette was studying its surroundings to ensure no passerby's witnessed the hell he was about to unleash onto this ignorant, imbecilic insect. As James observed the shadow man, the urge to run away blossomed in his brain. Darren gazed blankly at James, pondering on how wonderful his face would look attached to his mask. In his vision, young adults were better than middle-aged men whose skin was already wrinkling. James felt very unnerved by how Darren just stood there, observing his prey like a shark swimming around a diver in a cage. When Darren stepped into the lamplight, showing his skin-stitched mask to James, he yelled back, "Alright you win you-you freak! I'm out of here!" James jumped back into his car and locked the doors behind him. "What-what even was that thing! Was that a mask? It looked like someone's face got ran over by a tractor! Jeez, I-I need to call the poli-AHHHHHHH!" The rest is silent, as Hamlet said before death. The last thing James saw was Darren's shadowy presence slither towards him then thrust his crowbar into his driver side window. After which, Darren did what he believed god sent him down here to do, murder with illicit efficiency. This poor delivery driver stood no chance against a man who has killed more people than the amount of women who have slept with Hugh Hefner. The autumn leaves began to fall and land on James' car. Darren picked one up, then crumbled it within his hand. He let the remnants sail away from his hand back into the breeze like James's spirit back into the Garden of Eden. He inhaled deeply, in a state of walking meditation. His mind was filled to the brim with apathy, the only concern persistent was getting this individual into his house without seeming suspicious. Darren did what he did best, he adapted to the situation.

Darren began to whistle as he disposed of James' car down in the valley in front of the neighborhood across the street. While on his walk back, he tossed his pizza GPS locator into the pond right outside the neighborhood across the street's entrance. Darren walked idly with James hoisted over his shoulders in trash bags he brought with him in his backpack. He looked like one of those hikers climbing the alps with their entire arsenal loaded on their backs. The midnight mist emitted serenity. Darren found pleasure in strolling through the fog, watching it part ways as his legs churned forward like a locomotive without a conductor. He made his way up to his parent's bathroom. It truly was a beautiful bathroom, that's why Darren always runs his baths in here. He believed the serendipity received from the vibes this room produced was hitherto the Devil recharging his batteries down in the depths of hell. The lit frankincense sticks reminded Darren of how the ancient Babylon's would offer heaping amounts of incense to their God's for good grace in the year ahead. Similarly, Darren used his bath time to call upon the Parthenon of Gods, not the ones outside our realm however, the ones dwelling within his subconscious. Darren was a Carl Jung enthusiast, which spoke volumes considering he respected people very little in general. He was on the Genghis Khan train of thought, viewing most 'civilized' people as nothing more than mindless cattle. Sheepishly shopping for the newest products and expensive experiences. Living their whole lives in a sort of a hamster wheel rotation, the 'tail wagging the dog' as Dan Carlin would say.

Nonetheless, the moonlight outside glistened over the porcelain bathtub. The magic of the moonlight cast a contagious white light onto the rims of the tub. Once the array of Yankee and Fire-wick candles were lit; it created a creamy dream within the candle bowls. Bats outside screeched with intensity, emitting their propensity of echolocation everywhere they went as Darren proceeded to run his bath with the bags of blood he acquired from his freshest kill. The bloody bags rested along the white porcelain bath rim, labeled "James the Delivery Driver." He pinned his name tag on the empty bag on top of the closest door as a souvenir of sorts. James's face was too acne-ridden for Darren to consider it useful, the joy of taking his life was a token enough. Darren began humming 'Cool Cat' by Queen; he really admired Freddy Mercury. Darren did not understand his 'way of life' when it came to dating men, however, his love for his artistic excellence triumphed any partisan feelings he possesses. Darren continued to hum while dumping his final bag of blood into the bathtub, even singing through the high notes which were his favorite parts of the song. He found his music soothing to the ears, as with the wonderful Adele. When Darren dumped the blood into the tub, the bathtub's color went from crystal clear to blistering red in seconds. The color of Crimson glided across the slick transparency pulling a thick, velvet curtain over the tub's curve-less edges. Darren dumped the final bag down to its last drop. He started from miserable, went to musical, then to whimsical the moment he entered into the tub. Like the night finally changing into daytime after ages of no sunshine. The curtains swayed back and forth, dancing to the tune of the music the wind outside produced. Darren stared at the ceiling without regard of his past or future, only observing this present moment.

The frankincense burned with intense vigor for what seemed like infinity, like time never existed to begin with. This frozen-in-amber moment was blissful. James's blood was still somewhat warm, how Darren liked it most. He started seeing stars on the bathroom ceiling, when he submerged, he experienced peak euphoria. The tale of Elizabeth Báthory sprung up in his daydream, the very tale that inspired his mother, then himself, to attempt this temptation. She proclaimed about her ability to retain her youthful beauty by bathing in other people's blood. The 'Blood Countess,' as they called her, established an everlasting precedent for the wretched and demented. For the Darren Hansens within the population. After his first encounter with blood bathing, he made it a routine. A routine he soon became addicted to. It used to be a ritualistic muse, now it's more of an opioid he cannot control the craving for. Like a rabid vampire in search of someone's blood to suck, Darren was triggered to kill when he heard that initial knock on the door earlier. But, it was Courtney. However, he could no longer contain his urges when the door was knocked again. Yet this time, it was someone within his boundaries of killing. He feasted upon the opportunity to take James's bloody carcass back to the basement to be dissected, drained, then destroyed. For once in Darren's idle mind, he lacked control over his desires. A normally tightly wound assassin who disregarded people as nothing more than 'NPC's' found it increasingly troubling trying to withhold the urge to absorb every victim he slew. Darren's vision was kaleidoscopic, vibrant colors and glass shapes paraded around his peripheral without aim nor direction. His mind was an open abstraction, allowing all sorts of thoughts and possibilities to enter inside. He had passed completely into the Iris, he had experienced complete transcendence. The incense continued to burn slower by the second; time ceased to exist. At that standstill, with the thunder and rain pounding against the street, Darren achieved total peace. Albeit, a very fleeting peace. Any regular heroine user knows that chasing the dragon is always a mismatch against their favor. Yet, they will persist to try again and again, thinking perhaps this will be the time they can latch onto the fleeing beast. Darren opened his eyes while still submerged under the blood, unsure of whether anger or aggravation were the first emotions he was feeling. He had been blood bathing for so long that his 'tolerance' was too high to keep him high for long periods of time. His kaleidoscopic vision slowly lost its initial grandeur, there were no more beautiful streaks of colors or glass objects to look at, there was only red. He jumped out of the tub like a still-plugged-in toaster was thrown in there, spraying blood all along the outskirts of the white porcelain. Darren didn't care though, he scrubbed the tub clean each time his ritual was performed. His OCD would not allow him to leave behind a filthy bathroom, nor would his mother who takes great pride in keeping the house cleaner than spotless.

Darren looked like a red silhouette standing by the bathtub, he stared at himself through the mirror as if observing himself in third-person. He wished there were more mirrors in the bathroom so he could see himself in every direction he looked. The spider-web-shaped crack in the lower left half of the mirror caught Darren's attention. It showcased his own shattered self. His shattered soul gazed upon a reflection that correctly reflected itself. The scattered thoughts that continued to toss upon Darren's consciousness seemed to settle. He sought the root of his unnerving anxiety, to which he uncannily already knew the answer. Tommy. His intense paranoia reached its peak as he contemplated his options. The thunder outside screamed even louder, while the rain was much quieter, struck the shingles on the roof louder as well. Each drop touched upon the roof of this house like droplets of Darren's thoughts dropped on an open pond. Not causing roaring torrents, rather, idle inflections that spread across each domain of his uncharted body. While still dripping the color garnet onto the floor, Darren looked a little deeper into the incision within this slit of glass. He saw all the possibilities of Tommy sacking their great empire as Rome toppled Carthage or as the Mongols conquered the Khwarazmian's. The little shit just couldn't keep his mouth shut forever, Darren suspected. He suspended himself upside down in his mental lair as Count Dracula awaiting to suck the despair out of someone did. The possibilities ran endlessly, like his thoughts were on the longest walk. He had considered for twenty years how he could 'accidentally' get rid of his insolent brother. But within strife, he found the stride to triumph. Darren gazed at the separation of glass in between the broken mirror, seeing the culmination of the parts that make his brother whole. A flash of lightning gashed through the night sky, and inside Darren's mind. He did not need to even lay a finger on his brother to inflict terrible angst. He saw the pieces of Andre and Courtney connected elegantly to his brothers restoration. The boy who became more bold the more love he was given could be reformed back into the mortal man Darren saw him to be. To keep his angst at bay, he needed to instill into his brother that one misstep will take everything he's ever loved away. By no exaggeration. Darren did not care to stand on his brothers body when he had fallen down. He truly only saw the linear line of keeping his way of life in tact, by all cost. All measures, even if wearing your brother's girlfriend's face like a baklava to show you're just as much of an animal as a leopard or a great white shark. Those thoughts did not depart him, Darren thought long and hard about his previous strategy. He realized he did not even need to murder his own brother to set the precedent. In all his years of experience, he learned that he could kill someone without actually inflicting death upon them. Darren rinsed himself off in the shower neighboring the bloody bathtub. Now that his ritual was complete, he could commence his comedown. His trip leaped off of a tall balcony before the shower anyhow, yet consider a massive meteor colliding into the moon, causing fragments to spew in every direction. To this effect, he was condensing an already determined catastrophe into something more manageable.

His hatred radiated off his body, piercing through the veil of atmosphere around him like an infrared beam through a crystal prism. Within the roaring torrent of his intense anger, he remained stoic, refusing to budge and give into his emotions like the once great Spartans. Darren continued humming 'Cool Cat' from earlier, except this time, singing instead of humming. Each note Freddie Mercury hit was bliss incarnate, Darren joined in when he got to the part where he said "you used to be a mean kid, making such a deal of life. You were wishing and hoping and waiting to really hit the big time. But did it happen? Happen? Nooooooo." Darren tried his best to hum on par to the great Mercury, but understood that he was the king of killing, not singing. However, he did like hearing his voice. Darren was a man who believed expression was everything. Even if it regards releasing your inner femininity once in a blue moon, he highly valued expressing who he truly was within outwards into the outskirts of reality. The four years he had been idle were harder than any other task he'd accomplished. It would be dangerous to say that within their 'hiatus' they did not occasionally take lives in their free time. Yet, their return was like Rome converting the Republic into an imperial empire. Shedding the dead wood was necessary to achieve the fruits of their labor. The prospect of almost getting caught that fateful night shook Darren and his father intensely. Enough to make them quit for a little while, but like asking a shark to become vegetarian, it just wasn't in their nature to change their ways. To be docile towards other humans was not within their rubric of living life.

Darren continued to sing in the shower, allowing his revelations to wash over him like the rain outside. The storm was still going on strong without any chance of dying down soon. Darren consumed his hubris for a moment and considered that Tommy was a worthy opponent. To treat him like the 'cattle' he encountered when on murder sprees was endearing, but not very helpful. Darren understood that Tommy was created from the same flesh, bones, soul and blood intertwined within his system. Anything he could do, theoretically, Tommy could to. Darren could never admit to his brother that he actually admired him, he admired killers, yet also admired resilient leaders. He knew his brother was one of those latter half individuals. To even be Salutatorian while coming home to deal with a family like theirs was commendable in Darren's book, even if he disregarded all forms of education brought upon by the school system. "The place where artist and abominably average people develop their insatiable hatred for life" as Darren often told Tommy. He did not find school to be an institution that fostered any real form of creativity or intellectual thinking. That's why he didn't show up to accept his award for 'excellence in the classroom.' Why would he? He believed all people should strive for excellence, what does a paper plaque have anything to do with that? Does that laminated piece of paper make him richer or get up quicker every morning? Needless to say, he threw it away when it was given to him in class the following day. He despised the participation trophy era he was conceived in. He wished he was a part of the gladiator age in Rome or riding on horseback alongside Alexander the Great while jamming his spearhead into the chest of Acheminid's in abundance. Darren wished to be a part of a century that allowed killing as commonly as the ancient civilizations did. One day, he believed, that metropolis would be achieved. Anarchy is always an option, not just an obvious result of chaos. This thin veneer of reality surrounding humanity could easily be dismantled. Just like Heath Ledger in the Dark Knight revealed, "madness is like gravity, all it takes is a little push". Darren admired the character Heath portrayed greatly. Not so much so he wanted to be like him, yet, he viewed his ideology upon condensing the joker's uncontrollable chaos into a more controlled and calculated version. Among other inspirations, Darren kept that quote in his heart. While he didn't consider himself mad, he agreed with the sentiment it presented. He believed all people were inherently born with the desire to conquer and kill. With the cultivation of civilization however, people have become socially inept to others feelings and grievances. Darren cannot stand this, in his words, 'soft population.' Where were the remnants of the greatest generation? Was any semblance of the great Achaemenid Persian or Roman Empire still alive in our time? He thought not. He turned the shower off at this final thought. Darren accepted his place in this generation, he would be a modern-day Achilles without the weakness of being dipped into the river Styx. Darren viewed his whole essence enveloped by the Styx, even around the Achilles tendon. He grasped the concept of taking other people's life, yet never his own in return. In his brain, that day would never come. Until it does, what is there to convince him otherwise that he is undeniably impervious to anything life had to offer. He walked the earth as a God walked among a Parthenon.

After his long shower, he invested more time into looking at himself in the mirror before declaring "If that cock-sucking cockroach continues to stand in my way, I will step on him so quickly he won't feel a thing! Let's continue this charade with grace shall we?" Darren smiled, not widely up to his eyes to indicate real happiness, but as more of a reflection of what he wishes to feel. Some say to force a smile upon your face can rewire your brain into producing more "happy chemicals." As most "woo-woo" beliefs Darren came across, he disregarded it. But as time went on, he found himself still trying to bring that damned smile across his clean cut face. This was not Patrick Bateman peeling back the mask of sanity, this was someone embracing their evil face. This is who he truly was deep down in the darkest part of his heart. Darren grabbed a Mr. Clean sponge from under the sink where his mother kept all of the toiletries and began scrubbing the bathtub clean. He was still smiling, but less forcefully than before. He emitted gratefulness for another day of murder without warrant, hoping another twenty years of this lifestyle would treat him better the more it progressed. He considered his addiction more of a motivation rather than a hindrance. Yet as all men must learn, a man's ambition must never exceed his capabilities. Winston, in 'John Wick Four,' believes in worth rather than capacity of capabilities. Some individuals would argue otherwise. Ask Genghis Khan if his worth as a fatherless child when he was abandoned by his tribe and left to die was exceeded by his ambition. If anything, his low worth created his ambition. Nonetheless, they both still stand. For Darren to continue killing with considerable carelessness, he needed to excel in every other avenue and keep these rules in his back pocket. Because, if not, who knows when rubber meets the road. His momentum may move him rather than the other way around. The gravity of being pulled into a situation is much graver when you cannot change its course or direction.

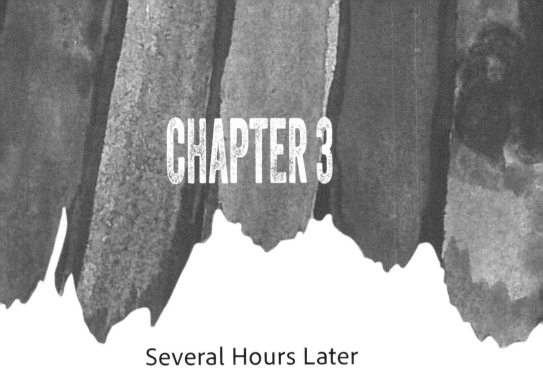

CHAPTER 3

Several Hours Later

Courtney slept so peacefully, I wish I could have entered inside her mind and seen what she was dreaming about. Maybe about the clouds, or perhaps frolicking throughout a field filled with sunflowers (her favorite flower). Her little nose crinkled as I got out of bed to let out a midnight tinkle. I wondered if she was playing with a little bunny or a unicorn while in dreamland. The rain outside definitely added to the sleepy tension littered around my room, I had trouble leaving my door let alone reaching the bathroom because I was still so drowsy. The mental taxation of keeping my sanity in place almost became too great some days, yet like a noble knight who must fight even when death is standing inside their door-frame, I pushed forth. Through the groggy haze, I peed a little on my toilet seat. *Doesn't everyone?* I thought. Before I was able to lay back in bed, I heard the sound of saw blades going to town on what I presumed to be something strong enough to resist its teeth. "Darren," I mumbled, uncertain of if it was worth journeying downstairs to discover what ungodly nonsense he was up to at this hour. I heard Courtney jolt awake as if being shocked with a stun gun, which made me angry that the visit to her peaceful kingdom was breached. I went back to my room and told her it was just me peeing, and consoled her back to sleep. If it weren't for the TV blasted on max volume, then she perhaps would have heard the horrible noise eroding my eardrums. Yet she went back to peace. I was almost envious of how elegant Courtney was created to be. Completely overshadowing me, who was created with insatiable angst and anguish. She was the light, and the joyful child looking for it when the night arises. I decided to be brave and investigate the noise so I would not have to worry about my queen being interrupted from her slumber once more. I felt like Dante and Virgil entering the inferno, I knew better than to go down into 'Darren's Lair.' He was prone to keep things there that made the hair on my hands and neck stand up. But keeping my queen asleep was more important than my anxiety. The wrath of her being awoken once more or worse, discovering Darren down in his lair, was too much of a consequence to risk allowing that to happen.

The staircase banister boards moaned as my feet touched them. I swept them quickly to condense the creaking, yet that endeavor did not pan out as I expected. I created a xylophone of plank boards, bringing an odd ringing in my ears as I made my way to the basement door. It was ajar of course, Darren has the consideration level of a toddler who just discovered the word "mine!" He could have just closed the door and saved us both the trouble, but that's not how my brother did things. He is usually more uniform in his approach, only accommodating himself while not wasting a spare second considering the needs of other individuals. To Darren, Galileo might as well developed heliocentrism around him instead! I passed by the giant bookshelf bordering the walls near the garage door. I would be lying if I didn't add that I stopped for a quick glance. It wasn't common that I came downstairs. I reveled in Darren's new books and the ones stolen from under my bed. "That little bastard," I muttered under my breath. My breathing was reaching increasingly intense speed, the same speed Julius Caesar displayed against the Roman's during their Civil War as a matter of fact. I had a bad feeling about what I would find Darren doing down here in the middle of the night. The lights were not turned on, he preferred to work in the dark. Alone, he was only accompanied by a candlelight. That made my endeavor of entering his lair all the more unsettling. I tiptoed through the corridors hoping he would not hear me. I did not want to startle a serial killer with a saw in their hands, there's only so many options they'd choose to do with it.

"Darren... wha-what are you doing? You do realize you left the door open, right? If Courtney finds out what you all have done...... then we're fuc..." He stopped sawing whatever he was carving into, I could not see through the darkness to discover what exactly it was. He calmly put the saw blade down, I couldn't see it but I could hear the light tap of the blade hitting the chestnut desk he kept in there. He said "Shut your stupid mouth Thomas, why did you even bring that tramp inside of our home? Do you want us to be discovered!?" The dim candlelight provided enough illumination for his smile to carve through the darkness. "Can you just keep it down? I don't have the energy to deal with this. For both of our sake, it would be best if we did not get caught. I say 'we' loosely, I'm bound by blood to you guys, not by actions. What are you even doing anyways? It smells horrible down here, like you doused a dead deer in detergent." "Don't worry about it, I will have my little project out of here by dawn. Killing isn't as easy as it used to be, once a fiery passion now feels like throwing coal into a locomotion to keep it going. You wouldn't understand the dedication it takes to be great if it smacked you over the head with a bombing strafe. What makes you think you can come down here and tell me what to do? You are the little black lamb inside this family, never forget your place. You're lucky I don't go up there and have fun with your woman, there's not a damn thing you could do to stop me, Thomas. I'm like Genghis Khan and the Mongols, if I wanted your queen she would be mine. Her face would make a great addition to my collection." I crinkled my fingers into a fist, ready to erupt with a volley of punches on my dumb-ass brother. While restraining my anger, I replied, "Courtney wouldn't sleep with you even if you were the last person with a dick in this universe. Stop saying that shit, I will never let any of you touch her. She stays out of this!" "Thomas..... I could walk into your room right now and have my way with your woman. And what? What could you possibly do to stop me? Hit me? Thomas, if you ever touch me, so much as look at me unwarranted, I will beat your face into your brain with my baseball bat while you watch me take your sweet ride for a spin. Don't get cocky. I'm still your big brother. Anything you have is because I allow it." I tried to close the discussion. "Okay, not-so-grim reaper, I'm going back to sleep. All I'm saying is keep it down, and if you ever harass my queen then you will make a killer out of me." Intrigued, he responded, "Is that a challenge, Thomas? You know..... a good game of cat and mouse is too much to pass up on. Okay, riddle me this, why don't we wager over this matter like men. I say you keep trying to find a way to bring me and the family down, while I diligently pursue you as a good tomcat would a bunch of pesky little mice. If I catch you though, I will kill everyone you love until you're the only one left. How's that sound? You know, you can still stay out of our affairs if you want to. It'll be much more blissful for you if you just let go. You've been a bystander for so long, why don't you go back up to your room and be grateful I have no reason to kill you yet." I contemplated long and hard about my choice following his words, maybe it was me being increasingly tired of everyone telling me to shut up and not express myself like my feelings are not worth a damn. I ran away from intimacy with Courtney because I could bear sharing this despair with anyone other than myself, and because of that, I suffered in silence, forced to live a life of quiet desperation. For years I've sat in my room and accepted who my family is and what has become of my life. But within this moment of slightly intense anger, mixed with confidence of a long-standing notion to express myself in my entirety, I said "Shut the hell up you stupid bastard, your own mother doesn't even love you. You wanna play, let's play. Have fun sitting in a jail cell forever you maggot, you'll be eaten by a bunch of your own kind when you die! I'm not afraid of you any-more. If you guys weren't so insatiably insufferable to live under the same roof as, maybe you would have outlasted a life of serving time for your crimes but nooo. You're all awful, you deserve to burn in hell for what you've done. Jail isn't enough, but it's a start. You're on, I'm so sick of your shit! Your brilliance and your ambition will not be your downfall, your ten-foot-tall belief in yourself will be!" Darren paused before replying. "We will see, I believe in myself so much I have already given you and Miles a head start, I hope you didn't think I wasn't dumb enough to uncover your boy's little 'murder board.' Your brother likes to leave his door unlocked when he brings that little bitch Meghan around for dinner. You could never contend with me, it is you Thomas who should have shut up and stayed in his room. You have no idea what I am capable of, do you still accept the terms of our wager? You are still allowed to bow out by all means. Would you like to be a king who continues ruling, or a once-great warrior who lays buried in the dirt. It's your choice." "It's not really much of a wager, it's basically the same game we are already playing. Except now there have been consequences laid out before the both of us. I step away from your territory mostly, as you do to mine. Yet this evil is beginning to ruin my life, I can't just stand by any longer. Goodnight Darren, you still have a chance, too. It's never too late to change your ways. There's always a choice to be made. No matter how far astray from the original destination you've gone."

Darren stared at me through the candlelight flame, unsure if any more words were warranted. A usually stoic person, Darren only spoke more regularly when irate or sparked with interest. Instead of turning on the saw again, he pulled out his hacksaw. Within the crackling flame, my brother grinned a little. Not enough to exhibit any positive emotion, it seemed to me as more of a 'you've become a worthy adversary, someone worthy of my respect, little brother.' As I walked up the dark dungeon stairs, Darren startled me by saying "Not all those who wander are lost, Thomas, but all those that drop are not promised to return to their feet," before slipping into the darkness again. I did not want to be unnerved, but I was. I did not understand why my pride screamed louder than my humility. Gambling with a human gremlin seemed stupider then traveling to Jupiter with no space suit on! Yet an uncanny confidence also sat amongst my shivering heart, almost eighteen years of this torture has made my patience dwindle remarkably thin. Especially now to have more to lose than ever before, it's different when it's just me. But to believe Darren would kill my friend and girlfriend over the slightest indifference was an understatement. I counted on it. Even with all this knowledge, I did not care. I could no longer be a canary inside of a cage, I desired to be set free. If they wanted to kill again, then I would have to take it upon myself to stop them. Even when the odds were against my favor, and despite the cost. Darren did not ask me to a game of cat and mouse, he signed me up for a series of life or death. The best of seven seemed to be the winner. I heard a quote once that "The bad guy had to get lucky all the time, the good guy just needed to be lucky once." Probably a drastic misquote, but the notion still stands. I bet against my brother because sadly, I am a product of this environment. Instead of feeling the need to cry and vent, I kept myself from bending out of shape. The insidious creature dwelling inside the dungeon my heart harbors wanted to be released. As much as I differed in every way from my family, I was also just as much like them then apart. I challenged my brother tonight because for once in my life... well... I wanted a fight.

I dragged my feet up the staircase step until I reached the bedroom. Courtney was still sleeping, as elegant as can be. I slept at the foot of the bed so I did not awake my sleeping beauty. Also, a part of me was daunted by what Darren had said about taking my woman. As much as the beast wanted to be unleashed, I very much was still afraid of my brother. His capability time and time again deters me from uprising. He has the capacity for Assyrian level evil without so much as blinking to even see what he has done. While my good soul chose to discern his derogatory comments as mere insults rather than facts, my inner monster made me sit on the edge of the bed like a dog or a leopard on a tree. Guarding the best thing to happen to me with my life as a mere passerby. I had trouble falling back asleep, my brain kept replaying our conversation over and over again. I have now taken it upon myself to be the hero in my own story, even if it leaves me bleeding in the streets like Superman after battling Doomsday to the gruesome end.

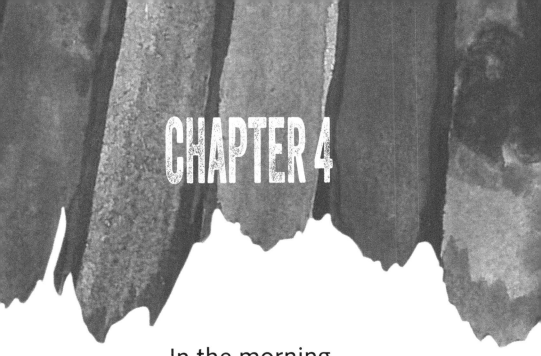

CHAPTER 4

In the morning

After a wonderful morning of lovemaking, I escorted Courtney out of the front door. The doves did indeed sing along. She felt like I was rushing her out of the door, which I was, but I persuaded her that I wasn't. I elaborated by saying I would be seeing Andre today. She did not appreciate me choosing Andre over her, yet she understood. I said before opening the front door, "Courtney we hung out all night. I will see you again tonight, alright? See, that's only an afternoon of loneliness." She kissed my cheek then replied, "Yet, every minute is loneliness without you.... my dear. Goodbye Tommy, I hope tomorrow morning maybe you'll sleep in with me. Perhaps I'll be more in the mood for that thing you wanted to try..... See ya!" I couldn't stop smiling as I closed the door. If she was normally the stars that light up the night, today, she was lightning! It made me sad to see her go, but I put my foot down on today being the day I decide to show Andre what my life is really like. I've avoided it for four years and taken a lot of nonsense to avoid speaking about it. But now. It's time. I made sure Darren was away at work before I called Andre. I don't really know what he did at work, all I know is he came home looking rugged and covered in dirt every evening. He usually wore a neon zip-up that had sweat stains swimming downwards starting from the armpit area. *What a grungy person*, I thought.

Andre finally answered after the last ringtone came on. He seemed to forget our proposal from yesterday. He said, "Come over? For what?" I reminded him of our conversation from yesterday and it hit him like the light of day. "Ohhh yeah, my bad bro, I'm high on mushrooms right now. I forgot you brought that up." I replied "I didn't bring it up, you did you goof after ringing me out, what was that all about? I know I didn't answer your friend for a couple days but damn. You really went cold turkey on me real quick. "Yeah... sorry bro. I had to show you the Brooklyn side of me real quick. I love you, you're my favorite friend. But leaving your girl/ my other best friend on 'delivered' all damn day until she begs me to ask you what she did wrong is obviously a problem. You don't get to just pop in and out of people's life when you feel like it Tommy. That shit hurts. You do realize both Courtney and I don't know where the hell our real fathers are? We are the product of abandonment; don't you dare put us through that shit again. I'm sorry to be so hard. Just stop running away from us. Okay? If you desire loneliness then just say so, don't lead us on a rope just to force us off the plank. We deserve better than that." I bit my tongue, instead of justifying my actions. I wanted to show him so he could determine for himself that if my absence was worthy instead. I said "You're right, Andre. I will not walk out again, even if I did so to keep you away from certain annihilation. Come over, let me show you what I've been hiding for four years from you and my future wife." "Future wife? Sheesh! If you keep disappearing into the veil, then I may need to gain a taste for white woman and take your queen to a kingdom beautiful enough to be inside her dreams! You're on a fine line, mister!" "Yeah, but I also got game. I maybe unnecessarily introverted sometimes, but this guy got some good-good last night even when his girl was mad at him minutes before. Boom. Eat that Andre!" "Ew, gross, I don't want to imagine my two best friends having sex. That's gross. Have you considered she perhaps used you for your sword then sheathed it back in its place when she didn't need it anymore. You know, I bet you she's still mad at you." "You really think so?" "Of course, she's still mad at you?! Are you stupid? Goodness gracious you are gullible, you really better have a good excuse so Courtney doesn't kill either of us. Hell hath no fury like a woman scorned, you tool!" I pleaded, "Nooo! Courtney cannot know about this, what I'm showing you today is between you and I. Andre please, do not tell her. You think she's mad at me now? Holy hell if I tell her this then I'm screwed! I can't, not yet. I have to play my cards safe." "You're really going to risk losing the most perfect girl in the world for your inability to be a man and tell her something straight? That's ridiculous, Tommy, however, I will do my best to matador your mad bull back towards the other direction." I couldn't tell if the mushrooms were talking or if Andre was really speaking from his sober heart. Either way, it rung several bells inside my head. The intense pressure to be this perfect man for Courtney momentarily subsided, allowing me to finally see the full horizon. How stupid was I to wonder if someone would still love me for being a part of a situation I did not ask to be involved with. The guilt I possessed was mountainous, so much so, I felt as if I was just as bad as the murderers themselves. Yet, as Courtney shined a light into my dark room, Andre too shined bright. Allowing me to see past the seething darkness for longer than usual.

"I'm excited for you to come over, my friend, I hope your words stand against the test. I hope you don't run from me either when I reveal who I really am." "You're the one prone to running, I will not leave under any circumstances. I might revile you for a while, but Tommy, you're my best friend. Maybe I'm the dumb one, but no matter what you do I'll always forgive you. As long as you didn't punch a woman or something then we'd maybe have to exchange hands first." "No.... I can promise it's not that. Just come over you buffoon, this has been a ten-minute conversation that could have been condensed to two if you just hurried up." "You act like I haven't been getting dressed already, chilll, I'm sorry I forgot. You and your girlfriend have made me go crazy these past few days. Let's get this over with so I can determine what is the damage control." "Probably too high for me to pay, Andre. But nonetheless, it's finally time. Whether you stay or flee is not up to me, I have to put this out of my hands." "Okay, brother, I'm proud of you for opening up. You're a very reclusive person, it's one of the qualities I like most about you. But you're a real nuisance when shit hits the fan, your introvert-ism is a true boomerang sometimes. I'm on my way though, sorry it took so long, I didn't realize talking on the phone while getting dressed is more time consuming than it seems. I'll be there soon." I ended the call. My stomach quivered, I'm sure my kidneys and liver could feel the seismic shift within my intestines. For the first time ever, I would let someone see my world in its entirety. Not another drop of lying would be needed after I showed him who my family was.

I ran to Miles door and knocked the beginning portion of Mozart's Requiem so he knew it was me. It was customary of us to knock in a familiar rhythm, the other members of our family have a tendency to barrage rather than knock anyhow. "Tommy, glad to see you buddy. Are you ready to get star-" "I'm inviting Andre over to show him the murder board, I know you're going to be irate. But just listen, I can't lose him or my girl because of them. If I have to let them in to keep them then there's no debate. Once upon a time there was, but not anymore." Miles looked at me with wide, Anime-like eyes. He seemed unable to produce an answer. My dumbfounded brother gazed at the ground and said "I hope you know what you're getting yourself into... what you're getting them into. If anyone discovers that they know then our family will not hesitate to slay them! You think I would ever tell Meghan? Hell no. I-I-I don't know about this one Tommy. You know what happened to Rome after it gave up on its fundamentals? It crumbled. We've survived, and the people we love survive because of the laws we follow. To break that cycle, you might cause a downward spiral. Just like Mimir told Kratos after killing Heimdall in God of War Ragnarok, 'I don't know if we're breaking fate, or if fate's breaking us.' Be wary." I responded, "Isn't breaking fate a good thing? This 'fate' we're in has made us miserable? We have seen things no human should have. How come I get to watch every god damn parent pick up their kids from school while I walk home wondering why the hell mine don't love me enough to, or see families sit at the dinner table eating together through the car window while I'm forced to watch my family embark on a killing spree! Tell me, where's your fate there, huh? How come your god who arranged this fate can't even show his face and explain why! Screw fate, I am changing it. What has fate ever done for us?" Miles considered, then responded. "Given us the opportunity to be better.

By fate's terms, we should be killers too. But we're not, why is that? Did we earn that, or was that given to us from something beyond our comprehension? You tell me, then we can discuss what fate has done. Our situation sucks, no shit. But they're people who suffer everywhere. Especially in America. How do you think someone like our Dad is even created? Imagine you're sent to fight in a war that does no good for you, only your government. You can't even say your country because that would imply the people who inhabit it would benefit. But they didn't. Life is always fifty shades of grey, never black and white. Yet I can confidently say this society played a part in how a violent, insatiable, 'oppressed since his day of birth' man would behave in this day and age. Don't be so benign is all I'm saying, fate is like a spiderweb, it's not linear. God gives you a spirit to have free will and the ability to live with your choices. Whether good or bad. Dad could've turned out very differently, so can you, so can I. Hitler was once a poor postcard painter, with no particular special qualities. It was only when he served in the First World War, and saw how Germany was treated after the war that made this borderline imbecile turn into a rabid fascist capable of mass destruction. It takes one bad day to become insane. I don't want you involving Andre, Tommy, but I can't tell you what to do. Just like how you put your trust in me, I put mine in you. You're the only one I can trust in this house. Proceed with caution at all times." "You can trust me Miles, I'm not making a lighthearted decision. It's a decisive one. I need those two, they're the best.." "Just don't let your feelings override your intelligence. Like Bertram Russell said, 'a man cannot be expected to walk a tightrope forever.' Don't fall Thomas." "Are you just a quote fountain today or are you on mushrooms again?" He interjected, "Hey! Psilocybin is a medicine! Not a drug! Show some respect! I feel like the freaking Buddha right now, my partner and I have made groundbreaking research with 'magic mushrooms.' We tried LSD but it is too intense on the brain for long term use. Mushrooms are so much better. You should try it sometime, I bet it would change your life." I retorted, "I can't believe you're even a scientist you drug addict, I will stick to my marijuana, thank you very much though. I'm too traumatized to try something even harder, I feel like I would freak out." "But Tommy! That's why Psilocybin is so different! It's not heroin dammit, it's doesn't activate your trauma like a ON button. It's an entirely different thing, it allows you to fully see your complexity like a observing the solar system within a planetarium. There's no comparison. You just have to try it for yourself--"

"Put a pin in that thought, go get your friend. You better hope Darren doesn't come home." As I was walking out the door, I commented, "I know, so let's make this quick."

I trotted down the steps with sweaty hands, I felt like a monster with palms too hairy to hide. Before I opened the door, I explored my reasoning for being scared. I took a deep breath and allow him in, physically and mentally. What's more important, holding on to your pride tightly, or letting it go entirely? I accepted letting someone into my domain, I wanted to share thoughts I could only share with myself for so long. "Hey Tommy, isn't it crazy after being friends for four years I've only been here like once or twice?" "Well, you're about to see why," I responded. "Oooo, so ominous, I like it. Let's get this party started." "Can you act any more excited? Jeez, are you high or something? I wish you would've brought some ganja over for me," Andre commented. "You act like there isn't a whole joint waiting in my car, I figured we'd need it after you show me this 'thing.' I see by that smug smirk on your face that Courtney came by last night. Grrrr. I swear Tommy, you've put her under a spell or something. Even when she's mad at you she still wants to see you, you better not blow this opportunity Tommy. Cause if not I'm picking your chick up." My sarcasm came out in my tone. "Stick to your class, Andre, you said you don't even like white women. I've already told you many times I'm surprised I'm the guy who's with her instead of you. But you've made your preferences perfectly clear so steer clear of my woman player, you'll find your Egyptian queen eventually." "God, I love how sensitive you get, all I'm saying is seeing how she treats you it has broadened my view. You're safe though Tommy, I love Courtney, but she's just my friend. We mess with each other like siblings, not as romantics, and I like it that way. She's a great friend. She always calls me when she needs help with her homework or has a girl problem she can't talk to her *boyfriend* about." I feigned surprise. "What?! Like what? You better tell me you dork." "Hell no, the way that there's a bro code there's a girl one too. It's called best friend confidentiality. Since there's a bro code, I'd tell you if Courtney ever cheated or betrayed you. You're a lucky man, she hasn't. Yet." "Okay ominous Andre, can we get this over with now. This will be unpleasant I imagine." "Let's go! Show me!"

I knocked on Mile's door the beginning sequence to Beethoven's Moonlight Sonata. When he cracked the door ajar, we slipped into my brother's dark room. Miles greeted Andre in a very upbeat way, clearly the mushrooms had taken full effect. Miles was a more timid by nature personality, but from what I could observe, he seemed remarkably out of his shell while tripping. An inkling of desire dropped onto my blank psychedelic slate. Perhaps I would receive similar pleasure and effects if I tried these magic mushrooms. "Hello Andre, how ya been, buddy? I know we don't see each other much, but thank you for being my brothers friend. You don't realize how much it has helped him. Speaking from the heart, I am appreciative, and I'm sorry to let you into the dark side of our life." "Well... thank you. I don't handle compliments very well but it is held in my heart all the same. Why's it so dark in here?" Andre asked. "Sort of, I just wasn't ready to see your reaction yet. It's Tommy's decision to show you anyhow, I believe he should be the one to unveil what's behind the 'curtain' sheet." I walked over to where the curtain covered a big board. "Yes! Holy shit, you are the master of suspense! I've been ready for ten minutes now let's go."

I took a deep breath, unprepared to lay my closeted skeletons bare. I still remained unsure how Andre would respond, but I could not wait any longer. My best friend deserved to know. With a wall full of atrocities, Andre latched onto a picture my parents took when they were younger. A picture of my mother, elegant as ever, holding two severed heads while smiling vibrantly. I presumed my father, who took the photograph, wrote on the bottom right "Regina's first kill all by herself! I'm so proud of you my love." Miles had been swiping scrapbook photos of my parents since he discovered our mothers skin-bound scrapbook in the attic one day while playing hide and seek with himself. In their early years of the killing spree, my mother combined her love for photography and murdering into the same thing. They've taken dozens of photos during their prime time, Darren has taken up the hobby as well. Several of his photos were also displayed on the wall. But Andre gravitated most towards the picture of my mother. He was horrified, like the wretched Wicked Witch of the West having water dumped on her. His facial expression implied he was scalding from within his insides. There were too many pictures and lines connecting them for Andre to really understand the root, but the images were all too surreal for him to grasp what was happening. The pin points around Helen, Georgia really sold it for him. "Tommy! That... that's your mom! Why is your mom holding human heads?! Why?! Are-Are they the same people.... Oh goodness gracious. I think I'm going to faint." "I hope you're jok-oh Shit! He's not." My brother Miles jumped up from his chair, he yelled "Put him on the bed!— no not face first you idiot! He needs to be able to breath, who taught you how to do this?" We caught Andre's body just before it hit the floor. "No one taught me how to do this! I've never dealt with this situation before! I don't have the capacity for this Shit!" "Well then sit down and shut the hell up for one second! Damn, do you always talk this much? It's not cute, it's annoying..... and abrasive as hell! Grab me that ammonia salt in the mini fridge." "Salt?! Are you going to cook my friend? What the hell is salt going to do?!" "Damn it Tommy pass me the salt! He's going to be okay. You wanna know what your biggest problem is Tommy? You think you know every goddamn thing in the world! You've been through a lot, you're going to stand strong for your ideologies. I get it, but you should be more open to accepting you don't know everything. I didn't give you friend freaking table salt, I'm not a moron. I gave him ammonia salt, salt used to trigger an inhalation reflex. You can thank me later when you get your head out of your ass." I hated being proved wrong, especially by such drastic measures. But the message definitely stuck. I regarded my brothers advice as valuable, but I did not have time to ponder on it. Andre was awaking from his unconsciousness, and I needed to figure out what the hell to say to him. He blinked repeatedly, as if seeing a bright white light before passing into the other-side. My brother gave him some water and told him to sit up slowly, like an earthquake sometimes there are aftershocks after fainting. Andre could not bring himself to look at the 'murder board' again. He feared he might faint again. "T-Tommy. Is this a joke? Wha-what the hell was that?! Why do you guys have this?!

What-what are you trying to tell me Tommy? That your family is a bunch of killers and you moving here was no coincidence? Because if so... I don't know how to process that." I took a sip of that water my brother handed Andre, unsure how to put my words together. I said "Andre. I'm just going to give it to you straight. My family are serial killers. My mother, my father, Darren. But not Miles and I, I've never killed anyone. I don't know if the gene skipped us or what but we are in trouble. We have been for years, Andre. That is why I have been so distant with you and Courtney these past few days. My family decided to take a break when we almost got captured a couple years back, but I guess the feeling of fear subsided, they have started killing again. I believe they were doing it anyways secretly yet that's not the point. That is why I have been so difficult lately, I've pushed this problem into the back of my mind for so long, now that it has resurfaced, the grief feels more ravenous like a Leviathan rather than a giant viper like it once did. Being a kid makes the depth of your understanding less prominent, it hurts worse being old enough to understand what our circumstances really are. I'm sorry I had to tell you this way, I-I just thought I would lose you and Courtney if I told you the truth. I feel stupid for having lied to my best friend for so long. I hope you don't treat me differently." Andre put his hands in his hair and began to pull strands out.

He winced while counting out loud from ten to zero. Once he was done, he straightened himself up, and wiped away the tears that started flowing when he pulled his hair for the seventh time. Andre gathered his fleeting clarity, then said "Tommy, this is a lot... I thought you were going to tell me you cheated on Courtney or something. This is magnitudes different. I-I-I....don't know what to say. Can-can I hug you?" Miles wiped a tear from his eye, he acted like I didn't see it but I did. I considered it an indifference. The numbness I feel in my heart because of my situation overtakes me sometimes; within the paralysis of telling my best friend something horrible about myself, my sense of empathy was nonexistent. I nodded however, unsure of why he felt the need to hug me. Yet I let him nonetheless. Andre hugged my brother as well. That was the first time in a long while I had been hugged by anyone inside this house other than Courtney. As futile as it seemed, I really did need it. Andre asked Miles, "Tommy tells me you're some sort of behavioral scientist? Have you made any headway on your family's case? Is this a state of psychosis? Perhaps insanity?" My brother replied, "Neither, in my eyes, it's just who these people are. Individually spun up in their own webs of course. Nevertheless, their roads have led them down the same path." Andre asked, "What use are the roads then if they lead you down the same path?" "Because there are other roads. Our family have followed a dangerous one, one anyone can get sucked into. Yet there's always a choice, even if you're already heading down that road, to turn around and start over again. With the right mindset, and more time in the lab, I believe my team can provide a solution that allows all people to experience 'abducting you from the road you're on, and putting you on a new one. One with a better direction.' We could cure our family's insatiability." "Miles! That's incredible! You could cure a lot of people's insanity if that worked! But does something like that actually exist?" I interjected, because my brother had a tendency to be very bohemian when it came to this issue. I view myself as a realist; Miles says it's pessimism cloaked with a nice, white coat. "Not as of now, Andre. What Miles works on in his department is psychological science. Borderline woo-woo, his optimism cannot save us from the truth. The results he has shown me are promising, but on a personal level. Nothing yet has convinced me we can rewire our families thinking with any sort of compound. It seems like science cannot solve this issue." Miles corrected his crooked glasses then said, "You only look at the numbers, little brother. I have lived several more years than you. I know more about Ancient Greece than you do about anything you have in mind combined! You know why he hasn't seen any results Andre? Because he himself has not tried psilocybin's mind-rewiring effects. He can't speak about some..." "Wait-wait-wait, you've never tried magic mushrooms, Tommy? Oh my god, that explains so much. That's why you always have a gigantic foot up your ass! Damn son, we need to fix that!" Andre added. The tide was thrashing, encapsulating the life raft my pride clung onto.

I swallowed both of their comments, and tried to not take them too harshly. But I did. I said "What would you know about why I hate this forsaken planet, Andre? Why I hate getting up every day just to see a world where nothing's changed. You found out more than five minutes ago my reasoning for being clammy. But you wanna know the real reason? It's because I can't stand other people! Why would I want to transcend this world just to come back? I'd lose my mind." Miles interjected, feeling the strong need to defend his life's work, "Your mindset is what holds you back. You don't realize that it's not an issue or a limitation to transcend then return, it's the entire reason to transcend to begin with. To experience something so much greater than yourself, then to bring those revelations back home with you. You don't transcend to leave, you transcend to elevate your current standings. To leap forward your intelligence leaps and bounds ahead of people too afraid to see what awaits on the horizon. You can call my research woo-woo, but don't discredit what I do. You deliver pizzas to overweight American's and make them feel good about their day being a fat, lazy, discarded remnant of a person. I study the human fucking mind trying to find answers as to why people like our parents exist. You are the equivalent to the 'dreamy' Steve Jobs, while I'm the Wozniak in the background here to save your ass from your own spaciousness. Do you even know what part of the brain the cerebellum is in? Or what it even controls? I thought so. Slander me as a pseudo-scientist but what I do is real. You dreaming of the day your balls will grow the strength to drop themselves so you can singlehandedly reprimand our family is more of a pseudoscience than anything I work on. Don't blame other people for your lack of awareness, Andre is not responsible for the hand you've been dealt. You are. It doesn't make it fair, or just, you don't think I wanna be a kid again? Where the pressure of fixing your fucked up family isn't always on your shoulders as if a bench bar is tied to them? I wish, Tommy, and I wish you got to be a normal kid too. I don't want to turn this into a therapy session, God knows we're overdue a few of those. But you have dragged Andre into this affair now. If you weren't already acting in accord to total perfection, then you are now. This isn't chess, it's battleship." We took a step back from the conversation, and I felt the heat simmering in between us three. Not in the form of any hostility towards one another, more-so of an awareness of the malevolence this evil within our family possesses. How it latches onto you like tentacles and pulls you down into the darkness alongside it. Like the Lochness Monster never to resurface, the myth is almost as daunting as the reality. It didn't really matter if it was really real or not, what did was the infinite "what if" presented by the very idea of such a creature existing in our era. The Hansens were the same way, it didn't really matter what they have already done. What would always live in my thoughts, hiding in the dark like the familiar Lochness Monster, was what could they do next. 'What if' they decided to say "fuck it, let's gut the two son's we have, too! We can snack on them with supper while I sear some rib-eye steak!" Nonetheless of how Andre and Miles were thinking, I felt the rumination of bitterness spindle quickly in that room.

"Okay... that was intense. I-I I hope you don't mind that I recorded all of this; just the audio though. Tommy told me he had something important to tell me so I thought I'd keep it for his wedding. Yet, dear heaven if I ever shared this there. What should I do with this?" I threw out the first suggestion since I was still too numb to deal with conscience thought. "Get rid of it, we don't need to listen to three idiots babble about bull crap, I can turn on the Stooges if you want that." Miles spoke up though, slicing my sentence in half like his mind was wielding a lightsaber. "Tommy, you always talk about writing a book of your experiences living here one day when you 'get the chance.' Well... here it is! Maybe you can record your entries until you're ready to put them to pen and paper. As your brother, who loves you very much, I'm happy to say God gave me brains. Not artistic ability. That's all you." I responded, "I don't know if that's supposed to be a backhanded compliment or not. But thank you. You're right...you always seem to be Miles. I'm sorry for ragging on you for what you do, you're a brilliant person. You're gonna change the world someday. You too Andre, you're a great friend to not have run home by now. Because you both have shown me what great people do when times are tough, to believe in something greater than yourself, I think I am ready to try Psilocybin. I want to be able to understand my past better. I've buried a lot of it back when I realized I had the capacity to analyze what was happening around me. Before then, it seemed like mindful bliss. An era of endless road trips, and a state of euphoria that lingered for weeks at a time. But these years since then, being old enough to understand my situation does not dampen the darkness. It enlightens it. I'm done running. Running is what has brought me here, of what use is running if it leads you into the same situation standing still would have?" Miles and Andre shared a momentary glee. Once they realized they succeeded with their peer pressure, they hugged me. Miles said, "You deserve to know who you truly are. Don't repress it, do the harder thing instead, accept it." The murder board seemed less scary than usual, it seemed more of a matter of fact that surreal reality. Stalin said it best, "One death is a tragedy, a million is a statistic." Staring at these pictures of people I sat next to for dinner with on occasion, whenever a family meal was allotted to the 'outsiders,' made me feel these frozen in amber moments only captured a fragment of our family's wrath. The statistic visual was given new meaning for me, I could no longer feel as numb to their rampage as once before. The embers still burned though. An endangered animal can still gore you to death, but the beast becomes idle the more time passes on. The more times it is not fed and left to rot within the dungeon inside your head, it just seemed to hit all at once. Person by person, it all became too mundane. Until the days I could walk in on bloody bodies or chopped off heads, without as much as a glimmer of hesitation. My insides were with the maggots like those kids my mom killed four years ago, but my mind had transcended through the veil of guilt surrounding it. At least for their situation, for my own, it seemed more of an eternal dilemma.

Andre even gazed upon the murder board once more, not able to stand it much longer than last time. But his determination to try showed me how quick the human mind is to adapting to new situations and surroundings. When you're living within those scenarios, it doesn't seem so. But when removed and placed into a more unfamiliar environment, the animals' senses are heightened. Like a boxer right before he's about to go out. My father told me, 'Those are always the most dangerous men in the world. The ones about to fold, the ones who had something to fight for and to die for were the worst for any boxing coach on fight night. You give a good fighter a beat down, and you will see what kind of individual they truly are. Do they fold? Or do they show you that they can take it? Who is the Incredible Hulk afraid of at night? Well, I'd assume it would be of something similar to his size and might. But with ten times more ferocity, fanaticism, and fearlessness for encountering beings equal to it.' That's how I would describe my side of the situation, I cannot imagine how Andre must feel being the outsider looking in the windowpane. I can only explain what it's like inside the hurricane, analogies for Andre would be his best bet of understanding what it is like outside of the storm. Putting words in people's mouths is not only rude, but corny, only if you really knew what they would say in that situation.

Andre filtered through Miles's bookshelf, remarking that, "A person's bookshelf is considered a window into their mind. You can learn a lot about someone through which books they read. I see a lot of Stephen King, stuff on biology, psychology, phrenology, anthropology...... there's The Republic by Plato, and a lot of 'enter the criminal's mind' novels. I'm surprised you don't read more poetry, it's quite enlightening if entertainment isn't enough of a virtue for you." Miles lifted his eyebrow, unnerved to meet someone paralleled to his intelligence. He smiled, greeting this notion of opportunity, and opened his closet door where a mountain of books were stacked along the top bar. Miles said "The ones on my bookshelf are the 'need to read's', these ones are my 'need to read agains'. When you want to escape as much as I do, you keep a lot of books." "Wow... that's quite the collection. What did you do with the 'need to read no more's? I'm sure they have a special spot as well don't they?" "Ummm, kinda. I give all my though-roughly finished books to Tommy. And the ones he discards as 'not interesting enough to get lost in' are given to my other brother Darren. Not directly of course, I just leave them outside of his doorstep." Andre appeared alarmed, he had not encountered Darren much at all. Once or twice my parents have met Andre yet Darren refuses to leave his room most days. Darren doesn't care to meet anyone new, to him; it's just blood he wants, but cannot spill. Why entice a lion to an appetizer when it clearly wants the entire diner, I suppose. Miles took his glasses off, rubbing his temples then his eyebrows. Andre seemed unsure of what to say, yet as always, he found a way. Andre asked Miles, "What is your brother like? Tommy tells me he is your twin, that is all. In hindsight, I should've probably asked why. Nonetheless, what's his deal? Why is he so... terrorizing? If he's the one doing most of these killings then sheeesh.... He's got a real issue in the ol' thinking dome." Miles laughed at Andre's quick wit, it was certainly one of Andre's most prominent features. He could turn anything into a comedy, which aggravated me on the days I have no appreciation for such humor. Nonetheless, it was undeniably a talent I wish I had. Miles said, "Yes. Darren is my twin. I don't think words alone can describe such an individual. He is someone with an incredible intellect, yet possesses an utter disregard for other people. Megalomaniac is a good place to start. Hypnotic is another. He has this ability to entrance you in his decisions. His use of touch, sounds, gazing through you, understanding of human nature, and intense awareness for reasoning. It's undeniable he is one of the most prolific killers I've ever heard of, bias for being my brother cast aside of course. He treats murder like an art form, completely devoting himself to its evil essence. I've seen him study throughout the night reading books like 'Assyria,' 'Think fast, and Slow', and 'How to kill a Gypsy' just to name a few. Darren is utterly profound; it embitters me to be his twin. He shakes my foundation with how smart he is. I think we all believe in this dreamy delusion that evil contains some sort of self-destruct button. That evil humans will always undo themselves because they are flawed, or stupid, as some people would put it. I believe that's bullshit, if anyone met Darren they would disregard that soft sentiment. I feel his every pulse. Every thought. Maybe it's superstition, but being twins with someone is an exotic experience. We have a weird relationship. We respect one-another, yet stay clear from each other as much as we can. The most we've grown into hanging out is swapping books, he finds my taste "suitable." My self-help books are his favorite... in a weird way, his darkest ones are mine. I've read Assyria, there's some horrible things inside that book. Those people used to draw reliefs of torturing the souls they captured, the one that took my eyes off the page was of the King Sennacherib watching the citizens of Babylon be thrown onto stakes. He made one man wear his comrades head around his neck. What I thought was the most awful was that the king didn't need to watch. He wanted to. I agree with what you said earlier Andre. Books are a window into a person's thoughts and conscience, if you read several of Darren's you'd understand the man. He's not evil, he's a genetic mishap. Imagine Satan and Bloody Mary have a baby, will that baby lead the plucky republic against evil? Or will that baby most likely grow up into some sort of Lord Voldemort, or Darth Vader character? That's my brother. Why Tommy and I were skipped, beats me. I hope that answers your question."

Andre scratched at his goatee, interested in the conversation enough to look back at the board. He lost his initial fear from before. "Do you think genetics plays more of a part than environment? I don't think you guys were skipped; I think you both chose to handle your situation differently. The scenario of the drug addict dad leaving two kids behind plays in my mind. One of them becomes a psychologist, someone determines to understand the human mind and what makes people cling to addiction. While the other becomes a psychopath, someone unable to handle their path in life. Unable to handle the lot given to them by the gods. The genetics are all the same, but it's the brain who handles pain correctly that will vanquish one that doesn't. Your brother seems very intelligent, but intelligence is a spectrum. If your spectrum does not see between the lines of 'right' and 'wrong', of what use was your intelligence?" Miles itched his eyebrow, and then told Andre, "Well said. You know, you appear to have a superior intellect as well. Maybe one day you'll come down to my lab and let me play with your brain. I love learning about what makes a complex mind different than an average one." "You can't turn my friend into a science experiment, you do know that right?" I added, unabridged by that comment. "It's alright, Tommy, you're not my mommy. I can speak for myself. Sure Miles. If it will help your research then I can come by sometime. If anything, you should slip Tommy some of that grade-A Psilocybin you keep down at your lab. Now that would be a worthwhile experiment!" Andre said, making Miles laugh so hard he nearly fell off his bed. I wondered if I would be criticized my whole life for not trying to 'transcend' ever before. Not ever having the desire to try to. I didn't believe in that stuff. What did the mystical ever do for me? Why was I to believe some garden grown abomination would solve my problems? Mushrooms were a fungus, not a tool to pass into the Iris. In my mind, it was all hogwash. Harry Potter shit. All just people's intense reaction to what the mushroom does to them. Transcendence isn't a true virtue when we are stuck inside bodies that, by nature, are flawed to begin with. Who cares if our spirit changes, we still inhabit the skeleton of someone who is born with an intense capacity for evil. Nothing in my life makes me feel like transcendence is a possibility, the only limelight that shines bright upon the roaring torrents of darkness is love. I consider love to be the only true form of transcending beyond the worthless being I was created to be. I wasn't created out of God's love, I was created by two psychopathic parents who wanted to sleep with each other. "There is no transcendence, there is only nature. There is only the way things are, and operate. To observe life while filtering the fleeting feelings you feel before reaching the land of the deceased. There is nothing more, there is nothing special about this planet. You are given the luck of the draw the moment you are given into this world. Fortune favors the bold when all the glorious components of creating someone are fulfilled. Why isn't everyone Gandhi? If the Buddha is supposedly everywhere why are we still mindless monsters who operate on whims with no meaning!" I said, interrupting the silence that befell the room. Andre had his face in the murder board, fully accepting of what my situation was to him. Miles had been scurrying through his books, having Andre's dialogue replay over and over again in the back of his head. He wondered what his books said about him as a person. When I said what I said, they both seemed to synchronize or something. They both replied at the same time "you dumb ass! You haven't even tried it yet!" Andre patted Miles on the shoulder, clearly feeling what he was feeling right alongside him.

Andre turned back at the murder board and swiped a picture with my brothers face on it. Darren was wearing his mask, which made me scared. Andre was unaware how terrified I was at night with that mask on my mind. He put it close to my face then said "Tommy! Do you want to become this?! Do you see what shutting yourself off from enlightenment does to you?! Imagine if you were to kill me!! Or Court..." "Don't! Say that! Get that picture out of my face! I'm not a killer! I've given every ounce of my sanity not to butcher you both into little pieces and eat you up for a snack before lunch! I want to gut you open like a dumb fucking pig before crawling into your skin so I can sleep with you forever! I've given every ounce of my sanity to keep myself together but I can't control my urges forever! You wanna know why I'm such a distant prick, Andre? Because one day, I'm afraid I'm going to bash your goddamn brains in. I am a product of this god forsaken family, and I can't change it! I can't do a damn thing about it but sit and wait for this virus to take a hold of me." Angrily, Andre responded, "You are not them. You are the funniest person I know. You make me laugh when I'm sad, you teach me about philosophy, the Romans, the possibility of World War III. So many things. You see yourself within the shade, without ever considering you could step into the light. Light doesn't have to be casted onto you each time you feel the darkness. You can provide that light yourself. Stop following your own shadow, Tommy. If you think no one's sees you then you're wrong. I see you. Courtney sees you. Your brother clearly sees you. Maybe, consider for once, that it is you who needs to see yourself. I only recommended the mushrooms from my own personal experience with them. When your father is a no-good drug addict, you feel inclined to find out why. To find out if you are destined for that same fate. Psilocybin has allowed me to go a long way with discovering myself. You are not your parents Tommy, you are not your siblings. You are you. It seems to be one of the hardest things in life to accept. You're such a wonderful person Tommy, but you have a seething darkness inside your heart. Even before I learned of.... this.... You've always alarmed me with how hollow you can be. You should really heed our advice. Maybe what's holding you back from understanding how to defeat your family without means of violence or arrest is your inability to separate yourself from the situation. Tranquility isn't woo-woo. It's a privilege to pursue. I love you Tommy, but with what you've told me, you both don't seem to be stopping any more murders by being idle. It's easy to let more people suffer when it's not you who has to. But that's not who I am. Now that I've learned this I have to learn more. I want to help you." "I want you to help me too, Andre. That's why I brought you here. It's not just a formal conversation to bring this up. I need answers myself. I need to understand how to beat these people. If Miles would let me just take them into the nearest police station or slit their throats in their sleep then it would be easy." "Hey, we don't turn our back on family. If the position was flipped, I would only hope my family would love me enough to try and fix me," Andre responded calmly. "Fair enough, okay then. I can see the consensus is for me to find myself. Where do I start?" I asked. "Good, good! That is where you start! Wanting to change! Now step two, Miles do you mind bringing home some of that Psilocybin you have? I would love to trip sit Tommy and talk to him if that's okay?" Miles eagerly jumped in. "Say no more, I got it, but can you do me a favor in return? Take notes, I can give you a clipboard with some stuff I've taken on my Psilocybin studies so you can observe him with some sort of timeline to follow by." "Thank you, Miles! That's great! Okay, Tommy! Are you ready to experience transcendence once and for all?!" I hesitated before replying. "I'm not sure, I have never done so before. So how would I know?" "Well, you don't. You only know when you walk so many miles on foot, come to a screeching halt then realize you could be flying instead. It is only when you realize you don't want to walk or run anymore that you know you're ready to transcend Tommy." "Alrighty then, cheers to no more walking. How is this going to help stop my family though? This seems like an individual issue." Miles grabbed his notepad and asked me "Is it really though? Tommy, what I want to show you with your trip is that we could give this same bliss to our parents. Maybe even Darren! We could save so many people from pain, even themselves." "If this substance was so universally loved then why isn't the government dropping it off in cartloads across every pharmacy? Wouldn't there be a demand for such a great thing?" I asked. "The FDA won't approve of this any sooner then they will with weed. It's a loss cause trying to get a "drug" through the ringer. I am a scientist not a pharmacist. There's a big difference when you're sending billions back to the government. No one cares much for actual research unless funded from themselves. That is why these experiments are so crucial, who knows, this could break the barrier in between drugs and medicine. Our family matter first, but this research is bigger than us. We could make the planet a less aggressive environment for our kids one day. Imagine your daughter living in a world where people like 'The Hansens' aren't creeping around every ominous alleyway." "You're starting to sound like a mad scientist again, but your ambitions are what brought you here. I may harp on you for your job, but I respect what you do. Going against the grain to make the world a better place is what we all need. You could easily take your talents down to the big corps where you'll develop medicine to keep people dumber than washing your hands with water and sandpaper. This.... Is actually interesting. I don't know how valid your information is, so until I test it, let's hold off on this discussion." I added. "Agreed, I will pick up the Psilocybin later today. What are your plans until then? We can't raise any alarms or it's already too late. You know what happened last time I tried to bring them down... I, I can still feel that cold basement floor as Darren tortured me until submission. Even then, he didn't quit. They are merciless... that is why it is more important we fix them." "More important for them, or for you? Miles... don't put all your pride in finding yourself through fixing this family. Some grapevines grow forever. Our parents have been this way since before we were born... Darren's fate was destined by the gods, not us. I know you're hurt, and I wish I could fix that. But it is okay if we don't save this family. What if saving us was enough?" "If everyone thought like that, Tommy, there would never be anyone willing to do what needs to be done. I will consider what you've said, but this is my life's work. It is too late to not take this seriously, if I can't fix this family than who can I fix? My research will be for nothing if it doesn't work on this family, if it can't operate under extreme measures then the simplest of circumstances will cause problems. I need this to work, Tommy." "Okay Miles, but if one of them crosses the line it's go time. I can't take any chances man. The way you say this research has become your life, Andre and Courtney have become mine. They are... my family. I will not risk either of them being harmed. If anyone shows signs of touching my loved ones, they're done for." "Those who make peaceful options impossible only cause violent ones to be inevitable. Be careful to not gaze into the abyss for too long, you may yourself become the monster you ponder in the darkness to catch a peek of," Miles responded.

After one long-winded response after another, we finally settled down. Our intellectual discussion ceased its flickering flame. We returned to more docile matters, like what my heart wanted to do. I wanted to see my future wife again before I embarked on this 'trip.' She made me so happy whenever I thought about her, that happiness was soon followed by immeasurable guilt. I felt ashamed for the way I had been treating Courtney this past week. If I wanted to have a blissful trip, I needed to see her once more before jumping into wonderland. This momentary freedom from the hazy daze that is my life has provided me enough insight to realize one day, Courtney will die, with or without my family's assistance. To waste another second dwelling on the possibility of losing her when in any instance that is possible in all forms of existence without help from Satan's Assassin's seemed wasteful. It would not soften the blow if I lost her by always thinking about it, believing there's some sort of force field that envelops around you from pain when you're always in it. It does nothing. If anything, it amplifies it. It makes you feel that same pain twice, instead of no times. To push such a lovely soul away because I am scared to love another person openly is blasphemy. If I can't handle it, then I can't have her. She deserves better even if it's without me, but luckily, she doesn't have to be.

"What are your plans, Andre? Miles?" Miles gestured his hand for Andre to speak first, Andre greeted his politeness with a nice gesture of saluting back. Andre said "If I'm going to trip-sit your ass tonight, then I need to be high as a kite to enjoy my time. I will probably go home, meditate, smoke, then read up on Miles notes before I come over again." I nodded in agreement, Miles then said "Sounds good to me. If that's the case then I am going to go to the research facility to get a few things, if you don't mind, I'd like to take part in this trip if that's fine? What are your plans Tommy?" I sighed, a slither of nervousness flooded my nervous system. I did not want to feel like a lab experiment while I tried Psilocybin for the first time. But I improvised. I said "Fine, Miles, but you need to be lookout. If anyone in this house finds me on drugs, then I'm done for. Not only will that be the worst experience ever, I'm positive our father will beat the psychedelics out of my system. So let's face the music, we need to test the waters here. Put your TV on max volume so no one hears us in here, and keep your talking to a minimum. We can get through this easy if we just follow each other like a team. As for me, I need to see my queen. I've left her alone for too long now, I have a relationship to save." Miles patted my shoulder, then said "Great, now let's go. We only have a couple hours to get everything together, I want us to meet here before sunset. That's when our family... you know." "Yeah, I know. I've been on so many murder sprees I lost count at around fifty. I can recite their entire protocol like our father can lottery numbers. They will be gone for a few hours if they're in the mood to hit a couple houses. But let's go, I need to see my girl." "Okay Juliet, we will get going so you can see your Romeo. Let's go," Andre said, bumping fist with Miles while restraining their laughter. I smiled, uttering under my breath "Why do I choose to share anything with them? It's like explaining my pain to children."

Andre skirted off in his beauty of a car, leaving tire marks along the asphalt as he drove away. I heard him blasting "Rhiannon" by Fleetwood Mac. He had a thing for Stevie Nicks even though she was a white woman. In his words "Screw my preference, have you heard her sing?!" Andre wasn't wrong, she did have the voice of an angel. Her voice echoed in my mind long after Andre had driven away. He's the reason I listen to Fleetwood, I had never even heard of them before him. My parents didn't believe music was a soothing virtue, well, my father didn't anyway. So, all of my taste have come from the music I've found along the way, and for Andre, he was my vault of songs. I walked on the street humming Rhiannon while listening to the birds humming in the trees near me. It was really peaceful. Like one of my favorite artists, Logic, said in a song once, "Any moments we have free of this feeling we will not take for granted." Every chance I am flying farther than my feelings I dream it would last forever and whatever's after. I let Stevie's voice take away my anxiety, I faded away like that black cat strafing into the darkness. My street was so solemn, all of the houses were so beautiful. Then behind me, as I peeked around, my ugly house stood out like an apple on a peach tree. Everyone's lawns and gardens were so well taken care of, while mine looked like even death had died there. The stench of decay followed my every breath wherever I went, wherever *we* went. That house we live in used to look like all of these ones, until we moved in. Anything we touch turns into dust, wherever we go, death and decay are soon to follow. I saw a cardinal land on the street in front of me as I starting humming the part where Stevie says "takes to the sky like a bird in flight." It made me smile, not with the intent to convince someone I am happy when I'm not. However, all by myself, having this magical moment for me only to see. I smiled from cheek to cheek, emitting true glee. I appreciated this moment for as long as I could, knowing just like the bird, it would soon be fleeting back into the wind it came from. After walking through my neighborhood towards the exit, I called Courtney to see if she wanted to meet at the spot I first took her out to when we started talking. It was a wonderful experience. In hindsight, I realized in that one night I wanted her to be the last girl I ask out ever again. "Tommy? Whats up? I thought you were hanging out with Andre?" "I was, my love, but I really wanted to see you so I told him we can hang out later. I know this is impromptu but would you like to come to the cliff with me?" "Ugh, that creepy place we had our first date? Like right now? Ummm, okay! You're lucky I like you, because I was just getting ready to play with myself. Since somebodyyyy wants to be a big baby and not treat me right." I laughed in response. "You are absolutely the Devil incarnate; I would say Prada but you'd burn them right off! Haha, I'm sorryyy I am a polite person and feel bad after going ghost for a whole week. I'm not exactly in my playboy phase of time I apologize. Sooo, who were you thinking about? Was it David Hasselhoff again?" She responded quickly, "NO?! That was in a dream, you idiot, mhmm. It was one time! I was thinking about you...doofus. You're the only dude I think about when I feel... aroused. Gosh, you men are incredible, do you think about other people while..." I interjected. "Noooooo.... Of course not. Why would I even suggest such a stupid thing..." "You. Are. Disgusting. Thomas. ANYways. I'm going to touch myself to this picture of Magic Mike, then I will come by? Okay? Love youuuu." She kissed me through the phone before hanging up.

I hoped she was joking about what she said, yet I also asked for it so the consequence fits the crime. As I walked to the cliff my thoughts started running on the hamster wheel. I had a tendency to do that when walking, it cleared my mind. I thought about how there is such a disparaging difference between Courtney and I, she can have any guy she likes. I however, am on a life raft out in the open ocean while the tides roll in. Pondering upon the constellations with hopes one lovely lifeguard will come out to get me. I've seen for myself that in this world it takes men twenty-times the effort to achieve the results a woman can achieve while exerting two-times the effort. Even one or none if she's a walking goddess. I live in an era of time where the woman gets to decide which guy they want in their life, not the other way around like it had been for all of human civilization. I am not weighing on what is right, I'm not a philosopher, I can only observe through history how it's always been. When generations of genetic information are given to you yet the social environment of the world around you drastically change over the course of those generations. Then you have created an entirely different environment, an entirely different animal is discovered. I can't speak for all men because well, it's obvious, we're not all just walking, talking clones of ourselves. There is quite the variety. However, I can say with some confidence not as many men choose freely which woman, or women (given the culture they inhabit) they'd like to marry. Hell, even hook up with. They still do in some aspects, but not in broad sums as usually accustomed. We tend to settle far more than in other ages in history. What I've seen of this world is a wider variety of women choosing the men they wish to be with while more men are settling for women they, fifty years ago, would shun from even looking in their general vicinity. I can only say I am a fortunate soul to have found a beautiful woman who chose me. It doesn't make a difference whether you look for it or not, when it's real it hits you like a megaton brick. I've looked for a woman my entire life and have failed every time I tried. I only wish that was an exaggeration. The one instance I didn't look for anyone, being quite content with my friendship to Andre, he introduces me to a girl that changed my world. I know, it's not very important to discuss these things when I'm surrounded by insatiable terrorist who turn people's faces into cake batter. But it does matter, because this story has no meaning if I did not explain how redeeming it was for me to be finally loved by someone. It is liberating beyond belief. So much so it scares me sometimes. I get the irrational idea that I will one day lose the beauty I have found. Like a mother who holds their child, smiles, then cries inside thinking about the times they saw that mother on the news who lost her little Timmy to a runaway eighteen-wheeler. With the wild idea that maybe this fate will take your baby too. It is a burden to love someone, because to do so means you are willing to be completely shattered when they disappear. For the moments of being there for them when they're scared, even when you're scared too. For the moments they feel insecurity while you lack the emotional maturity to properly assess their feelings, for the times you see them leave after a bad venom spewing session wondering to yourself "Will she come back? Or is this the time she doesn't?" I would never trade Courtney for anything, especially feeling the misery of not being loved the way you should by your own family. It is not negotiable whether she stays in my life, I would rather handle the pain it takes to lose her then to never even experience what life is like with her. To love someone other than yourself requires an intimate knowledge of human nature and human history. Love requires reason, while simultaneously asking you to provide more compassion than intelligence. Love requires so much more than most people are even capable of understanding, let alone appreciating and applying it correctly. I throw myself in that sad category alongside the other men who live in quiet desperation. I say this to cast some shade on the situation, if a miserable cabbage minded person like myself can find love, anyone can. I hope when my story is told about everything I went through in my life, I want the highlight to be how I remained a vigilant lover to the woman I truly loved. No back door shenanigans or bragging about cheating on one of the only things that matters to me. I would want people to see for themselves that even in peril, you can figure out how to love again. If you cannot stand tall, then be small for a while. If you cannot bear being small, fall to the ground and contemplate. If thinking isn't your thing, then merely talk to your idle self. You may not like the answers you receive, but it'll be the truth. Once you correct your idleness, contemplate what it is you will do about it. When you've figured that out, stand back up. Even if you still feel small, you stand as if you are ten feet tall. One day, you will walk among the giants and wonder why you're able to be as high as them.

The sky-scraping trees seemed to wave at me as I passed them by. There are many deer out here today, I watched a bundle of them cuddle together when the wind swooned down with violence. Even in nature, family sticks together, I pondered upon the nature of my family. About how, better yet, they strayed so far away from what nature wanted from them. I did not want to consider that who they were was their nature. The way that nature unfolds all around us made me believe there was some sort of ordinance. As I walked by these deer who comforted each other through the spurt of cold wind, my heart opened its doors and was warmed up thoroughly. I considered chaos, how maybe just like these deer, just like these trees all around me, just like the river spewing water down gigantic jagged rocks five hundred feet from me, maybe all of this was coincidence, mere chance on a roulette table. Nature is not any set of ways upon how the world works, however, each life form operates under its own unique nature given to them. What makes a "peaceful" lion attack an "aggressive" one, or a "senile" human batter someone with far "superior" intelligence than them? Is it this universal randomness we all generate? Do some hands get played, while others wait their turn for generations? Was it mere chance I was put in a family as insatiable as my own? It couldn't be, at least, I did not want to believe it to be so. It is more comforting to think I have suffered for some reason deeper than my intellect will ever understand. Was it more divine to say Courtney was fate? Or to think I capitalized on a chance any man could have had if they were in my place, at my location at the right time, but didn't? I was the lucky individual who Andre introduced her to, I could not pick whether it was more important to see it as fate or an offbeat ordinance on the universal scales tipping over towards my favor.

I waited by a tree continuing to let my thoughts run free while praying Courtney remembered where to go. This grotto was very special to me; when I first moved here I was afraid on where my family was heading. We had just escaped damn near captivity from the police while I was only still a kid. I did not know why a god would send me here to deal with these modern day barbarians. But he did. I ran away from home a lot as a child and into adolescence. Yet I never had anywhere to go. When I ran away several times upon arriving here in Helen, I found this place one day in search of a secluded area to off myself. I figured the guilt would outlive me, I did not want to see another dead person for as long as I lived. The images tormented me every time I closed my eyes to sleep. I wanted the torment to stop. This cliff spoke differently to me, as I sat upon the edge waiting for the courage to throw myself from it. She caused me to become calmer, to just watch the river flow without any interruption. For some reason, this spoke to me. Even as a younger person than I am today, I realized like the river flowing through the jagged rocks that no matter how many obstacles stood in this waters path it continued onward. Like Bruce Lee once said, someone I looked up to dearly for being a undersized warrior, "Be formless, shapeless, like water." As I watched the river roll on without regard as to what stood in front of it, I took that message with me. It's one thing to hear an idol say something incredibly profound, it's another entirely to see that applicable advice applied into real life. Ever since then, I come to this cliff whenever I need time and space to think. There are these beautiful train tracks in the distance that I took Andre on a couple times to smoke some 'Siberian Haze.' I tried to take Courtney on them one time to which she said "You have a better chance of receiving a threesome then seeing me walk across that thing." I've had some great memories here at this cliff, whether intentional or not. Sometimes the greatest moments and memories are the ones you stumble upon.

My philosophy session was interrupted when I heard Courtney shout from in the distance "Tommmmyyyyyy! Where are you?! My feet probably smell like pine needles now, ugh." The sound of my sweet queen broke me free from my dive into the abyss. I wouldn't say I quite reached there, more like looming along the outskirts of the cavernous trenches. If I enter too deeply, then I might start to see things then shriek like a lady in distress. "I'm over here, Courtney, just stay there I'll come to you." I kept crunching leaves under my feet as I walked towards her. The sound was satisfying. Almost as satisfying as seeing how beautiful Courtney's outfit looked on her. She was wearing a white dress with little bumblebees and honey-combs on them. Not the prom kind, more like those people you see taking pictures in a sunflower field. "You know, we could have just eaten out somewhere like a normal couple? I look too cute to be out here," she whined. "Well, we're not a normal couple now are we? You look marvelous my dear, besides, it's just you and I out here. Going out would be nice, but I enjoy spending time alone with you." Courtney giggled, then kissed my cheek. She said "Okay, lead the way my prince" before taking my hand. As much as I liked being 'the man,' I liked when she asserted herself as well. What can I say, I'm a product of the generation of men I discussed earlier. I took her to the cliff side, and proceeded to sit down on the ledge. She was took scared to sit next to me, so I took a moment of bliss along the edge before getting back up. "You know I don't like when you do that, you could fall!" She said, nuzzling against my arm. Courtney was too gentle for me, for the whole world even. If I could childproof every part of existence for her I would, but even then, is that really living? "Okay baby, I won't do it again, I promise. Come sit with me. Let's watch the sunset like we did when I first brought you here." I held her in my arms as we watched the sun fall into the horizon. The stars were not yet in the sky yet they were wildly present within my heart. I embraced Courtney tighter as the sun dissipated into the darkness. She rubbed my arm with angelic gentleness, then turned around to ask me "You know when you first brought me here, I thought you might kill me, is that bad?" Out of all the responses I expected her to say as we stared at the sun fall that was the farthest one from my conscience. "Well okay then, damn, did I scare you or something?" "Uh, yeah! Who brings a girl out here on a first date! Major serial killer energy, dude." "So why did you not say something? I'm speechless as to why you stayed if you felt I was going to kill you, jeez." "Because you were, and still are, pretty darn cute. I figured if you were going to kill me then I could die happy having my last look at life be of your elegance. Besides, your creepiness was circumstantial, not of your character. Why would I still date you if I thought otherwise? If you just took me out to dinner like a normal human being I think our first date impression would be drastically different. You goofball." I smiled as the sun fell down. I'm not very good with other people, but meeting Courtney showed me I just needed to be good with one. Two, considering Andre, yet we are not sleeping together so it's a different kind of love I have for him. I replied "Fair enough, in my mind I wanted to take you someplace that it could be just the two of us. Okay, saying that out loud now sounds bad. It was better in my head, but you get it? I hope?" She smiled softly, one of those smiles that didn't come from the face but from the heart. "Of course I get it... I feel like you forget men aren't the only ones who have crushes... when Andre told me about his 'new friend' and how smart he was, I was very interested. Without even needing to meet you, Andre's words provided a bright enough picture of who you were a person.

I don't know why I fell head over heels for you. You're very timid and shy. But I liked those things about you. It gave me the impression of underlying confidence, of the ability to be reserved. The guys I've dated in my past are attractive assholes, athletes with concrete between their ears and between their legs. I've dated…" I interjected, "Okay we can skip this part… I get it." "I'm sorry honey, I forget you hate talking about that… I just think it's funny to reminisce on who I've been with. And how those terrible people led me here to you. You are the absolute best part of my life, Tommy. I know you get uncomfortable talking about these things, but you are everywhere all at once for me. I appreciate my individuality and independence, but none of that matters when I'm with you. I just want to feel you. Everywhere, all at once. You are the man I want to watch all my sunsets with." It took everything all at once in my body to stop me from crying like a little toddler. I reflect so often on the negativity I have allowed into this world by being a byproduct of my family's insanity. Yet I rarely ever consider the positivity I have left behind. I treat Courtney as if she is my gift to me from the gods, without actually understanding this gift is not self-serving. This gift goes both ways no matter how much I fail to see on what end it extends to me. I similarly wanted her to be the only woman I speak about these things with, and the only woman I ever feel these things with. We held each-other until the stars came upon us. I put on "The Little Things" by Colbie Caillat, who was one of Courtney's favorite artists. She told me once that her mom used to put Colbie on when taking her to school in the mornings. I tried to remember those things for nights like these, when it all came full circle. "Don't tell Andre about this, please, I will never hear the end of it," Courtney said while swooning within my arms. "Why is that?" I replied back, unsure of what she meant by her comment. She turned around to face me directly, crossing her legs around my undersized waist like a mechanical claw around a small stuffed animal. "No, Thomas. Because I don't like to be seen as a little sentimental infantile. Andre and I are friends because we share a similar love for intelligence. I respect his opinion very much… I don't want him to think of me like that.." "What is your issue with vulnerability Courtney? You know Andre loves you very much, you're not just some tool to pass school with. You're his friend.

He cares about you. I'm sure he would love to hear about how you sway in my arms as we listen to music that soothes your mood. What is wrong with that?" "Can you not just promise me that? It means a lot to me to be seen as strong and confident. It's not obvious to you, but I live in a man's world. There are plenty of opportunities for a woman like me, but I hate the mold put onto me by society that I'm just this little girl who needs a man to save her like a damsel in distress. Andre is the first friend to actually respect me, to not just use me as a possible hookup or just because I'm their 'hot' friend. I'm not some prop, Tommy, I'm a woman with actual use in this world. I just want to feel that way.. allow me to have that even if it only exist in fragments." Courtney said, wiping tears from her eyes. I put my arm inside my shirt so I could use the sleeve to relieve Courtney's tear ridden cheeks of being wet any longer. Her skin was softer than an angel's feathers, I wondered what created such a wonderful thing. Fate, or chance. I said "Okay, my love. I got your back. Just the two of us, remember? Let's just enjoy this moment. I will keep all of your vulnerability up inside me so no one can see it. My sweet baby. Come here my big, strong Valkyrie. You can be strong outside these walls we've built up, but just know, you can always be yourself around me. I'm not like these other mongrels you've encountered before. I'm a barbarian bred with Shakespearian and Marcus Aurelius' DNA." Courtney did just that. I comforted her speedily beating heart down to idleness. She continued to caress my arm while singing along to her songs. I never wanted this moment to end. There was no better place in existence to live than in this very situation right here. God could have come down from heaven and granted me three wishes yet all of them would've been used to make this moment last forever. Nothing else mattered besides spending time with my future wife. She twiddled with my arm hair then said "This. Is why I love you, Tommy. Not because of your charm, or anaconda cock, but for making me feel safe when I'm scared. All of my life I've wanted to be a big strong woman, a woman powerful enough to fight against the oppression some men instill into this world. But you're the first man whose ever let me feel comfortable being myself. I don't have to stand tall, or talk about topics that don't particularly interest me but interest my colleagues. I can curl up like a little girl in the arms of someone I know who truly loves me. Who really sees me for who I am. Thank you, honey." I took my jacket off so she could lay down on my lap. She looked at the stars, wondering which one was the one her mother would point to and call the Northern Star when she was a child. The stars were awesome, yet my eyes could not gaze toward the sky. My observation was on the wonderful woman in front of me. Those moments people say it feels like a dream to be with someone whom you love sound so obnoxious and over the top. But I can't even explain how correct those sentiments are. Every day I woke up newly astute that she was still my woman, every time I got lost in her eyes I wondered why those same eyes saw me as her guy.

"This is the perfect night Tommy, thank you for taking me out here. It's getting kinda late though, and if you were to kill me right now would be the perfect time. So if you'd like to head back soon that would be swell. I got some homework to finish before I go to bed." "You mean you still have some Hasselhoff to finish before you go to sleep?" "You're stupid, I mean it. You know, since I won't get to sleep with my prince tonight. Would you like to have some fun before we call it a night?" "In the woods? My love, I cannot for the life of me fuck my queen in sticks and leaves. You deserve better than to get dirty." "But I like being dirty, does my appearance make you think otherwise?" "Youuuuuu are dangerous. Get away from me, Satan, I-I still can't allow that. Here, take my jacket, so you have something to lay on." "Oh geez, every queen's dream is to hear that her king has a jacket for her to lay on." "You asked for this didn't you? We can totally wait until tomorrow when we're, you know, at a house!" Courtney said, "But that means I don't get any pleasure now.... that won't work. Will it?" before reaching into my trousers like a bee entering a flower. "Okayyyy then, I guess this is happening. Can you please just be gentle you Viking warlord. You can't use this sword if it's broken!!" "Oh don't worry, I'll be gentle" she said back as she gave my little gentleman a kiss. I will leave the rest for the imagination, as for me to discuss these things only serve myself. I don't imagine I'll ever publish a book about my experiences until I'm old enough so I'll keep this memory locked away in my mental safe. I have no need to recite memories that are though-roughly stained into my brain. Let's just say we had fun, and I got the job done. Even though sticking two dominant type people into a sexual scenario is always fun, for me it's like losing battle after battle then finally the war is won. God damn that girl can work her body, she has the sexual prowess and stamina of a animatronic. I'm usually the fool stupidly stuck in a daze after we're finished as she's already up and ready to proceed with her day. Courtney smiled while standing over my shuttering body, she said, "You did good kid, we really left it all out on the field that's for sure. Keep fucking me like that and we might get married tomorrow." "I think it was you who fucked me, did you study about the Kama Sutra in your spare time or something? Damn." "You did good though, champ. You made me squirm like a little worm, god gifted you with something fierce down there. I hope I'm the last lady to take that thing inside me. You've probably split a lot of ladies with that thing, jeez it's ginormous! Does it have its own colony on it?!" "You already know that you're the only woman I've slept with, yet with those moves you put on me I can see several men have had wonderful nights with you." "Wow, rude. I may have had my fun, but ain't none of them packing what you have. Do you know why I'm good at what I do? Because no man before me could make me... you know. I tried to make it happen myself, it sorta worked. Putting moves on an acorn doesn't help me much. But damn, putting moves on someone with an elephant trunk down there is wayyyyy different. I see that there are levels to everything. Consider you have saved yourself for the best one, I had to travel through latter rungs of unsatisfactory sex before reaching you. It's like, wow, I met this excellent person who truly loves me. By the way, has a god damn infinity stone packed in his pants. I mean, I'm speechless. I've received your penis for three years now and I'm still... speechless. I almost cried because you were just going to town down there. My little lady appreciated all your effort, she can rest easy now until I see you again." I could not help but laugh. Courtney had such a cute way of referring to things. I did not know why I was blessed, I always said it was because I treated woman right. Even when those same women broke my heart over and over again, I never changed my ways. I was never a player, I was the played.

As we got up to head back to the street, Courtney sheepishly grabbed my arm. She said with worry in her eyes, "Tommy, I heard something." "What did you hear, my dear? I didn't hear anyth- okay. I heard that," I said. It sounded like someone skipping rocks, or a squirrel dropping nuts. Courtney grabbed me and said "Uh, yeah! Let's get out of here!" I gazed upon the constellations overhead hoping that noise didn't come from a person. Because if it did, I already knew who it was. We made our way through the woods with intense swiftness, with Julius Caesar crossing the Rhine River type speed. I asked Courtney what she had heard originally, to my dismay she said "I heard another person, someone mumbling something." I tried to keep as calm as possible, but my thoughts ran wild. I turned around and nearly froze still like a Popsicle stuck into the dirt. I saw a figure standing in the pathway we just walked away from. About the same distance as when I saw the river earlier. I was utterly mortified. I told Courtney to keep going though without mentioning the human-shaped monster lurking in the backdrop. I made sure she was in front of me so whatever was behind us would choose me over her. The wind whistled while we ran. I was uncertain on how to handle this situation, if it really was Darren, I needed to bring Courtney as far away from him as possible. Darren was not the type for negotiation. If Courtney discovered his identity, then we would both be kissing the leaves. I made a decision that I felt was best for me, but for her first. I told Courtney "Don't stop running until you get to your car! I will be right behind you. Don't look back for any reason!" Which was a mistake, not because I defied the odds, but because I lied once again to someone who has completely put their trust in me. But that wasn't important now, I'd rather be chewed out while alive then dead with truth fading from my eyes like the light inside them. I strode further away from Courtney until I was close enough to the ominous figure. His mask was corroding off of his face, he appeared as if he was deteriorating from the inside out. I said "D-Darren? What in the hell! Not cool dude!" He replied, "That's one." Then he slipped away into the darkness he was brought out of. "Grrrr. Stupid prick!" Why did I agree to play this game anyways? Am I really as insatiable as him? I believed not, but how many times has life shown us the difference between believing in something being real vs. that thing actually existing?

I watched Courtney drive off, ensuring Darren would not follow her. I did not know what the hell his deal was. I believe we are playing two different games. Did that maniacal freak really watch us? I sure hope not. He would have been horrified with what I was doing to that woman. She looks cute, but doesn't act like it when she's in the mood. Darren was a disgusting degenerate if he really spied on me all evening. How many evenings has he secretly been in the backdrop to ensure I'm not out blabbing to others about our little secret? This time seemed personal though; I should have never agreed to play this game. My own arrogance was as insatiable as Darren's. Our brotherly bond was not just on paper, I hated him so much because I see much of myself in him. I recognize that it takes one bad day to become that person. I put on my music and began cycling through my thoughts. Tonight did not go as expected, as usual. I felt terrible putting Courtney in danger, and for allowing my anger to get in the way of being a better man. It was dumb to turn back around, I know what it means to her for me to still be alive. My death has no valiance if the life I saved would rather have died than not have me here. However, I am tired of running, I must confront the monster head on. How can I protect my princess when there's a three-headed dragon thrashing around our kingdom? I agreed among my own audience to not take her to that spot anymore, even though the moments there were so blissful. I hate that dumb bastard for ruining every good moment I have. I can't even enjoy spending time with my woman while living in a constant state of paralyzing fear for possibly seeing Darren appear from the mist into my window, or snatching Courtney up while I'm not looking, butcher her and claim it was an accident. What was my father going to do? Beat him? Hit him over the head with an axe? Darren is my father's pride and joy, he could do no wrong in his eyes. I know I skate on thin ice when it comes to keeping my queen alive. I did not want Courtney involved at all, I already break her heart enough with the dumb nonsense I pull off to keep my families lies behind closed doors.

I changed the topic in my thought process, the melancholy was not going to help me have a good first trip. I put on Eddie Murphy's 'Party all the time', and proceeded to get lost inside the melody as I walked on autopilot. I started singing along with the song without regard as to how dark it was. My music carried me through the gloomiest of situations, if I wasn't listening to it, I was working on it with my guitar I bought after saving up enough money from Darnell's. I thought it would help boost my appeal to Courtney, which it didn't. I ended up getting good with it on my own after learning she didn't really care for the 'guitar guy vibe.' I would play her my music sometimes, but only after she told me she loves music that is made from the artist's heart. She's not particularly fond of the music intended to get woman to find men more attractive or 'deep.' Basically, she was saying she was too smart for such nonsense. Ever since then, I started making music for myself. Courtney could play piano like no one I've ever heard of. Even on audio. The way she plays Beethoven or Mozart's 'Requiem' is profound. Her proficiency is amazing. I've heard her play several times when I get the opportunity to come over to her house. I've wiped away tears several times while she wasn't looking as she played the piano. It tends to trap me in paralysis like a magnetic field is surrounding me. Courtney's rendition of 'Aeolian Harp' by Chopin is the only time I ever got caught crying while she was playing. That song is so beautiful to me, and to hear her execute it perfectly was stunning. I remember she said she was sorry when she saw me wipe my eyes dry, then got up to hug me. I told her "Why are you sorry? That was amazing." Courtney smiled and said "Well thank you, but I hate making you cry. I would rather break my fingers and never play again than to see that sweet face sad." I don't know what I said back but I'm sure it was something with enough poetical prose to make Shakespeare faint from his writing chair.

CHAPTER 5

I made it back to my house with a little less doubt that life would forever be bad. If I got to end every day with Courtney the way tonight did, minus the teeny tiny terror of Darren appearing from thin air, it refueled the dwindling light inside my eyes. Time spent with her was my soul's rejuvenation from the torment it experiences daily. I entered inside the front door and put the folded clothes my mother left for me on the staircase banister into my room. Before I went into my brothers room to check on his progress with our trip session, I ran downstairs to hug my mother. Being with Courtney reminded me that my mother was once a kindhearted woman like my girlfriend currently is. It reminded me that life tends to strip even the most beautiful parts of ourselves if we do not restrain against evil intertwining into the fibers of our being like grain on wheat. I looked at my godless father while I hugged my mother, who was preparing dinner for herself and the old man as usual. I felt compelled to hug him too. Wasn't he just once a little boy who strayed away from god's plan?

My mother raked through my forearm hair with her fingernails, then said "My sweet boy, did you go see your girlfriend again? I can smell your smile from here, it's masking my marinara sauce, my darling." It wasn't affecting me though, that sauce stifled throughout my nose. It filled me up with a rush of childhood, when my mother made banquets for the whole family. My father was unmoved, he kept his gaze directed at the television. I responded by saying "Yes, I did. She makes me so happy Mom. She makes waking up every day worth it. I no longer feel like a senseless wanderer, every step I walk feels in for some direction. Some purpose bigger than my own." My mother stirred her sauce, giving me a dollop of the sauce falling off her wooden spoon. It tasted delightful. She said, "I am happy you feel that way, my son. I would love if you could bring her by some-time to try my food. I hear all about this wonderful angel, yet you never let me see her for more than a few seconds when she comes by. Your mother deserves to know who her son is dating, doesn't she?" I presumed my mother had a point, but she also wasn't a normal parental figure. We weren't the secret sharing type, while my affec-tion for my mother remained high. To see her slice a man's neck so she could suck the blood rushing from it was disheartening. No child wanted to see their mother as the bloodsucking monster hiding in their closet at night. I loved her very much, yet I would never be able to look at her the same since the day she slayed her first victim in front of me.

"Perhaps, but if I'm your son, you will let go of my hand. Letting me live my own life is the greatest gift you can give a child, isn't it?" I said, stealing another swipe of my mom's homemade marinara sauce. My father looked in my direction with his usual disdain-filled face, and added, "You should listen to your mother, if she wants to know something you tell her. Don't be a sneaky little shit Tommy, I raised you better than that." I was amazed he even had the audacity to say that. I said back, "And you should hit my mother a little less, maybe she could think straight long enough to kick your couch ridden, potato chip eating, backseat driving, arm-chair quarterbacking ass to the streets where people like you belong! I guess we don't all get what we want in life now do we? Don't ever tell me how to talk to my mother, your own mother didn't even love you, who are you to tell me the first thing about being a good son to mine!" I probably wouldn't have spoken so valiantly if I didn't just have my encounter with Darren, but I lost my energy to give a shit. I grew more tired every day of my father's insolence leading us to a rock and a hard place. To watch his face twist as I spewed those words was satisfying.

His reaction, however, was not. He flew like a rocket out of his chair, then ran towards me with supersonic speed. My mother intervened, as she usually did in my defense. Yet my father wasn't having any of it. He shoved her out of the way like a windshield wiper would an insect. My mother hit the dining room table hard, hard enough to send her into near unconsciousness. My father got five feet from my face, then said, "Do you see what you made me do?! I will kill you right here on this kitchen floor, you were always my most disappointing child." I did not want to admit that I was startled, in my future novel about my life, I can . He tortured my mother, and I was too weak to ever do anything about it. This time, I felt encouraged to act differently. Which, in the end, is always a mistake when your opponent is ten times stronger than you are. I grabbed my mom's wooden spoon and smacked it across my dad's giant, egg-shaped head. The spoon split into two separate pieces, one flinging off towards the cabinet doors where we kept our food, while the handle stayed in my hands. Appalled was a nonsensical description considering how I was really feeling. I did not have the words in my head to elaborate the dread I felt in that very moment. My impulsivity would be the death of me one of these days, I wondered if today was that day. My father smiled, and relieved me from my thinking by smacking me so hard in the face I felt electricity shoot out of my sweating palms. He stood over me with hatred looming in his flaming eyes; my ears were ringing. Yet what I did make out of what he said was, "Talk to me like that again and I will throw you out of the goddamn window. How dare you think you are capable of standing against me? I am your father! I will not tolerate your behavior any longer! You don't deserve to be my son." My father walked away from me and my mother, unfazed if either of us were okay. I crawled over to her then hugged her, smearing blood and tears along her cherry blossom colored shirt. I could hardly muster the courage to stand up, my body was able to but my pride wasn't. He smacked me so hard I saw stars as I fell down, yet my ego took broken bones over a bloody face. I hated that bitch, but I also hated how defenseless I was against him. I meander through life too much as the guy too afraid to say what he wants to say, because in this home those things got you beat senseless. I hobbled towards the staircase, on the edge of my deathbed it felt like, hearing my father scoff, "You look like Mohammad Ali after fighting Frazier.... son, you sure as hell can take one just like him too. Good job getting up this time." He shouted "Regina! When you get up, can you clean this blood off our floor. It is disgusting. I don't want to step in that shit."

What a depraved monster I thought. I counted the days until I was able to put him in his place. He just had to be the most menacing individual on the planet. The souls of Genghis Khan and Charles Bronson live inside that monsters mind. I waited for the day the gunpowder arrived to stop the Steppe invasion awaiting outside my doorstep. I knocked on Miles' door to the tune of Aeolian Harp by Edward Chopin, the song Courtney so eloquently performed for me when I came over. I think about that song a lot when I'm sad, or unable to see the sun. He opened the door and hushed his impulse to scream when he saw how bad my face looked. Once he pulled me in, he began wiping my face off with a rag he had lying around. "Damn dude, I heard from up hear how hard he hit you. Are you okay?? Why do you always gotta say some shit man.... If you keep letting him hit you like that there will be no brain left inside your head." "I don't want to talk about it... okay? I just can't take it Miles. I can't hold my tongue anymore." "Well, he's going to chop it off if you don't. You gotta learn to roll with the motions, we can't help them by killing them." "What is your obsession with helping them? They're terrible. Our mom is the only one I will give optimism towards." "Because they were supposed to be my family! I got robbed of that. There's probably millions of kids robbed of that, maybe not to the severity of our parents, but suffering is subjective. Pain is all the same when magnitudes are taken out of the equation." "But they aren't. You're right, Miles, you could help so many families if your research is groundbreaking. But you can't save this one. Do you see the scars on my face? Their disillusion concerns me Miles, we aren't even family in their eyes." "That's not true, Thomas." "How is it not?! Look at my goddamn face! Is this what a loving father does to his son?!" "NO! Okay!! Does that make it feel better? I assume not! I know they're monsters Tommy, but we could change that! Why are we arguing about this right now, you need to be in a good state of mind before you trip." "I don't know if that's such a good idea Miles, my head hurts really bad. My brain might be bleeding." "Yeah, it might be, these mushrooms might be your one way to repair your broken brain. Stop poking bears, you're still a little lion. You're defiant, but you should stop trying to be something you are not. You are not a killer, Thomas. You are an artist, one who should spend more time trying to write his novel than getting into slug-fest with our father!" "It wasn't even a fight Miles... I hit him with a wooden spoon before he sent me flying into the stars heading towards planet Jupiter with one swing." "Why do you insist on letting the same dog bite you over and over again, you're never going to beat him. Can we just begin this trip now? Where's Andre?" "I haven't called him yet, I just walked in the goddamn house to talk to my mother then got slapped in the face. There wasn't exactly time to talk!" "Okay smart ass, can you just bring him here please. I want to get this experiment started as soon as possible." "For one, how is Andre going to come inside without being seen? Secondly, I still don't know how this is going to help us stop our family from becoming more rampant." "Tommy, did you listen to anything I said earlier? I told you that if this can cure your dark urges, then maybe it can work on our family. I could rewire their brains so much so that the urge to murder may dissipate entirely. As for Andre, he might need to climb up to my window." "Miles, that's insane, how ca..." Miles interjected, "You never even tried it! You impotent little mole rat can you please! Just! Do this! Okay? It's really not that complicated." "Why can't you do this, you douche?" "Because dumb-ass how can I observe myself while I'm tripping? Besides, I've done it enough times to elaborate my own experiences. This one's on you. I need to analyze the effects on someone with trauma like my own to test my theory." "Fair enough. I will call Andre, please tell me you brought some snacks." "You act like I'm a barbarian, of course I brought snacks for my little bro's first trip. Here you go. But I'd eat that stuff now, you won't be hungry while you're tripping." Miles handed me a white grocery bag with a clown holding a sign saying "Deejay's Gas Station" on it . The bag gave me the creeps, what convenience store thought a creepy clown was a good mascot? Nonetheless, the bag was filled with all sorts of snacks. My brother's damn near identical memory was key when I needed it; he never failed to pick out the snacks he knew I liked. There were even two blue Mountain Dew's in the bag. I was beyond happy. I pressed the two drinks against my radiating cheeks. It relieved a lot of the pain I was currently feeling. My father sure knew how to throw a punch, if I truly was Ali then by all means he was Frazier. Maybe even Foreman if he still were in his prime. My father had fallen off the wagon hard, yet he could still hit like nobody's business. I bet he could walk in any gym and box up the first person he saw. The army trained him right, that's for sure. Imagine giving a demon the same training as an elite soldier and the discipline of a marine corps veteran. That would be the best way to elaborate how my father is as a person. A spawn of hell with years of dedication to performing one thing: murder. "Can you just go with me if I lie to Andre about what happened tonight? I don't want him going downstairs to bark at dad and get treated worse than I did." "What are you even going to say, make it something bad-ass and I'll go with it," Miles responded. "Alright then, I'll say Darren took my favorite book so we brawled in the hallway. I'll tell him he should see how he looks when he says how bad my face looks." Miles and I laughed, sharing a good moment together before I descended into the abyss of my sunken temple. I did not want to journey too deeply into the true essence of who I was beyond the locked doors imploring in my mind. The doors protected me from seeing me in a too revealing mirror. I chose to not think about my past circumstances for good reason. If I think about the past for too long, I might be drawn back into that energy again. That mindset again. Yet I grew tired of running from who I was. If this trip would get me closer to accepting who I really am, then I need to take it with grace. As I stared at myself through my brother's closet mirror, still semi-bloody and semi-certain of suffering a concussion, the transparency of being an entirely different person than I was when I was a child humored me. The etchings of a beard across my chin didn't seem real, neither did the stains of black and blue bruises along my face. The years within life definitely took a toll on me, yet I wasn't even twenty yet. I wondered what I would look like when I reached my father's age. Would I be the same depraved man, or would I be something completely new? My inner river was overflowing, the emotions inside me brewed with vigor. The spindling string of my sanity was slowly unspooling, the deep seeded anger I've felt since I was old enough to understand the universe was exerting it's inertia onto me. I smiled while looking at the mirror one last time, in this battle between good and evil, I see that the forces are equal. It is our oppression of one to choose another when the war never even began. Good and evil can never exist simultaneously in harmony. Wouldn't it be better to be a warrior in a garden rather than a gardener at war, I can't quite remember who said that but the message was profound. My final thought gazing into that mirror was putting the pieces of my shattered self back together, to see the whole creature hiding behind the curtain. The little things I saw in between that made me into who I turned out to be were paralyzing. It was finally time to take a trip into the mind I try so hard to hide from. Maybe then, I will no longer feel like a prisoner in my own situation. In my own body and skin.

Miles opened his window for Andre to crawl in. I could tell by his face he was appalled that I made him climb up a tree to enter inside. His reaction over the phone alone enough told me his stance on the situation. He plopped into my brothers room, brushing leaves and debris off of his jacket sleeves. He said "dude, that tree is intense! I felt like the king of Zulu conquering that tree". "You know about the Zulu? My man! Can we talk history or what?" "Miles. I am a proud black man, of course I know of my history. I could name every great African in history. To the Zulu even down to the kings and queens who ruled the Egyptians for a little while. That was one faucet Miles and Andre could connect on, they started talking about Joseph Bologne, otherwise known as 'Chevalier de Saint George's' and the legendary general for Napoleon Bonaparte: Thomas Dumas. I did not know as much as them in history. I considered myself smart, yet one of my idols Stephen King said a genuine genius would never consider themselves as such. So I assume that speaks volumes on my intelligence. Anyone who considers themselves smarter than the population were usually dumber than it by tenfold. Out of all my conversations with Andre and Miles, they never have proclaimed their intellect. Except when rubbing it in my face. Which in my mind, measures how far their smarts actually reach.

I walked around the room as they talked about Nefertiti, an Egyptian queen who apparently was quite beautiful in her day and age. Andre argued that even today she and Cleopatra would be far more attractive than half of the people on this planet are today. I did not really care about the conversation, my mind was lashing out like a violent lightning storm. There was lions, tigers, and hyenas picking me apart as I stood in a Colosseum all alone. They ate the steaming steaks chained around my neck, then go for my own flesh. What did this mean? I wasn't a psychologist so I didn't know, but it gave me bad premonition for how this trip was going to go. I paced around the room with hazy clarity, my fingertips flexed as my breathing became less automatic. As if my body was preparing for what was to come. How would my body know what this substance is supposed to do to me if I haven't even tried it yet? Was this really god's energy, or was this just natural? The way of nature has instilled millions of years into me, all things that have ate these mushrooms have passed down their genetics through generations. Perhaps my body had an inclination of what was coming. Miles asked, "Have you heard of the stoned ape theory Andre?" Andre replied "Terrence McKenna came up with that, right? Yeah I've heard of it." "Do you think it's true though?" "To be honest, no. It sounds incredibly complex, life seems so much more simple than that. In my opinion, we use theories and religions and shit to hide our inability to understand what really is." "What really is? So apes evolving from psychedelics to make the modern human is more complex than a god having immaculate ability to create entire civilizations with just his hands?" "Exactly, they both seem far-fetched right? I don't just say neither are true, who are you or I to ever understand the truth. All I can say is I feel life isn't that complicated. We are intelligent animals. We have risen through the evolution of time and are now at a point of stagnation, because there is nothing else for us to accomplish. We are the only animals smart enough to provide everything we could ever want, yet are the only ones dumb enough to still search for more. To withhold an abundance of properties for people in need just so that person can die with a feeling of wealth and prosperity. Life isn't that hard to understand for me. I see it as we are merely the most advanced animal, there's no specialness to us. We are just the ones with the ability to think, use our thumbs, and plan for the future. Give every other animal that capability then see how special we are. We're not. We're dominant because of a selective byproduct of nature, not because of our overhauled thought process. Take me to any universe other than this one and I bet we see life in a higher virtue. Perhaps dogs would walk us." Miles surely seemed stunned, I don't think he's ever debated anyone who actually understood more than his own intellect. All the geeks he contends these things with are usual to hold onto their biases and beliefs until the dire end. Andre spoke only from what he'd observed, and offered the valid point that he doesn't know. A feature not common in today's 'gotcha!' culture that decides you need to be right at all times when you speak or not at all. Andre did not accept these judgments. He spoke from a place of understanding. I liked listening to him speak about things he was passionate about. You can tell he thinks about these things in his free time, that he has a mind equal to Julius Caesar. Miles said after his moment of pause, "Alright Andre, I like the way you think. Even if Terrence wasn't correct on if apes taking psyche-delics made us into the humans we are today. I say his theory because what if he was onto something. What if the humans we are today all took these plants. I'm certain that we would evolve into a higher life form entirely. Imagine a hive mind where all humans think alike, and can aim for the same heights." "Isn't uniqueness what makes life so interesting?" Andre responded. "Absolutely, we don't strip that away with opening our mind, we allow ourselves to join together because of our differences. Because we will realize that no matter how different we are, we are all the same entity. We are all cut from same cake, different flavors and sizes of slices but it all comes from the same batter. I want to live in a world where people like my parents can't exist. I don't want there to be senseless violence inside of families homes anymore. The world deserves better, the children of now deserve better." "You're right, Miles. You really are. But this force... you can't oppose it. You can only choose one. If you dance between the embers too long it will consume you! You cannot walk along a tightrope forever. To be good, or to be evil, is its own virtue. The virtue of choice. To dwindle in the middle of them is the worst fate imaginable." I munched on my snacks and tried my hardest to relax. I felt like they were going to battle until dawn if I did not inter-vene. I said "Guys, your philosophies are charming, can we just move on to the part where I trip and feel better?" Miles chuckled to himself, hiding his smile in his shirt collar. He told me "It does not work like that Tommy; do you think I'm wielding the infinity stones here? This 'trip' has a destination you must choose to arrive to. It will only show you the side of your subconscious you cannot normally travel to. You, Tommy, have to observe and learn what the 'shrooms show you." "This sounds like a lotta woo-woo, what's next, am I supposed to meet some sort of guru who guides me through my trip?" "Some people do, while others don't create subconscious characters. Those people experience themselves everywhere all at once. Able to see themselves through childhood all the way to their doom, in several different instances. I've had one of these experiences, it's quite profound. But it's rarer in nature, most people cannot escape the veil surrounding their subconscious. There's always this problem and this trauma to resolve. But with enough patience, I believe all people can reach the 'higher' state of thinking." I did not know if what he was saying is true. I was not a doctor nor a performer of the mystic arts. What he was saying sounded crazy to me. But in a few moments, I can tell him myself how I feel about his laborious experiment.

Miles handed me a clear, vacuum-sealed bag with several giant mushrooms inside. He told me "Make sure and eat the caps, they're what get you the highest." I sat on my brother's bed, contemplated what the hell lead me to this very moment, then ate the mushrooms whole. They tasted terrible. My mouth puckered; this awful flavor stuck to the sides of my cheeks. Even bits of mushrooms were stuck in my teeth. Ewwwwww, yuck! I withheld the urge to vomit by thinking of Krispy Kreme donuts. Once I mustered the willpower to swallow down the colossal mushroom ball dwelling inside my throat, it made me jitter. Not as if being electrocuted, but more like being tased on the lowest setting. My teeth were beginning to involuntarily clench about ten minutes in. Miles kept writing stuff down as I laid down, so I asked him what he thought so far. He replied, "Subject appears slightly sweaty. His eyes are dilated about trifold, completely engulfing the iris." I was surprised to be feeling different so suddenly. I did not think long about how quickly this would hit me. Andre's face changed shade and shape, going from hexagon to decagon then to triangle. I wasn't scared however, I felt like I was really high. Except my body was pulsating some sort of wavelength. Words wouldn't do it justice, but even my feet were radiating as if plugged into a supersonic battery. Twenty minutes in, my head rocked back and forth; there were so many waves hitting me all at once. I could feel the force life exerted onto each individual creature, giving it it's uniquely special abilities. I turned back to Miles, which made my eyes water. Not from sadness, but from brightness. I wiped my eyes as I watched all kinds of colors flood through my brother. He was like one of those mosaics in a church. My sense of time was fading too, I did not know if my ten or twenty minutes was actually hours. I asked Miles how long has it been, but no words came out. I was unable to speak. My imagination sped past me at nine thousand miles a minute. Yet the part of my brain that produced words was unable to work. Andre grabbed my shoulder and said "Tommy? You okay man? You're starting to sway a lot. Maybe you should lie down." My brother differed however, he said, "Keep him up for as long as possible. I need him to explain as much of this experience as possible." Miles began taking more notes, asking me multiple times "How do you feel? Tommy?" He would snap his fingers, trying to get my attention. I still did not have the mental faculty to speak. I touched Andre's hand with my own. Before I knew it, I faded into the darkness. It seemed more like she pulled me into her black water. I could not help but scream, but no one was there to hear me. I drowned in the darkness. I kept swimming upward but submerged deeper with each stroke. "Where would this lead?" I wondered. Andre and Miles both looked at each-other as I fell back into unconsciousness. "What the hell was that?! Is-is he still alive!" Andre said, touching Tommy's neck before Miles said, "He's not dead, he's experiencing something far worse. His worst fear." "What do you mean, worst fear? What the hell is wrong with you?! I thought you cared about him?" Miles responded angrily, "I do damnit! That's why I did it! Tommy will walk around his whole life trapped because of his trauma. I am providing him a solution to that trauma. I would never hurt my brother, Andre, I'm trying to save him." Andre backed up, rubbing his temples with his trembling fingers to alleviate his brain from any more discomfort than it already was experiencing. "Damn you, what did you do to him? How much of those mushrooms did you give him?"

"I gave him what is considered a heroic dose, which is ten grams."
"TEN GRAMS! Holy hell, I'm never going to see my friend again. If
I do his brain is going to be mush!" "I would never do something to
my brother if I hadn't done it myself. It is a tremendous experience. A
toll to bear in its own way, but the price he is paying now is too much,
Andre. You wanna know why his face looks like that? It's not because
he gets along with our father so much. He is a prisoner within his
own family. I have a chance of changing this family's fate. You gotta
trust me Andre, I want what you want. Tommy's safety and survival.
Let's work together and bring him home safely." "Okay. Okay. What
do you need me to do?" Andre asked. "Keep an eye on his heart rate,
tell me when it accelerates and when it declines. I'm going to try to
map out Tommy's trip so he can explain it to me when he wakes up."
"That's genius, you really are smart. Let's do this."

CHAPTER 6

The soles of my shoes clammed onto Miles's floor, like being dragged under the surface from a planet-sized magnet. My eyes were not open, yet they felt as if they were. The colors framing his room into place started swirling; leaving me entranced within DaVinci's vision. Before even realizing it, I phased out of my conscience! Like static to a television before activating its scheduled program, I was turned on. Stuck in place with memories slowly loading in as static sparks fired rampantly. Without relapse, I wondered perhaps if this landscape was tangibly present beyond my brain! Andre was nowhere to be seen, but as I stood there still loading into full awareness, I regretted joking about Naruto rather than asking how this 'trip' worked or what to expect. As my mental windshield unfogged, I saw I was nine houses down from my own! The Milner's property stood crooked as if imitating a famous tower in Italy; even their doorknob sat atop in the far right impossible to reach. I knelt down, smelling one of the universes sacred treasures- freshly cut grass. However, this was no ordinary yard, green fingers were pointing down the street towards my house! An intense breeze blew between the leaves drafted in the wake of dark draping clouds roaring above my neighborhood. Lightning sliced violently into the sky, slashing straight through ketchup-colored clouds with little resistance. The blackness began to bleed red plops of hot blood onto me! I could somehow feel my face singeing even though I was metaphysically transcending far beyond my brittle body. The nature of physics abided by its own laws in this realm. Following street signs led to inception, every house I passed by two more replaced them! Andre's advice echoed within the thrashing thunder above me, I properly conducted my crashing cabooses back onto course by instinctively running into the house beside me. I stared at the door, stumped at the sight of it sitting sideways, unsure if crawling through and entering was the best idea. As I hurdled through the door-frame then swiveled back around to check my surroundings, the entrance shifted back into being perfectly flat. As I peered a little closer within the darkness, I realized I was in my home! I glanced behind me, considering crawling back out, yet the door was replaced with simple, twig-like plank wood bordering around it's frame. My house's splitting staircase slithered off like a pair of silk snakes; leaving me standing in a bare room. Alone, surrounded by quietness, 'Roxanne' ran along the record player. Winding up with its snares, "You don't have to sell your body to the night." Window shutters shot open, welcoming red rain inside, and every commotion ceased to exist, allowing me to hear every voice more clearly now. My family's voices, Andre's voice, even Courtney's voice! Reality was cackling in my face, before transcending into waving parallels transferring me into the kitchen! I was enthralled, it was full of life and prosperity. Something that was rarely experienced within these four walls. The dinner table was stacked to the brim with five-star entrees that would've made Gordon Ramsey gargle on his lamb sauce. Everyone's laughter bounced off one another like a live game of conversational pinball. Darren and Miles looked completely unison, fulfilling the two perfect halves of humanities yin and yang. All uniqueness suppressed within his chest, but his eyes.... they were completely black! Dark matter coursed behind his forehead; showing he descended down a familiar abyss. However, this one did not call out to me trying to entice encouragement into scourging its depths of darkness. This one resided solemnly within the absence of light, feeding on nothing but self-absorption. My parents looked normal, too normal. As if standing in a fun house mirror contorting their horrible qualities into outstanding ones. Not even a wink of my mother's alternate identity was present, I could only feel her. Mike's anger experienced total dissipation; his default frown rose into a glistening gleam of teeth. Andre leaned over and passed Courtney our 'KFC Big Chicken' saltshaker to season her steaming steak. "Well, what a surprise Thomas, didn't expect seeing you here. The normally bed-ridden has risen!" Darren chuckled while chowing down mashed potatoes covered in cheese and chives "Hello angel! Come sit next to me, I was just telling Andre how DELIGHTFUL your mother's cooking is! How have I not been invited here sooner?!" Courtney chimed while chewing. "I agree sweet pea, this is just, delightful. Some would say even to die for, perhaps?" Darren said, flashing me a familiar wink. Darren lifted from his chair reaching deep into his pants. A fully loaded gun emerged out those pockets. He smashed the trigger without hesitation, he blasted Andre's jaw off into scattering shattered pieces hurling towards the wall! The struggling cabooses carrying my train of thought finally derailed into destruction. He sat up howling as his mouth flickered up-down and side-side like a Nintendo joystick. Courtney, now crying laughing, attempted to fly a piece of steak airplane into the hole his lower face was once located at. "Come on! Its rude to chew with your mouth open!" It was excruciating to witness, Miles collapsed to the floor with tears still flailing off his face.

I ran out of there instantly, heading for the only place I felt safe, my room. Instinctively curling into a ball and beginning to bawl. Escaping the looming truth protruding through my skull! That it was humorous believing I had any chance of doing this myself. As the clouds outside above separated, light peeked in. Peering within my minds dispute to escape this loop. Giving me momentary freedom from the Devil's relenting tempting. Remembering how the sun always shined even when it was night-time, for my faith not to be with me always is nothing less than failure. Andre's dorky voice saying certain Star Wars references traversed into me. I thought of Yoda yielding hearing Luke's lack of inspiration, saying "do or do not, there is no try." Goddamn those few words dug so deep, I began latching onto the very ideas formulating in my brain. That 'trying' was what got people in fourth place and given a participation trophy. My door shimmered in similar light being casted into the bedroom. I sprawled to my feet and tried coming back to life but was cruelly halted. Grabbing the doorknob made it grin with grimace! I drew my hands back before losing fingers in its attempt of snapping down. The knob discharged the most disturbing crunching noise ever to be heard, it was pure grit against several rows of teeth. "I would try that again if I was you" the doorknob said smiling. "What the-" I said back. The knob replied "Although I enjoy a good flabbergasting, finish if you will. Out of everything that just occurred during this trip, I feel I am the most usual. *I was thinking how he was reading my mind* "Before asking, my knowledge comes from being a projection of your subconsciousness, if you haven't noticed, everything here is." *Why.* The brain turned train dragging crashed cabooses was beginning to flow smoothly on lumber tracks. Everything I was receiving felt like a spike stabbing straight through the heart of glass protecting my ideas and feelings. The doorknob said "Tommy, your sanity is precious. You should know once lost; it is almost never retained. Evil has a horrible tendency to undo itself, becoming its own vigorous wick midst the land of candle wax. This great pressure was hoisted upon you, and I know you didn't ask Santa Claus for this 'gift' to be given. However, your only hope is survival. You cannot win". "I-" "Let me stop you right there. Possibly, your predicament outside this conversation is very closely intertwined. You seem to be comparably stuck in a locked room. Like a junkie, the hardest step is looking in the mirror and realizing YOU allowed this. We are all created within our own afflictions, despite massive hate for being placed around crime ridden circumstances. The purpose of life is to find out what's worth struggling for, and what's worth dying for. YOU, need to decide what's important, this fear will forever leave you frozen as a shadow in your own actions. I am only a reflection of the things you think when taken away from the exuberance of reality. Your circumstances dampen your potential. To think, and to act, are two totally different entities. There is a reason someone like your brother is dangerous. He balances the construct of maintaining his ability to think for himself and execute the exact act he planned out so accordingly-." I slapped the knob hoping every voice in my head would just go dead! The knob smiled, then said "One more thing...good luck." I was tripping so hard I could not tell what was real and what was a product of the psychedelic's. I wondered how a doorknob was talking to me, and how Andre could be shot and still talk. This psychedelic experience was going horribly! I ran out of my house without doubt heeding the needed advice. *Should've taken it kid.* Recalling those dreaded words said to me in the basement by my brother, refusing to believe that the fear of him had become attached to me. Like Andre pointed out: Insecurity reeks profusely while brilliance is riddled with carbon monoxide, mostly unnoticed.

Street signs scattered back in place, replaced from where I had originated. Yet, I wasn't alone. My brother Darren stood menacingly about two houses down. Amid the distance, I felt his, hatred. Utter distaste for being brought into my psyche, no signs of delight demonstrating that even in mentality, he was ultimately more powerful. His ambiance radiated sounds of bone rattle, clacking profusely carrying a chain of every soul he's ever collected! My remaining innocence was crushed in his hand, happily crippling any form of ignorance still lingering. Embalmed into a gyroscope and swapping essences, I for once truly understood what occurred within his head. There was no appalled abundance revealing massive lack of empathy, or twenty-seven voices telling him to commit sin. However, murder was his expression of hiding as the phantom in an opera. Openly enjoying it, behind the physical and metaphorical mask embellishing his inner monstrosities. Pursuing me, all that spun inside his inner record player was George Washington Jr.'s soothing serenity. "I hear the crystal raindrops fall, on the window down the hall, and it becomes the morning dew. And darling when the morning comes, and I see the morning sun, I wanna be the one with you. Just the two of us." Freezing. Sheer coldness coursed throughout each individual artery. Images of rose petals in a bathtub and harps paraded his head space. He savored every second thinking this was his chance to finally kill me. The only personal connection he ever developed during his display of exempting maniacal mental warfare onto reality. I wish I could say I felt his heart shiver in withdrawal but no, there was none. His resided deep indoors where sanctuary preserved obscure vanity under a draping rain forest canopy. There were no rustic thoughts convincing or diminishing his well-being, evil had crafted the most beautiful diamond. I retracted, compelled by the geometric force gravitating my entire spirit towards gazing into his abyss. Not quite back into my own skin, more so third-person spectating. I flicked my character's joystick and button mashed fleeting in fight or flight. Even in my mind, my abilities were suppressed. Conforming to his collateral conquering once again, reminiscing Jay-Z telling me in life there was winners and losers, drug dealers and abusers. Maintaining the median was meaningless. "It's useless running, you rodent! You're cornered, checkmated!" Exhausted of fleeing from his words, my mind pixelated to my arriving here. Being abducted, little by little, watching consciousness fizzle back into modern era. I awoke to Andre hovering above me bug-eyed, stuck staring shocked like I died! "Dude! Are you okay!?" Andre said, with frenetic energy spindling out of his mouth.

I replied "We're.... we're all gonna die! No... I'm not okay. That was awful, what the hell was that! Was that hell? Why does my brain feel like it's still loading?!" Miles took some final notes on his clipboard, then told me "I am sorry Tommy, I gave you a lot. I wanted you to see something special." I rubbed my eyes, still feeling foggy like waking up from forty-eight hour slumber. I said "Miles... that was horrifying.. what was that place? How long was I gone?" "About six hours, and that was your subconscious. A place where all your underlying thoughts live. What did you see? That might help me decipher what you are feeling deep down below the surface." "It was awful, I saw Andre die, sort of. Courtney was there! Everyone was eating dinner and being really weird. Then Darren chased me though our neighborhood while the song 'Just the Two of Us' was playing. I don't know how I was able to hear it though, there was no stereos on the road." "Physics doesn't work the same there as it does here in reality, at least as to why dark manifestations can appear even when they're severely irrational. It sounds like you are afraid of Courtney meeting them for real, as she may end up liking them. As for Andre, it seems you fear him being caught in the crossfire of our family's actions. Darren, is quite obvious. Even though dad beats you constantly, it is Darren you fear most. My reason would be because you don't understand him. Dad might as well have a sign as to why he does what he does. Our brother, however, is a million times more ominous with his malevolence. I can see why he brings you great anxiety. Could you feel their anguish as well..?" "You know... I did. I could feel everything. Like my mind was everywhere all at once. I need to lay down

in my bed, my brain feels like it was slammed against the pavement."
"That tends to happen when you take ten grams of pure Psilocybin,
go get some sleep. Andre you mind climbing out the window again?
I apologize in advance for making this request." Andre laughed, then
said "Yes, it's okay. Tommy, I love you bro, I hope you'll call me when
you're feeling better. I wanna continue learning about this journey
of yours. I can record again so we can practice for your novel!" Andre
hopped out the window with excitement tingling down his spine,
he seemed so stoked as if this was the most important thing he's ever
encountered. I was still hazy. I walked out of Miles room and entered
into my own with the few remaining brain cells I had left. I laid my
head down, trying to forget everything that was said in my head the
night before. The persistence and belligerence of these ideas made
my brain hurt even more than it currently was.

Before my brain could even warm up to idle, an intense stomping
surfed towards my door, crashing into my door like a massive tidal
wave! Darren stormed in then screamed "Get up! You're coming
with me, now!" "fuc-" Miles ran out of his room, attempting to
stop the commotion. Miles said "Darren, don't do something you'll
regr-" you stay out of this Miles! I warned you and that fucking kid
about poking around in our affairs!" "Just rela-" ""I'm not going to
kill the little rat, Miles, not yet... I need him to see my seriousness."
My mother walked up to me sobbing, shaking my face saying "You
have to stop, Tommy! He's gonna kill you! You have to stop!" My dad
paced back and forth in the living room, before throwing one of my
mother's favorite vases covered in orchids into the dining room cab-
inets. He screamed "I don't even want to look at you! Darren, do as
you please with the imbecile." Darren grabbed me by the collar and
dragged me outside with my father holding my mother back. Miles
ran back into his room, leaving me out in the cold like a sole snow-
flake in an orchard.

He threw me into the passenger side of his red Ford Ranger,
the interior door handles had been completely removed. I wondered how many unsuspecting victims felt the phobia of falling for
his charming persona and were caught like a fly on a honey strip
"Darren- I'm- sor..." "Just shut up okay, just shut it. Do you not respect
me, Thomas? Does it not rattle you to the core that I would slice your

spleen out of your body and not even save a moment to blink? You think because we are related, I will ignore the fact you have been telling your little fuck-buddy everything you know! Let this be a reminder. I don't ask for forgiveness. Don't make me turn you into a souvenir, I will make you dead without even killing you!" His words solidified in the back of my mind that he truly valued no one but himself. My ego was slain inside my brain, I thought I had caught a step ahead of him yet his chess piece shifted twenty paces forward. Darren sped his truck to seventy in a thirty-five, blasting "Born to Run" by Bruce Springsteen.

As we floored throughout our town's back-roads, there was a sole person walking their dog on the side of the road. Darren slightly smiled at me and said, "watch this." He swerved sharply to his left and crumbled the unsuspecting pedestrian and his dog within an instant. I was gazing at the blood- spattered windshield while Darren's smile softly swooped down, "Damn it! Dumb bitch busted my front headlight." "Wh-What the hell is wrong with you!" I screamed before puking out of the window. The sight of the blood smearing along Darren's windshield make my puke taste like pennies. "What? They were in my line of sight, I couldn't help it; I think there's some goddamn fur on the grill. Wonder if it's from the guy's scalp or his dog," Darren chuckled. I was mortified to even look towards his direction, my body was condensing coldly deeper than glacier depths. "Tommy, I hope we understand each other now. I just showed you how little I value anyone's life, especially yours. I will make you crunch under my tires and not save a split second to miss a nod to the beat of my mp3 player. You are free from my grasp, but listen and listen closely. If I find myself fishing down the wrong well again, I will break you, Thomas. Did you actually think you could win this game?" "You know you won't win right? No matter how much you take from me there will always be someone who prefers justice rather than anarchy? There will always be people like me willing to stand against people like you. Do your worst to me, Darren." "Do not ask for something you cannot cash-in. You compel me. I have never faced a single challenge while engaging in my art so to finally have that rush of consequence, well, it completes me, Tommy. Never forget you are a canary contained within a cage while

I am the tom-cat, remember that! Anything you think you under-stand about this family is because I allow you to know it! You think I haven't seen Miles's little wall of mysteries?! He's just as crazy as you are and doesn't even fucking know it yet, to think he can 'cure' us like it's not our decision to do what we do. Hilarious. I will take you back now, but just know, you asked for this." For once in my life, I wasn't met with fear from him. However, visual stimulation of seeing him, them, once and for all defeated.

I leaped out of the passenger door once we arrived home, imme-diately going up to Miles room to chew him a new ass for not pre-paring me for that any sort of warning. Miles creaked the door open, not prepared for my bull in a china shop rage. "What the fuck, Miles! Did you know he knew? He knows everything! Man, this is not good," I said angrily. "I told you to stay out of this, Tommy! He's become, erratic. I've never seen him lose his composure like this, he seems hell bent on fixing this 'problem'. My advice is listening to me this time, STAY out of this. Because of you now he's breathing down my neck about our research, I need to work overtime if we have any chance to do this with as little casualties as we can" "as little casu- LOOK around! This has gone on since before we were even born, there is no 'saving them'. We have to take action despite the detriment of consequence, if we falter to those who put us through fear we are the weak party not them! This ends Miles, I will find answers." "This is everything to me! If anyone has felt the wrath of the Hansens, it's me! There are far worse things than death can cause. Like forever living under the umbrella of torment provided by the people who were supposed to love you.... You just have to believe me, go hang with Andre, get the answers you seek. But please, give me a chance to fix this." I left his room uncertain of my position. I had one brother completely shatter my desire to see them live, while the other reminded me that worse could occur if our decisions moving forward were not executed with perfection. It was truly the divine feminine of crossroads, I was desperately in need for answers. I spent my whole life conformed to the idea I should shut up and stay out of everyone's way. The time now, was to act on my crime of silence.

I called Andre, hoping he did not pull a McLovin on me, but for once in my life someone pulled through on their word. "Yooo, I got some FIRE stuff man, you wanna come over to try it with me? I could only imagine the bad vibes you feel there, especially if you're still tripping sack." "Hell, yeah man let's do it, can you come now?" "What kind of question even is that, of course I can. I'll come nab you and you can pay for snacks since I got the drugs, Bucko!" "Fair enough, lemme grab my wallet and I'll be ready." I trotted downstairs, hoping Darren had left to murder some poor person within his proximity, anyone he could place into his cross-hairs and track with predator-level intimacy until the will for watching them live dwindled into the bottomless pit. My dad sat glued to his recliner watching 'The Great George Foreman' from when we last interacted. I tried tiptoeing down the stairs so I could avoid any possible halt my father might sporadically present. Yet, he was aware and awaiting my arrival. "Thomas! If that's you, Come here." "Damn it" I muttered. "Yes, father." "I hope your brother slapped some sense into you, if I find you mouthing off to that little bitch of a friend again, you're dead, you hear me?" I said, "You shut the hell up you brain-dead beast, you have some nerve. I'd be careful befo-" My dad was instantly on his feet, I never even saw his shoes move. He picked me up with insane force with no speck of struggle. "You... are a shell of my son! I am disappointed to call you my own. You're on your last leg kid, I will end this myself if it comes to it. I..." In the middle of his sentence, the doorbell rang. "Oh.... saved by the bell huh. I'm warning you Tommy, you're walking on the thinnest of ice right now. Don't! Push it."

He set me down and sat back in his chair, pressing play on Foreman knocking down Micheal Moorer. My mother brushed me off, then said "Before you go Tommy, we're all eating dinner together tonight!" "Okay, sounds great." "Yes, it will be, because I want you to bring Courtney! It will be so much fun!" "I don't think that's a good ide-" "You will do what your mother asks or I will beat your ass black and blue again! You just don't listen do you, Thomas?" I scurried out of the door, legs trembling like I just took that knockout punch that sent Moorer to the floor. Andre could see my disdain from his driver side windowpane. "Did someone just die?!" "I think I almost did!" "WHat?! WHat happened!" "Darren is what happened! That fucking lunatic! He's onto us man, how? I don't even know how he knows, he's a freaking demon! He's utterly ruthless, he's not going to stop until he gets what he wants, he was born a conqueror! Darren is trying to set me up, I know he is! I don't know what his ploy is but I can tell you where it starts! My mother wants Courtney over to eat dinner and I know Darren played a part in that! He knows ,Andre! We shouldn't have done this!" "Tommy! Calm. Down! Your brother's not Lord Voldemort, man. I understand he scares you. I do. Let's change the topic though, I know this is important so I'm going to share something very sacred. So that you know no matter what happens, I am in this until the end. You're not the only one on this planet who is suffering, by all means is this, extraordinary. But I too understand pain, it is permanently scribbled over the scars across my body. I feel my mind racing when I see people out in public with their fathers, stressing how I have to be there for my child! The fear, of not. Kills me. I know that doesn't help but I'm trying to say its human to confront your demons! We all have some cloaked persona of maliciousness that tries to heed us from our path to happiness. It's about letting go, letting go of what you know. What you think you know." "How are you so calm through this... I told you my family were murderers a day ago and you still haven't snapped. I expected after the first day shock wore off you'd leave, but you've really invested into this, why?" Because my father almost killed my mother..... in his rage for being denied a place to stay for his continuous bad drinking habits, he barged in and nearly punched her face off. I was about thirteen years old, so I did what I thought was smart: smash a chair over his head. Unfortunately.... I broke his neck with one of the chair legs. He died on top of my mom. I didn't suffer any consequences because I was ten years old, and it was obviously self-defense. Yet, the immense guilt I live with to this day is not something some judge could condone on me. I value intelligence because it allows me to live with the terrible things that I have done. My father wasn't a monster, only a product of a generational turmoil that he could not escape from. For me, to escape is what I live for. Being valedictorian is not important to me, what is important is that I accomplished something awesome even when the odds were set against me. You can do the same too, Tommy. I believe in you immensely." I felt the numbness return, how could someone live with such a decision. At such a young age too. I said, "That is just... awful. I am so sorry you had to live through that. I-I will continue to fight too then... even when my lips are dripping blood and my chin is black and blue. I will fight for justice amid the persistent evil around me. I will bring Courtney to dinner, and play the game so I can see what Darren is up to. I know that Courtney is safe in our home, for some reason, my family seems to like her. I'm gonna text her now so she can get a head start of getting dressed." "Well, be careful my friend. That's not enough time for her, but you can sit and watch her get ready. It's the little things that make a relationship tick. Let's smoke this doobie and I'll drop you off at Courtney's after. I can't wait for you to get a car, it's gonna be awesome cruising down California with you someday!" "Yeah... I can hardly wait for that day, Andre."

CHAPTER 7

An hour previous

Darren, who usually kept cool under annoying circumstances, was enraged. When he heard Andre and Miles whispering as he walked to his room with a woman, it pushed him over the ledge. Over the hedge would be more appropriate considering he did indeed want to leap ten feet into the air. He thought the promise of killing Tommy through their verbal warfare was enough to scare him, but he instead needed more drastic measures. Darren did his best to compartmentalize his emotions while spending the rare moment with a woman. It didn't take long for things to get freaky. By the copy of 'The art of Seduction' by Robert Greene sitting ajar on his fully furbished bookshelf, it appeared Darren studied affection as proficiently as he did slicing someone's head off of their skeleton. Darren dangled his cat o' nine tails whip in front of the brunette woman. She seemed pleased by this disposition. He decided to have his way with her, unleashing his frustration with each whipping motion. She laid complacently and ate up the affection Darren displayed onto her.

After a brisk intermission of kissing, Darren said "Are you ready to have some fun? Marley?" She perked up, then said "Why, yes, yes, I am." "Well good. Let's get to it then." They played passionately, almost as if they were bunnies in love. If you didn't know Darren was a psychopathic killer with no residual interest in humanity, you would say he was capable of intimacy within this moment. But, as most moments are, like butterflies in the breeze, they're fleeting. Darren played with her until her eyes were closed, then, ever so slightly, slid over to grab his globe from his dresser. Once he was certain she was in a moment of complete bliss, he bashed her over the head several times until pieces of her skin stuck to the weapon itself. Why he wanted her to feel bliss before death is only something Darren can understand. Perhaps, even he is unaware why. Like Frankenstein killing its creator, for another fleeting moment, Darren wondered why he even killed the poor woman. There was no reason to, yet, neither was the other hundred plus he had done away with previously.

Once that thought erupted in his head, he was reminded of why he committed these crimes. The momentary freedom from his hard-wired desire to kill anything he touches had ceased. He cleaned himself up, changing clothes while muttering to himself 'I'll clean her up later... right after I deal with Tommy'. He brainstormed about how he could instill his way of life into him, but his furious vengeance beguiled him. Not only did Darren want to scare him, Darren wanted him to watch everyone Tommy loved wither within the wind until only he was left. In the depths of the abyss within Darren's head, monsters were not the worst thing creeping down in there. It was actually darkness shrouding the true monstrosity, himself. Ever since that confrontation in their basement, Tommy had not realized what kind of beast he had awakened. Tommy removed the seal to the tomb and unwrapped it's sleeping pharaoh, reviving an astounding amount of wickedness within the cold descent of Darren's deep abyss. He had meant what he said when proclaiming this was a game of cat and mouse. Darren followed his prey endlessly, temporarily canning the need for bathing in blood to reach this high he's religiously seeking. He entertained this game stone sober, wasting no lack for exception or distraction. Entering an epitome of holding heaven inside a single mind state, except he directed demons to construct his ideal land of vicious incarnate instead.

Darren trotted downstairs, hoping to envelop his insidious snare around his mother's aura of calmness, which usually combated his calamitic tendencies. He saw his mother preparing dinner for the night even though it was only the morning still. She was a chef by heart, not by trade. Darren said "Hey! That food smells delicious, speaking of which, when will we be inviting Tommy's little slice of pie over for dinner? Haven't you asked him several times about bringing her over?" His mother smiled while rolling out handmade dough, then said "Why yes, yet Tommy insist on not bringing her over. I will respect his wishes. He will bring her by when it's the right time for him to. When you get a girlfriend instead of killing all of them, you would understand." "Perhaps. However, I know it bothers you to not meet his little princess yet. Tommy will have anxiety until the day he dies. He will not change his mind until then. If you want him to bring her, then you need to force him." "I will not.... but you're right. I do in fact want to meet this woman for longer than five minutes at a time. I will take your advice Darren, but I will not be belligerent like you would be. Be nicer to your brother." "Oh.. soon enough, he will be cowering to me like I'm an umbrella and he's a stray dog stuck in the rain." "That's terrible Darren... Why do you even care if Courtney comes over.....You hate everyone and everything on this planet." "On the contrary, I do indeed appreciate her company. She is beautiful like a princess, but does not carry herself as one would. That's a compliment in the highest regard considering she is dating a certified dumb-ass." "Ugh, Okay Darren. I'm done with this conversation. Will you just go get your brother so we can tell him to invite her for dinner? I want him to have enough time to dress nice, this will be so exciting!" "With pleasure." Darren responded coolly.

CHAPTER 8

Two hours later

"Thanks for the ride Andre, I will call you if anything happens during dinner. I already have an uneasy feeling about this evening. After that trip and that encounter with my brother, I feel like my life is in danger." "No problem buddy, glad to have you back. Against all the odds, even when I was worried about you these past few days. Hell, these past few years have been a trip. I just want you to know it has been an honor to be your friend. Knowing what I know about your family doesn't change how I feel about you. You have made me proud, even during the days you undoubtedly frustrate me.... Make this as good a night as possible. Tomorrow, we will move forward with what needs to happen. I trust your brother, but I trust you more. Whatever you say needs to happen, goes. Now go." I left Andre's car with a wide smile across my face, I wish it was stained there. Being at Courtney's house always made me so happy, it was as if I wandered through the wooden wardrobe to get to Narnia.

Once Courtney's mother, Natalie, let me inside, I immediately felt the refreshing warmth her home provided. She asked me, "How are you doing Tommy? The last time I heard from you was when you snuck into my daughter's window the other night. Hope you got what you came for, my sweet boy." "It's-it's not like that at all-" "Oh please, you don't need to lie to me. I am okay that my daughter is in love, just.... you know..... knock next time. Don't be conspicuous, and I will have no reason to believe anything bad is happening up there, okay? She's all I got, Tommy. Please take care of her, she loves you to the moon and beyond. I don't want someone treating her like her dad treated me. Promise me that, Tommy." I swallowed my saliva, certain that my words would matter highly in her eyes. I said "You don't need to worry about her, not at least with me. You've raised an amazing daughter, I will do my part to take care of her. I promise you Mrs. Martin that I will not treat her like her father treated you, I promise to be better". "Thank you Tommy, and call me Natalie. I think we're on that level now. This conversation stays between us... okay? I don't want my kid thinking I'm crazy or something. Which I am, when it comes to her. She is the best thing that has ever happened to me." "Me too," I agreed. "Awwwwwwww you guys, you're both so precious!" Courtney said, sitting on the staircase as if she was never there in the first place. Natalie jolted side to side like lightning had struck her down. She said "OH my! How much of that did you hear my dear?" "Just the part where you both were adorable. I just came down from getting dressed, are you ready Tommy?"

I sat there....stunned. She looked so gorgeous. So elegant. Just like Cinderella at her first dance. I felt wildly under-dressed. I said "Uhh.. wow! You look incredible... How is it that you surprise me every-time, even though I'm your boyfriend who knows what you look like, inside and out." Courtney's mom cut in, "Okayyyy... you've lost your knocking privileges. But my dear, you look so marvelous. Why is that when I take you out you dress like a sweatpants gremlin. Is this the first time you've met his parents?" Natalie said, giving Courtney a hug with much love intertwined within it. She said "No, no, we've met. But this is our first dinner together, so I needed to dress to impress." I smiled, feeling impressed to have her as my girlfriend. I said "I'm ready, let's get this over with." Courtney said before kissing my cheek "Okay Mister Grumpy, let's get you fed and in bed before you grow a pumpkin where your head should be." Natalie smiled, proud to see how beautiful her daughter looked. She said "Please bring her home in one piece, she is my pride and joy..." I told her that I would before escorting Courtney out of the door, not yet prepared to face this moment in its entirety.

The drive to my house was nice, arriving was not so much. The closer we got to my home, the more anxiety I got that something wasn't right. As we walked up the door, I pulled Courtney aside then said "Before we go in, I should just say my family..... probably isn't like any other family you've met before." "Tommy, My exes family consisted of a bunch of Hicksville haymunchers. Hit me with your best shot." In my head it seemed so easy to reveal my inner me to her endlessly emitting warmth. Yet I refrained, hoping I could continue to spare my demons from fighting against my only angel and get her through this night unharmed. "Just be mindful my family likes to rag on me, so, I'm sure you'll be in for a show." She grinned and took my hand waiting for me to walk her in, I stood there, hesitant, until Darren opened the door and sensed my frivolously leaking fear firsthand. "You know you have to come inside to eat dinner, right? At least don't keep your queen waiting outside while you ponder." My face discolored as a checkered finish-line flag, prolonging the inevitable would only make this feeling continue to drag along with me. We walked into sensational smells filled with widespread flavors, smelling like something similar to what came out of that 'Marie Calendar' catalog my mom always reads in the evenings after her daily chores are finished. I had never smelled such happiness inside our home before.

The living room was blaring 'Hotel California' from the record player while Darren plopped on the couch returning to sketching on his notepad. I peered over his shoulder, entranced in his focus to the paper, the way his mind presented his picture onto the paper made me realize my brother's mind extended farther than murder. It had me thinking I was living in the life of what my family was capable of instead of what they actually were. "Well hello kiddos, I was wondering when y'all would be arriving," My mother exclaimed. Seeing her dressed like she was interviewing for a slot on Martha Stewart made me crumble wondering when she would shed this snakeskin. For the most part, my mother was truly always this uppity, however there was always a sense of jet-lag only noticed if observed close enough. Dad and Darren were the only actors remaining in character. "It's so nice to see you guys again, you know how Tommy is, never bringing me by and all. Probably because he's embarrassed to be seen with me" Courtney joked before sitting in the seat across from Darren, who had plopped his sketchpad onto the dining room table. "I'm sure Tommy is just embarrassed to bring someone so gorgeous into our house, we don't make it easy on him now do we?" My mother said smiling, in the midst of our conversation I could see familiar maple red lipstick slowly start to smear off the corners of her lips. Cheeks growing more and more pale amid painted facial expressions. With ominous, I was the only one who could see her in true form.

My dad resided in his spot at the end of our table, contentedly eating and listening to our conversation. "So, dating a pizza delivery boy, that must be exciting," Darren uttered before impaling his steak with a meat blade. "I'm super anxious around Tommy in all honesty, the last time I met a decent guy I was a young girl entering high school. A naive one at that. I'm trying to convince your brother here how happy he makes me, but I don't think he's budging very much." Darren grinned widely staring at Courtney then back at me, "Come on, Thomas, how could you possibly be scared of falling in love? You should be proud to display her in front of our parents." I interjected quietly under my breath, "Have you met ours..." "What's that?" Darren interjected. "Nothing, I just think it's a pretty rational fear to fall for someone you call your significant other, to wonder if your capabilities exceed her wants and needs, it's stressful, you should try it." Considering my brother was an emotionless goblin, it was alarming to see his face with such an insidious expression. He replied "And you know what that's like? I've seen you try to love one other girl in your entire life that wasn't our mother, and seeing that this damsel in no distress is your now mistress, I can see you failed-". "Shut it ass-hat, At least I don't make every girl I come into contact with shiver in petrifying terror after taking them out." "The sight of diamonds make people shiver too, shit stain, don't degrade my intelligence debating your faults through my own," Darren retorted.

I glanced down at my mashed potatoes, throwing the conversation from my head space onto his dinner plate; wishing it would poison then end that animal's misery.. "Can you not right now, we have company," I said politely, trying to remain the only reasonable Hansen here. Darren, with intense grimace, said "I agree, you hush now, that's no way to act around a delightful young woman." My mother put particle sized pieces of pepper on her potatoes, then said "Imagine that, my youngest son teaching my first born something." Darren retracted mentally like usual after being insulted, "Yeah ok, the second I learn something from Tommy is the day George Milton guides Lennie Small in the art of murdering mice and men." "Have you ever considered for a split second about stopping being so arrogant thinking you can teach yourself everything when there's clearly room for you to be instructed?" I said placing my hand onto Courtney's inner thigh, irritated that asshole had the audacity to degrade me for being a better person than he ever could aspire to be. "You just haven't considered that not everyone in the world wants what you want Thomas, I remember since you were eight years old how you'd beg mom to let you read Romeo and Juliet over Julius Caesar because of how infatuated you were with the tragedy they called 'romance.' So, when mom finally caved, I grabbed the copy of Caesar and finished it in one sitting. Fact is, I grew up under-standing the people we strive and die to love end up stabbing us straight through our heart at the expense for their security. Not realizing words crafted better blades than daggers. I don't chase a woman solely because if I wanted to allow my power to be taken right from under me. I would just shrink into a midget then call myself Napoleon Bonaparte!" Darren exclaimed slamming his fist on the fine wooden edge of the table. My mother gasped, she said as she put her hand on her open mouth "My god Darren! Do you have to be so rambunctious?! I am so sorry for his behavior, honey. Why don't you take your plate up to your room, watch a documentary or two before you clock in for work, how's that sound?" I snapped back into defense mode, knowing Darren never took an evening shift. His nights consisted of whatever inhuman decisions he decided before-hand, as to why he strictly worked the morning schedule.

My mother's words made me reflect on the ones I told Courtney before entering. Reliving the idea of possibly not leaving this house in one piece compelled me to remind her how much I really loved her. "Before we go in, I just want to say your presence in my life is so divine. It's absolutely something I thought I would never find. I think about it all the time, about where I'd be on this path if you weren't mine? For me, I would say I'd be internally deceased for the rest of eternity. You fill my energy with something as sweet as Peace Tea growing from a Peach-tree." Courtney was visibly stunned, stared at me in awe. "Okay Mr. Ad Lib, Why do I feel like there's more to what you're saying, Thomas?" My mother interrupted my day-dreaming by saying "I'm just so glad you could make it dear, this nut couldn't try any harder to hide you from us! I know my son seems locked into rampage mode, but don't worry, he is so delighted to see you again!" I shuttered not really knowing what else to expect, an acute act availed.

Before I could defy, my phone vibrated with Miles's 'Into the Spider Verse' ringtone, I stepped out of the kitchen to accept his call. "Tommy, please tell me you are with Andre?" Miles said timidly as if held at gunpoint. I didn't know it yet but today would go down in history, just not in the way it was supposed to be. I said, "No man, you know I had to have dinner with our parents tonight with Courtney? You should be here too, what's up though? You sound more pan-icky than usual." "What are you talking about? No one told me any-thing about dinn-, Listen, I think your friend is in serious trouble. Why in the world would you ever challenge the spawn of Satan to a game you cannot win?! You don't think he hasn't been hot on your ass since you all the sudden justified stepping out of line! You need to fix this!" I was at a loss, not of words more so emotions to feel. I responded "I think you're paranoid man, I don't think Darren would ever take it that far I mean let's be honest. All the fucker does is cal-culate so he's smart enough to understand how hard I would make his world crumble if he ever took my only true friend away from me. You know that Miles." Yet life was like an Panasonic television set, you never knew when it would discolor into darkness. "Tommy, you should take this seriously, I would do it myself but I have to stay late at the lab tonight. Just tell them I need your help down here or something dammit." "Miles you know I can't do that, Courtney will-." "You'd rather risk losing your best friend for presentation on a dinner date?! I have to get back to work, you know you have to handle the mess you made Tommy." My palms were heavy and sweaty like I was going to puke Slim Shady's mom's spaghetti. I shot Andre a quick text to ensure he was ok before bracing to continue entertaining this freak show. I walked through my mind's corridor lightheaded, trying to rewire loose thoughts back into place. "Well hello darling nice of you to join us again." Courtney said, smiling widely. I could tell she felt so accepted in that moment. I hated the idea of tearing down these walls we vaulted over together. If I wasn't still so groggy from the Psilocybin then it probably would've happened in that instant.

My mother said "Your girlfriend is just delightful, Tommy. I could not pick a better one for you myself" before setting a plate of cookie crumble in front of me. "Sorry, I was on the phone with Miles. And thank you mom, I already know." "I'm happy pumpkin, we were just explaining to your lovely lady why we say grace for dessert, would you care to add anything?" "As a matter of fact I would, ahem, I would just like to thank god for allowing me to be sitting at this table with the most wonderful woman on the planet. Amen" Courtney leaned over and kissed me before proceeding to dig into dessert. "Take your elbows off of the table Thomas, but indeed it is quite the honor. I have to say Courtney, Tommy has told me nothing about you, I can't even imagine why he would hide this dime from my eyes!" Courtney's face turned as red as the sliced tomatoes on her Caesar salad, hearing my lies of telling my mom all about her dissipate right in front of her face. "Alright that's enough out of me, honey, would you like to add anything?" My father grumbled, the cookie crumble spoke before he could. He said "My son does get on my nerves from time to time, as you can see from his black eyes his brother would agree. But to see such a woman sitting at my dinner table brings me joy, joy that my son has done something right for once." Courtney stuck her head up from her silence, then replied "So that's how.... hmm. All those times I saw your face bruised was because of these two.. Could you at least not fight back? Or return the favor? Damn I guess that's better than saying you fell off your bike nine times since we started seeing each-other." My father giggled, so pleased to hear her say that. He said "Hmph. That's what I think, but he is a lover, not a fighter like his brother Darren. Please keep this one Tommy, I love her already."

I winced and said, "Than-k you, dad. Rea-lly appreciated that. Courtney, you look just elegant tonight." she rolled her eyes and blushed as my mom added "You are quite the Casanova aren't you?" I listened to them playfully conversate before feeling my phone buzz out of control like a honeybee seeking a honeysuckle. I had seventeen texts from Miles but what had my anxiety doing jumping jacks was Andre's message reading "Is your brother home? Cause I'm driving home from Darny's, and this Ford Ranger is persistently following me. I can't see his face, but it can't be Darren, right?" My stomach sank slowly past my knees and my body temperature dropped below twenty degrees, it was just too Tarantino to truly believe this was happening. Why was I casted into such radicalism? My rapid firing thoughts couldn't assemble themselves fast enough. In one ear rang my girlfriend's sweet laughter and the other fizzled with Darren's sinister voice. In that moment I knew I had to make a choice.

It suddenly clicked in my head why Darren excused himself from the dinner table. What I feared most as a possibility was now a certainty. I grabbed Courtney's hand, then said "Thank you mom for dinner, it was delicious. But Courtney needs to leave now, she has some homework to get done before tomorrow. Don't you, babe?" I gave her the look of a desperate dog seeking adoption. She withered, then said "Yes, I must be going. It was a pleasure to finally meet you guys. See you soon." She squeezed my hand extra tightly, fuming that I excused her from the fun she was having. I did not know how much of an extent of the situation I would tell her I was in, yet I could not afford to lose her. If she required my honesty then I needed to provide it. "Tommy what the hell?! Why did you make me leave! I was enjoying my time. Do you not like me meeting your family? Did I embarrass you or something?"

I walked around in circles, aware that this monologue needed to be snippy. My best friend's life was on the line. I kissed her with more love than I ever have given before. Then told her who I truly am. "Courtney I'm going to be five-thousand percent honest with you. You are just.... Magnificent. I would marry you right now if I could. How dare you think I would not want my family to meet you, I didn't want you to meet them!! You're not going to believe I word I say but I'm being serious. I already almost lost you once with my dishonesty...my distancing... my denial. I can't risk that again. Courtney, my family are a group of bloodthirsty serial killers, borderline cannibals if you consider consuming blood as body. Right now I think my brother is on his way to kill Andre for me breaking our 'pact' by telling Andre about what they do. I am sorry I lied to you for so long, I did not want to tell you who I belonged to. Because I fear you wouldn't love me anymore, I feared you might think I actually 'roll' with these people. I'm a product of them, I didn't ask to be born to such insatiable animals. But I can't get into this right now, if I don't go save Andre then I might become a killer too! I can't lose him Courtney, he's my best friend. And don't ask to come with, I can't afford to lose any friends. If I do, then it can only be one." Courtney stopped twirling her hair, she gazed into me with disbelief flickering within her bubbly eyes. She didn't pester me as I expected. Her response was to ask me, "Can-can I hug you before you go?" I felt like a dog who'd never been petted before. My heart burst into balloons and confetti. She whispered in my ear before leaving "We are so continuing this discussion when you get back." At least she left my cheek a kiss to masquerade her spine-tingling sentiment. She has a way of making my bones shiver and lips quiver separately then altogether in synchronicity.

Once I saw her drive off safely, I started running towards Andre's house. The scene was somber, as if I was tripping again. Except I was running away from my house instead of in its direction. There was a tinge of guilt and shame parading inside my brain. What if I caused a innocent bystander to die for crimes he did not commit? All in the name of making me suffer. Would I be able to live with that? Or would it consume me entirely? I stopped my philosophy session dead in its tracks. I could not have my mind clouded with any judgment other than how to save my friend from a ferocious force of evil. Luckily, and unluckily for me, Andre did not live far from me. Considering the school districts here are next to none, there's not much area for his house if it were outside the boundary. All of the houses in my school district were within a five-mile radius from my house. But that also meant Darren had a quicker window of opportunity to reach him before I did. I did not ask bothersome questions like "How would he know where Andre lived?" when I already knew who I was dealing with. If that was Darren's red Ranger, then he is already hot on Andre's tracks. I did not make a pact with a god or a deal with the Devil's, I basically traded my sanity to keep the ravaging Viking away from me, yet this pillager was bored. He was not one for peace offerings, the bloodshed itself is what he sought. It's hard to negotiate your life with someone who wants you to die. There's not much money or gems you can provide a man to exchange your safety when indeed, the murder is what he is in search for. He doesn't want your meaningless money, nor does he want to hear you plead your misery to him. Those things only tended to aggravate the little inner ball of rage swirling around at all times. I would know, I was forced to tag along my family's murder sprees for a decade like Barnum and Bailey's traveling circus! I've observed endlessly the lengths my brother will go to satisfy his desires, he would probably be a millionaire by now if he actually accepted any of the bribes people have provided in return for their life. Those things warped through him however, like passing through transparent glass. He could see the result of accepting said rewards, but the reflection it casted back into him restrained him from its temptation. I say all this to myself because I wondered what it would take to barter for Andre's life if I did not make it in time! I saw his house in the distance, the wind was whistling vigorously behind me. I ran so fast that the soles of my worn-down shoes were eroding along the asphalt. I did not see a red Ranger in front of Andre's house, which was the first good sign. Where would he be I wondered? Not for too long though, because I heard the grumble of his truck somewhere in the bellowing shadows.

I bolted towards Andre's door and spared myself the courtesy of knocking on the door first. I burst inside, landing on my stomach because I thrust through the door so vigoriously. Andre and his mother were playing Scrabble. I knocked over almost half of the board with my fall. Andre, of course witty on command, said "Dude! I was just about to play the word Contemporary! Good game Ma..... Tommy! What in the heck are you doing?!" I grumbled, still hurting from hurling myself into a coffee table. When I was able to speak, I said "He's... He's coming... we need to run."

Andre lifted his eyebrow, unsure if my paranoia had reached its peak or if what I was saying was meaningful. Since the Ranger

stopped following him I assumed he probably didn't suspect anything out of the ordinary. He nodded, then said "Oh, okay. Mom go
lock yourself in your room, put the dresser there until I come get you.
Tommy, what do we do?" I got up from the floor, shaking stars out
of my eyes as I shook my head side to side. I replied "I-I don't know,
he will not stop until the job is do..." Midway through my sentence,
the doorbell rang. " Oh no "it's him!!! It's him! Shit!" "What do we do
Tommy? Can we talk to him? My brain was scrabbled like the game
I tossed onto the floor, there was no fight or flight reaction. I told
Andre "Go upstairs, now! I will try to talk to him while you slip out
the window." Andre did not seem startled, if anything, he appeared
annoyed. He said "Tommy, I will not leave my mother here. Your
brother will have to take her from my dead body." "Andre, he has no
problem doing that!"

There was silence as Andre and I tried to decide the best response
to this unforeseen outcome. My brother did not ring the doorbell
again, this time he spoke through the door. He said "Thomas... you
need to let me in now. You knew this day would come sooner rather
than later." I froze like a stone statue, Andre barked back, "Go back
to hell you demon! We don't want what you're offering, okay? Now
leave, or suffer the consequences." I heard Darren do something he
rarely does, laugh. He snickered at Andre's attempt to deter him.
Darren replied "Real tough coming from someone speaking with
a wooden door between them and me. Let me help you with that."
He started kicking the door down like the big bad wolf without his
wind blowing abilities. Once chipped wood started shooting out at
us, Darren flashed his face through the sliver of open door. His mask
filled up my lungs with molten tungsten, it became hard to breathe.
Andre grabbed me by the back of my shirt and led me upstairs. As I
stared down the staircase, I watched my brother pummel that door
like it owed him a large sum of money. It was unbelievable to see
him filled with so much rage. He is usually the calm, cool, collected,
and measured individual. I must have lit the wick to a ticking time
bomb buried deep inside of him. One so deep even he did not notice
it was there.

Andre shoved me into his closet, then stood stiff by his door
waiting for Darren to ascend the staircase. I whispered for Andre to

come into the closet, I wondered what he was waiting on. The knee jerk reaction of seeing my brother caused my leg to fly up against the closet door. I've never trembled so intensely. Those moments people profess when seeing complete danger of freezing didn't seem accurate. I was frozen for sure, but the paralysis flooded my body with electricity. I felt each individual nerve in my body tingle, it was much more than the feeling of being frozen like stone. My insides felt combustible, as if the sparks inside my mind could set my whole life on fire. I was one can of gasoline and a Bic lighter from destroying everything I had concurred. Darren stepped into Andre's room, looking around and observing the person I had become so close to. Andre kept his distance, attempting to reach near his window. Darren gazed around, then at Andre, saying "I never knew you painted. How elegant of a display." Andre replied "Save it, freak-show. What is it that you need from me? Why are you here?!" Darren stared carefully into Andre's eyes, ensuring that he was locked in to the person he was talking to. Darren said, "I think you already know what it is that I want, I bet that princess has told you everything by now. I wanted to make him suffer for spilling our little family secret by killing you, yet, I see that suffocating him until he can't breathe isn't enough. He is a virus, and needs to be terminated. My plans will never work with a lingering worm like him still existing. Sooo... change of plans. Hand over my brother this instant, and I will spare your existence. Thomas should already know what a gratitude this is, I don't let anyone go. I never have, and have never intended to. But this is different, this is the first kill that is personal to me. Hand him over, and I will not harm you. You have my word." Andre stepped farther away from him. I watched his shirt twirl from the breeze blowing in through the ajar window. Andre said "Your word doesn't mean shit to me, you staple-faced barbarian. I don't give away friends, maybe if you ever made any you would understand." "Oh I do, Andre. You see this bat right here, this here is my best friend. It stands by my side even when it withers in the rain, will you do the same for yours?"

I did not like where this was going, so to save my friend from his untimely demise. I offered my life instead. I said from the closet "Darren! Don't hurt him! I-I will come with you. Just let me say goodbye to my friend first." Andre said "What are you doing

Tommy..... you can't..." Darren interjected his sentiment by saying, "He can, and he will. How dare he think he is better than us! How dare he try to turn us in after all we have given him! We could have slaughtered him the instant we figured out he wasn't a Hansen! But no! We gave him compassion! What did we get in return?! This! No more protection from your parents Tommy, you're mine." Andre looked at me through the blinds of the closet door, almost in a moment totally understanding my anguish. Why I have been such a terrible friend to him and Courtney. There is a moment to which each man can stand against injustice, or become a product of it. Andre looked at me in the eyes with the former on his mind. As Darren walked towards the closet door to pry it open, Andre said, "How dare people like you exist when the world deserves so much better. When my friend deserved so much better. You could not possibly provide him that, but I can." Andre attacked my brother with the same ferocity as a honey badger. The clash of the badger vs. the rabid raccoon unfolded in front of me.

Andre tussled with Darren onto the floor, where Darren stabbed him several times before he even had the time to react. Andre, enraged by this realization, snatched Darren's bat and began smashing his face in. Darren held his forearms up to absorb the damage, but they were torn to shreds. If you pushed anyone to the limit, they could become a killer. I witnessed that too many times in my life. I never expected it would be Andre I saw committing these sorts of atrocities. After innings of being pummeled, Darren snatched Andre's foot from under him. Then, he proceeded to pull a few screws out of his forearm, put them in between his knuckles, then punched Andre in the stomach like the Wolverine. Darren stood over Andre, peeled off the mask that was bashed into his face, then professed "Wow... you... you actually hurt me. I granted you the opportunity to live and you wasted that. You stupid basta..."

My urge to hide had died, the paralysis wore off long enough for me to push my brother out of the ajar window. Darren hit his face on the lifted windowpane as he fell outside onto some shrubs. My concern for my brother was quickly thwarted by the pooling blood coming from Andre's body. The paralysis came back, but I snapped out of its attempts of binding me. I snatched my friend up like a sleeping toddler, took him to his bathroom to get some towels for his wounds, then ran out of the house. I ran into the woods without much regard as to where I was going. The closest hospital was across town, across the train tracks behind Andre's house where we used to hang out. That's the direction I ran in, without much certainty as to if we would make it there. Let alone across. Andre winced with every breath he took, I reassured him he would be okay. But it looked bad. Really bad. My brother stabbed him several times along his body, there's no telling what damage he had done. Darren was a trained killer, I wasn't stupid enough to think that any altercation with him would not lead to death. Andre did not waste a second to challenge him, that has to be the first time Darren has ever felt pain during his raids. A hint of a grin formed on my face amid this realization.

I pressed the towel down on Andre's stomach, watching the white turn to red in seconds. The woods I was running in started to spin, the lightheadedness struck me like a runaway arrow. Nevertheless, I kept pushing onward. I put Andre down to rest for a moment then proceeded forward, stumbling over twigs and shit along the way. Once I saw the train tracks in the horizon, the haziness faded away. But then crept on me again when I heard a revving engine in the distance. The sounds of branches smacking against a metal frame illuminated the quiet night with fire-like vibrancy. I started to pick my feet up quickly, *how is that dumb bastard still alive?* The Red Ranger ran through every tree standing in its way, crushing them like toothpicks thrown inside a wood chipper. Darren drove forward with utter relentlessness, completely disregarding the damage done to his favorite vehicle.

I did not look back, I ran until I reached the train tracks, where I knew the bridge was too narrow for Darren's truck to fit through. Andre flickered between consciousness and not. When he heard Darren's truck destroying a whole forest to reach him, he asked me, "Is—is that. Your brother?" I ignored Andre's question, unabridged by the sentiment forming in my soul. I knew this day would come, yet all I did was run. *You should have slit their throats as they slept, now look what you've caused!* Yet running leads to tripping, and once you trip, you tend to fall. The seas finally parted for me, but the train tracks seemed longer than usual. The adrenaline must've been messing with my vision. I walked on the metal tightrope with nervousness fluttering around me like a band of butterflies. Darren tried to drive onto the railroad, disregarding how narrow the tracks were. His anger made him behave like an adolescent rather than a gifted individual whose studied murder like a Christian would study their religion. I trotted along the tracks, yet it was impossible to continue onward. My legs were the equivalent of strawberry jelly by this point. Daunted by this indecision, Andre asked me to do what needed to be done. Something I refused to do. He said "Tommy, I need..... you to drop me. Only.... one of us.. has to die tonight." I would not listen to it, even hearing the words uttered from his quivering lips caused me to involuntarily fidget. The paralysis was coming back to attack the parts of me not yet hit by her earlier wave of destruction. I told Andre "I can't leave you to die?! We can make it, save your energy dammit! Don't talk to me like that."

I pushed forward, regardless of what Andre said to me, my legs succumbing to the ground as if quicksand was in between the gaps of the tracks. Darren parked his truck on the railroad's ledge. I was not prepared for what to do next. He hopped out of the truck holding his baseball bat, prepared to smack a home run onto my best friend's face. I put Andre down to the sounds of him whining with deep despair, and my bones began tingling like striking a triangle with a nine iron. Darren shouted "Bring him over to me! Then you may leave." I withered within the wind like a dead daisy. I said "Darren, it's me you want remember? Let him live." Darren was not phased, he continued walking forward to us while scraping his bat's nails along the metal rails. Even while bleeding all over from head to toes, Darren pushed forward. He said "You're next, you rodent. Yet you're a personal burden. I need you to suffer before you are removed. Consider what I am doing to your friend merciful. Because what I'm going to do to you won't be. Dying is mercy in my eyes, the true terror lies in what suffering awaits at the destination death doesn't arrive at. You are my exception, Thomas. I don't want you to die to satisfy my needs, no, you deserve so much more consideration. It is indeed your suffering that will satisfy my deepest and darkest desires. So consider me allowing you a head start as something to be appreciated. Now run, as always."

Darren did not stop walking along the tracks, even if he fell through he probably would've walked back up again with his broken legs. His determination was bursting out of his mind like the Aurora Borealis. I had nothing for him, my fist were no match for his array of weapons. Andre touched my ankle with the hand not covering his smothered stomach, he was so gentle even when experiencing the worst torment imaginable: awaiting your excruciating pain to be taken away by a deranged executioner. He said "Tommy-I-I feel so cold. Can you... hug me? I want to feel....my friend, one more time-before I die." I turned away from Andre, too afraid to let him see me cry. I wanted to be strong as long as I could before I lost him for good. I knelt down and hugged my friend one final time. He whispered into my ear before leaning back "Thank you... for being my friend. You made a kid from Brooklyn.... feel so at home. Take care... of Courtney for me. She's my favorite friend in this world.... Next to you Tommy. I-I wish... I could hug my mom..." Andre touched me softly before I was thrown off of him by my brother. I leaned over the ledge, facing death and a magnitude of grief from the opposite edges. I tried to climb up quick enough to stop my brother, but I was too late. Darren crushed my friends face like hitting an egg with a sledgehammer. Some of Andre's blood splattered onto my cheeks. I could see red every time I blinked, the feeling of having your best friends blood on your chin was defeating enough. To be gloated on by my damn brother was a step too far.

As I climbed back up to the railroad, I was halfhearted and on the verge of tossing myself off the ledge. Darren did what he did best: pushed me to my physical and mental limit. He said, "This wouldn't have happened if you had just become a Hansen. It was your destiny, dammit! Why couldn't you just accept your fate like the rest of us?! You screwed the pooch, now death knocks on your doorstep. It's easy to ignore it when it's not your door death knocks at huh?" Boiling in a pot of toxic rage, melting altogether like a meatball in a fondue station, I said while clutching my dead best friend, "You worthless, insufferable reptile! I will kill you! I will kill you all!" I lunged at him with all I had left in me. Whether that 'thing' was fire, fury, fanaticism, or a mix of all three. I let him have it. I clawed at his face like an angry dragon, not stopping even when I saw blood.

I tore at his clothes, revealing his mystical tattoos he never shows anyone. In this indiscretion, I picked up Darren's bat off the tracks then smashed him in the side of the head with it. I wasn't swinging with lethal intentions, like my brother, the surge to make someone suffer was undeniably powerful. I made sure I was swinging from the non-nail side. Whether arrogance or angst to receive my needed vindication over my brother, I made sure he felt every tinge of torment he's ever bestowed upon me with each swing. He backed away from me, covering his head from any more damage. I flipped the bat over on the screw side one time for Andre, ensuring Darren caught another armful of screws before he took off with the bat still stuck in his arm. I had nothing left to chase after him, I watched him skirt off as quickly as he began following us. When the adrenaline died down, I was able to finally process the events that led up to this situation.

I comforted my dead friend, more so, comforting myself among his death-ridden presence. I shrieked and pleaded with him to return. But as I often do to no avail, no one heard me. There was no greater despair, hell, there was no despair even equal to this one. I talked to Andre, hoping he would get up from the rubble. I waited patiently for God to revive my friend, for him to release me from the burden that this was a permanent stain. A stain unable to be washed away no matter how hard the storm rains. *Please....just wake up....*

Doors were opening and closing inside my mind. Corridors that had remained locked and hidden away for some time basked in new-found sunshine. The dark hallways leading to those locked doors were now illuminated by flickering candlelight. The darkness surrounding Pandora's box was uplifted. The temple was fully visible now. The wind whistled then ran throughout my hair like the breeze sweeping through a weeping willow tree. Like the Stonehenge, I felt air flow into me and outwardly. The little garden where I've cultivated gentleness for what feels like generations, bloomed beautifully before diminishing into obscurity. Within these fleeting seasons, harmony was not an option. No matter how hard I tried to contain this monster, it refused to be spoken down to any longer. It bubbled to the surface of my sanity, lurking and waiting for its opportunity to roam freely. As I gazed upon my dead best friend, I let it do just that. For the first time in my life, I did not hide my inhibition to make each murderer I've encountered die for their crimes. It wasn't the suffering I felt they deserved, but it was too much suffering for all of humanity to allow them to continue living. *He was right, it took death knocking on your door to do something. What about all the other souls who lost their homes? You allowed this to happen!*

I battled with my guilt before picking myself back up from the rubble. My temperament felt different, the small ball of rage I've worked tirelessly to keep at bay was now astray. It danced within the wind, within the embers exhuming in my memories. Like Nero playing the flute as Rome was turned into ashes. All of my prerogative to be kind to all even monsters was out of the window now that the monster was under my bed. It's one thing to let that creature live near you, even walls apart, but when it lives inside of your thoughts. You are already doomed unless you pivot your course of direction with the upmost precision. I chose to let go, of my friend and of everything I will be. I told myself, "If this is it.... then I will use...... everything to end this." The remaining portion of grace I still withheld was used to close Andre's eyes so he could sleep in peace. I placed a leaf on his chest since there wasn't an abundance of roses around me. I continued to cry, yet this time this stream of tears emitted a different spectrum. I was not fazed by my sadness, I allowed my tears to fall out of my eyes like a samurai walking in a garden full of souls that have died alongside them. That sentimental displacement was the last sputter of good energy I had left. My thumbs began shaking, the jitters trickled down to all of my fingers. I was like a werewolf when the moon was finally full. Generations of marauding coursed inside me, I could see every tangent of murder in all of its possibilities. Was this how they saw the world? I wondered how far I would go down the rabbit hole, and if Alice would follow me wherever it goes? If Darren was Darth Vader, then I was Annikin on his way to transformation. There was a brief moment where I saw Courtney inside the kaleidoscope, but that quickly faded away. My thoughts belonged to the dark waters the Lochness monster submerged itself under. There was no steering this ship in any other direction, I gave that control up when I chose to let go.

CHAPTER 9

The walk back to my house was dreadful, each individual leaf crumbling under my feet caused me to shiver. The insidious omnipotence slithered around me, following my every move as a shadow casted at noon. Electricity was coursing through my clenched fists, the valley of anguish became deeper the farther I trotted in it. I busted in the door without any regard of who was home. Lightning strikes once or twice, yet in my mind they fired like fireworks on the Fourth of July. I felt a fragment of the insatiable hatred I imagine my brother is filled to the brim with. I wanted them all dead. I was not barbaric enough to ensure torment. Death was enough of a border I did not want to cross. Yet in this mind-state, there was no Thomas Hansen. I stomped upstairs, entered Darren's room to take one of his prized knives and a sword, then stomped back down the stairs to start the culling. I smelled the remnants of our dinner. I wondered if my mother was in on Darren's scheme. Or if she was truly as naive as she seemed. I did not care anymore about justification, evil existed here not because of me or my actions. Nevertheless, I played a part in allowing that evil to thrive here by conceding to their crimes. I could only afford to lose one friend today. The consequences of that mistake would torment me for the rest of my days. My mother looked at me, with shame supplemented by a smile. She said "Tommy, my love, why-why are you holding that... you're my sweet baby boy. You wouldn't hurt a fly..." I interjected "Shut the hell up mother, you're not allowed to call me that. I'm not your son. My mother would never hurt me as much as you have." My father slowly sank the recliner back down into chair form, turned off the TV then stood up. He said "You watch your tone with your mother, don't make me kick your ass again!" "Sit your ass down old man! I'm the one with the weapon here! You have some nerve to stand your stupid ass up when all you do is consume and produce garbage!" My father backed down, differing to my judgment just this once. My mother asked me, "Tommy, why are you acting like this... why are your eyes so dark... are you? Oh.. my. Do... do you have the gene?" "The gene? What the hell are you talking about? I'm here because your son took the only goddamn guy I ever cared about! Now I'm here to return the favor, I've allowed you animals to run free for years! Darren was right, it was easy to ignore when it's not my wife or friend taken from me. But you guys have crossed the line, you took the only friend I ever made. This crazy ass family ends, today!" My mother began to cry, she had never seen me act like this before. Neither have I, but sadly, like Eddie Brock when the venom suit was put on, I realized I liked it. The surge of power, the sheer bliss of seeing your mind in its entirety. To now shed darkness to the parts of myself I hated the most, I have the opportunity to feel the most myself than ever before. "What is it that you want from us, Thomas? Do you want us to turn ourselves in? Will that make you happy? Because you know we are never in a million centuries doing that. You will have to kill us all before that ever happens," My father said, shuffling over to the remote thinking that the conversation was over. I told him, "So be it." He opened his eyes wide like a white dinner plate, like his brain was unable to absorb what I had said. He replied "Hmph, you're kidding? Right? We outnumber you three to one, you really must be my dumbest son." He sat back down in the recliner with contempt in his face, feeling like he proved his point. I understood within this veil of insanity that logic meant nothing to me. My father could tell me ten times over how bad my idea was. But just like my father, I now understood the power of the 'dark side.' It is a compelling force for action even when logic guides you otherwise. I pointed the sword I stole at my mother, I told my father to get on the ground or I would slice her lips off of her skull. I told him as he dropped to the floor, "Death is merely a byproduct of what I wish could be done to the two of you. It should merely be the result of your prolonged suffering. You don't deserve it first. But I love you both, so I will bring it to you."

I told my mother to get on her knees, and to stop crying like a little toddler. I screamed "STOP! Your tears will not bring my fucking friend back, now will they?! Your miserable wailing gives me a headache! Spare me the theatrics, father, come here! You're first. Mom, you get to watch the rat bastard who broke you finally die for his crimes. I consider that graciousness used to the full extent." My father jerked up from the floor, pulling a dagger my brother had stashed away in the side of the armchair. He lunged towards me with the speed of a frightened cheetah. After years of being beaten to a pulp for speaking up, being dragged outside to wither in the rain after receiving bad grades, being neglected into oblivion without food and love from the only family I've ever known, being forced to watch my family murder innocent civilians so that one day I would turn into a relentless killer like them, and,, locking me in the garage for the weekend after refusing to kill another human on our first 'retreat', I was finally prepared to fight back. His arrogance was showcased in full display, like an exotic exhibit in the entrance of a museum. I held the blade in place, waiting for him to run into it. He could have stopped in any moment, but his belief that he would always topple me lead him right into my blade. So I think at least, I don't know exactly what anyone thinks. Nor would I want to know, especially for my father. My father slid into the blade, grabbing at it with his hands as if that would do anything but slice them open. In the midst of death, I guess the mind is not maximizing its full capacity. He continued to reach for me, only pushing the blade deeper into his chest. The crest of the blade rested in my hands. I leaned in close to tell my father "you will pay for every one of those people you killed, even my friend. You allowed Darren into this world, so his blood is on your hands! I taught myself to fend for what I need since I was old enough to read. When I was sixteen and everyone got a car, I walked everywhere! Night after night, my mother fed your useless mouth while her children starved! No more... You.... Have been bested."

I tossed the blade out of my hands with him still impaled by it. I wanted to watch my father wither while waiting for Satan to take him back where he belonged. My mother shrieked, her shrill voice sounded like a siren deep in my ear canals. My ears began to ring without any warning, the room grew eerily silent as my mother wept and held her dead husband. I could not bear to do what I did to him to her. She was my mother, vile but gentile at the same time. I told her "This didn't have to happen, you both could have been better parents. Neither of you ever loved me or Miles, all you ever wanted us to be was who you both were. Shadow's dancing within the fleeting sunlight. You never considered that we wanted something much different". My mother looked up at me with mascara bleeding down her cheeks, she looked like the Gothic version of her original makeup. She said "YOU! WHAT... WHAT HAVE YOU DONE!!! YOU FREAKISH LITTLE CHILD, DO YOU REALIZE WHAT YOU HAVE DONE! IT SHOULD'VE BEEN YOU, TOMMY! YOU MISERABLE, UNLOVABLE, MONSTER! NO WONDER YOUR FATHER HATED YOU!! THIS...... LIFELESS..... PERSON I AM HOLDING SHOULD BE YOU!!!!"

I broke free from my rage for a moment, shattered that she even had half of the personality to say that. I said "you.... miserable.... witch....YOU WERE SUPPOSED TO BE MY MOM! MINE! AS YOUR CHILD, YOU WERE SUPPOSED TO SHIELD ME FROM EVIL, NOT BRING ME INTO THE HEART OF IT! ALL YOU EVER DID WAS GIVE YOUR ATTENTION TO A MAN WHO NEVER EVEN LOVED YOU!.... Fine. You will get what you want. You will burn in hell right next to your lover forever. You are a damn dog who needs to be euthanized." After my mother hurled some more obscenities at me, she stole the dagger my father wanted to use on me out of his hands. Then proceeded to stab herself in the throat. She writhed, and held her neck with some success. Yet the spray of blood reached all domains, even my face. I now had three people's blood on me who I loved on different spectrum's. I did not know what to do with myself, I watched my parents lifeless bodies for some time. Wondering if they would wake up like those things from Evil Dead and try to get me! Yet, among all my disbelief that the slain were truly vanquished, they were indeed gone for good.

I walked up the staircase while keeping my head down, shame already started to infiltrate my brain. I did not want to discuss the situation, even with myself. I walked by the open bathroom door horrified to see my bloody face walk past it. I felt humiliated to be in my body. I opened the door to my room, and started to pack my belongings. I wasn't sure where I was headed but the train station sounded a whole lot better than being here when Darren came home. I went into my closet and nearly had a heart attack. Courtney was curled up in a little ball hiding in the corner! I fell back to my bed, then said "Jesus, Courtney! What the hell? What are you doing here?!" She stayed put, unsure of whether to move or not. Courtney said "I'm too scared to move Tommy. After you freaked out on me, you think I was just going to leave the conversation at that?" "Well I was sort of hoping..." "Thomas Hayden Hansen! Don't you dare do this to me again! Why are you covered in blood!? Where's Andre? What are you not telling me Tommy! Please?! Do... you not love me enough to show me who you really are?"

I sat on my bed, unsure of what to say next. I wanted to scream, but I had no mouth to speak. I said what I felt was best, even if I was drunk off of rage. "Courtney. What I told you earlier was true. It's all true... I tried to rescue Andre, but I didn't make it in time. I tried. I tried so hard to keep you both safe Courtney. And I failed. I failed the only friend I ever made. I got him killed because I'm too scared to resist the hell I'm in! I just want him back Courtney, I wish he would have killed me instead of him... I just killed my fucking parents because I can't control my hatred anymore! How did I become this person....." Courtney inched her way out of the corner, then over to me. She stood up and pressed my head against her stomach. While rubbing my hair, she managed to keep her clarity. Courtney wiped the streaming tears away from her eyes. She kissed my bloody forehead, even among my worst peril she was so formidable. So understanding. I wished I could feel her rub my head for eternity. She made me feel safe when the tide continued to crash onto my calm shores. Bashing the wooden pilings before they even had a chance to wither among the erosion.

Courtney asked me "Please don't tell me that's your blood, babe? Can I get you a paper towel or something?" "Uhh no. It's a combination of Andre's, my mother's, and my father's. A part of me does not want to wipe this off. But I know it's time to let go. At least, start the long process of trying to." "You're going to be okay babe. Yes, you may need therapy for umm... forever! I might need some too. But I'll still love you all the same. We... can heal together." "How can you be so calm right now?" "I used to practice going away to a special place when my father would put his hands on my mother. Whenever I feel pain, I find that place. The pain never goes away no matter how long you hide though, but to know you don't have to stand in the rain helps. You can decide at any time to actually feel the water, instead of just get wet. I'm too emotionally damaged to consider anything too outlandish in life. A family of serial killers would make an amazing movie if that helps!" "It doesn't, my love, considering I'm the main character in this visual nightmare. But I appreciate your concern, my sweet peach. By the way, did you happen to hear our altercation downstairs? If so... I just want to say..." "You don't have to say anything... babe. Grief is a hell of a thing. I see why you responded the way you did. My question is where did you learn to talk like that? That would be kinda kinky in the bedroom." "Okay, you can't be this cordial when we are dealing with an crisis. I just told you an hour ago my family were a bunch of murderers and you're just like 'okie dokie' let's discuss anything but that! Courtney, I told you something very personal today. Andre is dead because of me! We have to take this seriously Court-". "DON'T tell me how to grieve. You don't think I heard you. I've known for the entirety of our 'relationship' you've been hiding something. Did I expect a side piece? Maybe a one night fling you fudged the numbers on? Possibly, not really, but this? Jesus Christ! You don't think I understand your situation..... I can't ever understand it directly, but I understand the words that are leaving your lips. As for my best friend being dead, I am very distressed. But I'm also grateful the love of my life returned home. For every bit of hatred, confusion, and sadness I am feeling currently. I equally feel grateful. I feel grateful to know who you truly are, are we going to have to process some of these things together. Yeah, no doubt buddy. Is the mystery now over because I know you this deeply? I don't think so. There's so many more moments to be made. I love you, and who your family is doesn't change that. I don't care if their crazy! You are not your parents! If you're lucky, you emulate their good qualities, and conquer their negative ones. Don't be deterred Tommy."

I hugged her tightly and began crying on her waist. I released the guard I had held up for so long from not sharing this information with anyone other than myself. Andre chipped the wall, but Courtney made it fall like a line of dominoes pushed over. I allowed my misery to be released from me, within the span of a single day, I had lost my parents and my best friend. The torment I felt was unbearable, I knew I needed to pull myself together to finish the job. But I could not. I cried for so long, Courtney decided to sit next to me and let me lay on her lap instead of continuing to stand up. I told her "You shouldn't love me, Courtney, I-I am a monster. Just like all of them…. I was only created to-to…to destroy, to devastate, to follow the path my parents did! I'm worthless Courtney, my own mother said she doesn't even love me. How can I possibly be a normal person?! I'm broken, and I can't be fixed. Because… this is who I am! I can't change anything about me, why would God send me here Courtney? What did I do to deserve this?" Courtney stopped rubbing my head for a moment to gather herself. She sniffled, then looked away to wipe away her face. I wasn't quite sure if she did, yet I felt her fidget away from me when she sniffled.

Courtney continued to scratch my scalp, I don't know if she was some sort of wizard in her past existence but it's what she always did when I had an anxiety attack. Or a traumatic flashback. Like her inner instinct is to be kind and considerate to every living thing on this planet. No matter how much that thing distresses her. I hated the feeling of making my queen cry, but I was past my limit on withholding these feelings. I needed her to hear me, as years of screaming into the void with no soul shouting back left me internally distressed to exert my emotions with anyone other than myself. Courtney let me cry for a while, as I assumed she had nothing to say. Then she found the words. Courtney said while sniffling, "Tommy, I want you to look at me right now…. You, are not a monster. I can't explain why God dealt you this hand. You were created for nothing, not out of love but to be a tool in a scheme of murder it seems. Yet within that peril, you remain the most vulnerable, kind, amazing man I've ever met. I've said this before I even learned of... this predicament. I'm not trying to start a fire with flint, I'm expressing how I truly feel. You were not created to reap death Tommy, you're not just some useless junk tossed aside when done with. You're a human being... you're so much more than worthless. I had a problem cutting before I met you, everyone thinks you're beautiful until they realize you're loose a couple screws in the head. You never treated me as some weak deer to feast on because I was a girl with uncontrollable problems. You accepted me for my flaws. For all that I am. Something no boy has ever done before for me. People only love you when you're perfect it seems nowadays. I wanted to die before I met you, Tommy. Not hyperbolic, not 'I'm a sad, privileged teenager who feels so lonely,' no. I wanted to go. I know you do not want to hear that, but you need to. Because it's the truth. You're suffering... has given you an immense sense of empathy. You treat me so kindly even when I'm frightened, frustrated or angry. You just sit there and listen to me when I scream. When I have no kind feelings to offer in return. You make me forget that my father abandoned me, that I used to be a penis chasing gypsy rather than going after guys with feelings. That I almost killed myself out of selfishness rather than having the courage to express I was not okay mentally. You didn't yell at me when you found out like everyone else did. You merely listened to me, waited for me to be done, then asked me if it was okay to hug me..... then we watched Marvel movies while you held me like a little baby and fed me pizza rolls to comfort my sadness. What kind of monster does that?! You tell me. Your grief is blinding, my love. You are so far from worthless... it hurts to hear you even say it. I tried to ignore what your mother said, but that might've been the part of the interaction hardest to ignore. I wanted to run down there and punch her myself!"

I chuckled, appreciative that my little soldier was going to be by my side until I died. Which could be today, tomorrow, or when I'm off golfing at seventy. Whatever the case, I was going to appreciate this gift life has left me with everything I had left. I said "I'm glad you didn't, honey bear, you didn't deserve to see me like that... I never want to feel that way again, Courtney. I felt so close to becoming a Hansen... my bones are shaking just thinking about it." "I know baby, I can feel your body rocking right now. Please don't think about that.... Once this situation is handled, we can take this straight to the therapist? Okay?" She leaned down to kiss me, then said, "You know, " I interjected before she could finish speaking, certain by the look in her eyes that she was about to get crazy on me. Courtney looked at me, then my lips, then back at me again. She smiled softly, then leaned in for another kiss. I said before she got too illicit, "Babe, you know I can't do that right now. I-I don't think my little guy will work after watching my best friend be blatantly attacked by my brother. Besides, my parents being butchered a floor below me is too daunting to consider doing anything....I'm sorry honeybun." Courtney's lips quivered, as if my indecision slit into her veil of ignoring the situation. She said "You're right dear... I'm sorry to bring it up. You could just fuck my face if you wanted to, maybe it'll cheer you up." I was equally appalled and turned on. I told her, "Let me get back to you on that. What we need to do is get the hell out of here. I fear once Miles comes home he is going to be undeniably pissed at me. I did kind of just murder his entire life's work.... I had to stop them though, Courtney... I should have a long time ago." She nodded her head in agreement, then said, "You did the right thing. I don't know how many people have suffered because of them, but they killed our friend... that's enough in my book to put the bad dogs down."

I jolted up with a newfound surge to exist, this rift in tectonic plates changed my brains landscape. No longer did I feel contained in a cage by my family's angst. I saw this as my opportunity to truly be my own person. Not just a vessel extending as far as he can away from his origin. I wanted to be a real boy like Pinocchio told Gepedo. I told Courtney, "I need to take you home, then I must finish what I started." She flickered between gentleness and burning embers, her eyes told all. She responded by saying "What?! Tommy, you might die! Why can't you come with me? We can start anew. Away from this situation." "And risk bringing my brother to you?! Yeah, nooo thank you. Courtney. I love you. More than you could ever know. But there is no happily ever after if my brother is still out there! I have to stop him." "If Miles was supposedly the bridge trying to fix everything, what does that make you? Your need for vengeance, Tommy... it's alarming. You don't have to be the one who destroys your family. You did not create this evil! You did not allow this evil to exist either, you're still a child, Tommy. How are you responsible for fighting against your parents when you were still a little toddler!! Did you instill the thought for them to slaughter people? Goddamn it, Tommy! Why can't you see what I see-" "Because there is no God! That's why I did something about it. If I didn't do something, then my family could have taken you next! I've prayed every day to a God who refuses to answer me, or even show his face to explain why he has done this to me! The only grace he has given me in this life is my brother Miles, my best friend Andre, and you! Even then, he has taken one of those away from me just as quickly as he put it here! I-I am responsible for stopping my brother... I am a product of this."

Courtney appeared dismayed, like a disappointed parent. She said, "You frown upon a God that merely allows good and evil to exist into this world, it is people who choose their way. Your family chose evil a long time ago when they started killing, but God gave you the choice not to. If there was no God, you would be a heartless killer too. God gave you a soul strong enough to live differently. I would have never gotten the opportunity to love you. To understand you. To have hindsight and see why you were such a 'hide in the light' type of guy up until now. Even knowing what I know, I still love you. If that isn't God giving you... giving us...a second chance, then maybe he should show his face to explain his error. Cause I don't see it any other way. Let's go, Tommy, come with me so I don't have to mourn for you forever." The hint of Hansen DNA in my membranes trickled down my spinal column, causing goosebumps to flood my arms. I asked her, "Do you think I can't take him? Are you afraid I will die trying to take my vengeance against him?" She solemnly looked down, certainly unsure how to word her response to that. Courtney said, "No, Tommy. Because you're not a killer. A killer doesn't read me poetry over the phone to help me sleep when I have bad dreams. You're so different than anyone I've ever met, I see why. Tommy I don't want you to die.... It's not about machismo, or if you're man enough. It's about even taking the chance... when I'm with you it's like you are beauty and I am the beast. You don't even understand how happy you make me, if I lose you too... I-I" "Courtney... please. Don't say those things. I am not going to die. I have to do this. Not because I am foolish, but because I want a happily ever after with you. That fantasy can't take place if Darren is searching the world for me. I know he would. He will, if I don't end this here. Explaining this to Miles will be a whole other battle. But we will row that boat when necessary. Courtney, I'm taking you home first. We need to go." "This isn't much of a discussion. But okay, Thomas." "DO NOT call me that. Please. And you're right. It's not. I can only lose so many people before I break into Hansen-hood. There's no debate about this anymore. I've listened to everything you had to say, now, let's go!" Courtney folded her arms with haste, she did not like being the damsel in distress. Yet I figured she would like it less being dead. She did not know Darren as well as I did, there's no conception of quitting until the serpents head is severed. Anything less would result in death, or worse, ending up in Darren's hands to be tortured and toyed with until submission. Even then, he would continue his torment long after.

CHAPTER 10

An hour after

A mysterious aura overtook Miles while at the lab, he did not know why, or where it originated from. But he felt the urge to go home immediately. Like that queasy feeling when you need to leave before a big exam you did little to prepare for. He just knew he needed to be home for some reason, when Darren texted him a skull emoji for no apparent reason, he immedietly recieved this unerving feeling. The final touches of his formula were awaiting to be completed. Yet this sequence was heeded by his need to be back home. His girlfriend, Meghan, who was working on his formula with him, said "Miles? Are you clocking out early today? It's not like you to take a break so suddenly." He turned to her, then said "I know.. I just have this... terrible feeling that something bad has happened at home. I gotta check my inclination's validity to see if I'm wrong or not." "Alright, Mr. Scientist. Is there any way I can come with you? I would like to finally say hi since you rarely bring me by. Am I not smart enough for you?" "No, it's not like that at all. It's just, my family is crazy. I don't want you to be concerned about me the more you meet them." "Aren't all families a little crazy? You might be overreacting." "You wish I was, and no. I believe there are families that are built on a foundation of love, trust, and all the other good components under the sun. You can come if you want, but stay in the car." "Oh, so you can stick a dick in my mouth but it's too 'bothersome' for me to hang out with your family? How rude." "I'm afraid if you get too close to them you might catch their crazy." She retorted, "Well, you haven't." Miles calmly responded, "Guess we will see, won't we?"

Miles left the S.C.A.R research facility with impunity, this unfamiliar ringing kept singing in his ears. He wanted to turn his hearing off, the deafening sound rang continuously. Megan rocked back and forth in the passenger seat. She put on some music to soothe the tension. The song of choice was 'Sweetheart' by Franke and the Knockouts. Miles put on that song for her when they had their third date, a picnic in the rolling hills of Helen. He smiled, easing his raised shoulders down a notch. Megan sang along to the song, Miles did not drop a nod to the beat. The only thing he could think was that Tommy had gotten himself killed. "That kid, what did he do this time...." he wondered.

As Miles arrived home, he did not like seeing the door wide open. He knew his father would throw his children off a cliff like the Spartans if they left any door ajar. Miles told Megan to stay put, and he would be right back. She did not like that idea, as she has seen her fair deal of scary movies late at night when the cryptid's and cruelties of life come out. Yet she accepted it, she turned the volume up in the car then reclined back waiting for Miles to return. Miles approached the door slowly, and noticed a trail of blood leading to the staircase. Without much observation, the origin of the stains revealed itself. Miles dropped to the hardwood floor and did not return up for a moment. It wasn't just his heart that broke, it was also his soul. He hugged his dead mother and father, so certain that he could fix them and finally have a happy family again. But that just wasn't the case. Miles pleaded with them to wake up, yet hell had them now. There was nothing he could do but weep. Weep all alone like all the nights he sacrificed sleep for this dream. A dream that now was more dead than his parents. The same darkness that momentarily took Tommy, and forever holds bearings on Darren, had now infiltrated Miles's mind. Violent lightning thrashed inside there, striking with the same precision as infrared lasers.

Earthquakes tore apart the softness he contained behind his walls. He worked tirelessly to outsmart his circumstance, yet failed to escape who he truly was under the surface. Miles slipped into his new skin without dismay, once he accepted that helping them was worthless, there was nothing left protecting him from becoming a Hansen. Miles kissed his deceased mother farewell before turning around to see Meghan standing in the doorway with a twisted expression. She screamed, asking Miles with her crying pleas, "Oh my god! Oh my god! Are-are they dead??.......MILES?! Why aren't you saying anything?!" "Because, you dumb bitch, sitting and listening to you talk is making me want to vomit. I-I-I want to cut your lips off of that impetuous face...maybe dangle it like a little handkerchief. I must see what that feels like."

Miles stood up, holding the knife my mother killed herself with. It started dripping blood onto her dead body, like dripping water onto a dead garden. Megan backed away with ease. She said "Uh Milessss. Whattt.... are you doing? Why are you holding that knife? You're scaring me?" "Scaring you? No...No.. No, I'm sorry honey. I didn't want to scare you. I just want to rip out your throat with these here hands, tear out your heart with this here knife, then prepare your flesh for dinner with that there crockpot. I've always wondered what all the fuss was about from my mother. She always said human flesh was the best!" Megan tried to run away, but Miles was five steps ahead of her. He threw the blade at the back of her neck. It pierced through her throat like a knife into a loaf of bread. Megan dropped dead, she died before face-planting onto the hardwood floor. Miles saw bits of broken teeth on the ground, he picked one up and smelled it. He received a whiff of copper, and the smell aroused his nostrils. Blood began pouring out of Megan's mouth with no sign of stopping anytime soon.

Miles heard the door open, to which he flicked the blade out of Megan's neck for self-defense. "If you think trying to kill me will help anything, let me save you the trouble. I've been a murderer for eight thousand and thirty-seven days, you've killed one person. Don't get cocky". Darren said, submerged within the darkness of the fading moonlight. He peered over Miles' shoulder to see his parents deceased; he did not even twitch. He blinked indifferently, as if those people meant nothing to him like every other person he had come across in his existence. Darren asked Miles, "Is this..... what made you do... this?" He pointed toward the floor, where Meghan had become the equivalent of a leaking fountain pen. Miles gazed at my brother, for once seeing him for who he truly was. Not just a omnipotent force of nature, but as a person whose inner urges would never be understood. Miles said, "I found them like this... all of my work... everything I've suffered for, means nothing. What the hell happened to you though?" "Get a grip, princess. You may deserve to dwell on your bad decisions, but I don't. I have never wasted a second of my time trying to fix someone who isn't broken. But as for me, our brother is what happened. Him and Andre attacked me like rabid dogs. Had to put one of them down."

Darren walked into the kitchen, reminded of his mother's home cooked dinners. There was not a flinch on his face. Miles noticed this indiscretion, and asked him, "How can you not care that our parents are dead? You just stepped over them as if they're sleeping? They're dead, dammit!" "I didn't ask them to bring me here!! Neither did I ask them to leave. It doesn't matter to me where they are. I'm not an attached sociopath like you are Miles, I don't play Captain Save-The-Planet then get damaged when I'm reminded humanity is horrible. You killed your own girlfriend because what? You couldn't save mommy and daddy from choices they fucking made? You're dumber than a fucking idiot. They don't come dumber than you, do they? If you had any intelligent bone in your body, you could have fixed millions of brains. Not that I believe in that bull crap, but it's funny to see you succumb to your own stupidity. You preached to me time and time again about how dumb of a brother I was for indulging in what I wanted in life. While you... you... you capsized before you could even finish trying. You moron! I can't believe I share any sliver of DNA with you!"

Miles made his fingers into a ball while Darren roared with laughter. It was the first time Miles had seen his brother act this way. He wondered if this was Darren's first encounter with true humor. With something he actually found funny. The dredge of existence could not possibly provide that. Yet to see his brother become smitten by his indiscretions, that, that made him howl like a wolf under a full moon. "You're lucky I am your brother, and still want you to live. Get in the shower now. Clean yourself up, we're outta here in thirty. I will handle the bodies." "Let me help; I owe you that." "No, you don't. Let me set something straight, you're not a killer. We're not sharing any sort of sentiment here. You did something dumb, I'm here to help. If you help me get rid of Thomas, then I will make sure this mistake is washed away." "If Tommy killed our parents, then let's storm the horizon like the Mongols to kill him then take his girlfriend!" "Are you nine years old? Stop talking. I need to be objective rather than subjective. The last time I did that, the little rat almost caught me in a trap. No more games. I don't want his girl, I want him dead. I took his best friend to remind him that this game we play is played by my hand! How dare he think that he is more than a spineless idiot!" Miles responded sarcastically, "What's the matter? Tommy really did strike a nerve within you huh?... your pride must really despise having someone walk away from you. After all the boasting of a perfect kill record, you finally have been bested." Darren quickly responded, "For now, I will learn in the future not to play with my food. Superiority comes with its own pitfalls." Miles laughed, then said "Humility doesn't." Darren snarled like a snapping doberman, and said "Ummm.... are we really going to pretend your dead dog of a girlfriend isn't lying here drowning in her own blood? I hate you, not because you're my brother, or because you're a introverted, bipolar, sociopathic dumb-ass. But because you choose to time and time again think you're somehow better than me. You and Tommy.... You are the worst siblings ever. Now leave, before I throw you onto the heap of bodies too." Miles, in attempts to defend his shattered soul, said "I bet you killed our parents you obtuse douche-bag. If so, I will hunt you down until the end of time". Darren snickered, uncertain if Miles was being serious or not. He said "You would weep to be dead if you ended up in my clutches. Not a single person will ever hear of Miles Hansen again. Do you want to dance, and take that chance?"

Darren was colder than Antarctica during the winter solstice. He held the entire Bifrost within his withered heart. The image of his shattered self staring back at him in the bathroom mirror flashed through his memories museum. Miles felt the horrendous ambiance emitting from his brother's gaze, it is vile how much evil can live inside one individual. Even if Darren was responsible for their parent's death; the only hope of defiance would be to die trying, maybe inflict a life-ending wound while fighting. But most likely just end up giving him a scratch. To die for a scratch seemed like a sacrifice not worth obliging. Miles concurred to his brothers better judgment, albeit, with intense resistance. He trotted upstairs to shower off his parents blood from his face. Meghan's belonged to the floor, there were no remnants of her left on him. Darren decided which body to slide off into the darkness first. He would drag them to the basement, where Darren has contained countless victims.

Once Darren did the deed, he ran upstairs to wash the red from his hair. Besides being an assassin and practicing sadism, being neatly groomed was his third most important virtue. Darren walked by the hallway bathroom and heard Miles listening to music in the shower. He grinned ever so gently, certain that his brother was very much likable given the switch in circumstances. The normally timid, 'doesn't play music in the shower to avoid bothering anyone because that might lead to confrontation' kind of guy, was given a chance to beam brighter than before. Be not as you are, but as you should be, was what Darren was thinking. Miles had Rap God by Eminem on, which was unusual for him. That was more of Darren's genre when he was out killing in the night. Yet, psychotic breaks are usually causes for change. Miles enjoyed this newfound freedom, instead of swimming against the current as he always did, he now allowed the stream to push him down the mountain. He rapped alongside Eminem with precision, surmising that this is who he always wanted to be. Like knowing lyrics to a song you don't allow others to hear you often listen to, because then, it may shape too much of how they frame you.

Darren however, got in the shower and put on a playlist of Baroque music. The first song was Vivaldi's Summer, followed by Violin Concerto's Op. 11 and 12. The demeanor in which Darren carried himself versus Miles was radiant. Darren lived in a constant meditation, seeking peace in recognition that it is fleeting. The only time he felt the need to release his inner monstrosity was when he indulged in his 'art form.' All other facets of his existence tended to cultivate a state of complete mindfulness. Even his showers. Darren hated exerted unnerving pressure onto himself, nor exerting energy that didn't need to be used. Miles, on the other hand, in a state of euphoria from killing his first person, appeared more erratic by design. Like the wall bordering his shyness and inner desire to relinquish power was toppled. Miles rapped loudly, feeling his heart beat increase as he felt the music flicker through his nervous system. He activated neurons that have never been turned on, his days of living in a state of 'walking daydreaming' were over. He never felt more present with the current situation. He was not looking forward for once, the only concern in his mind was feeling everything this energy presented. Miles scrubbed himself erratically, using half of the bar of soap before throwing it onto the shower floor. Then he scrubbed his hair with the bubbles remaining on his hands. Darren's shower procedure was much more.... inclined to routine. He neatly washed his body with a fresh bar of soap, not wasting a single sud. Once he was done with washing his tattoos individually, he let the water wash his hands off. Darren didn't believe in mixing his body soap with his shampoo. The same way he neatly arranged his plate so that no two entrees were touching, he did not like mixing his soaps. He took his time on his hair, never in any rush to make sure his hair looked perfect.

Their showers ended around the same time, which was odd considering Miles entered way earlier than Darren. Yet, when considered, Miles was enjoying his euphoria for as long as he could while Darren remained focused on efficiency. Taking quick showers as with quick meals, quick task completion time, and quick thinking. Everything Darren did was based on speed, like the great Julius Caesar in his many conquests. They met downstairs in the kitchen to discuss further business. Miles remarked "Damn, you really do work fast. It doesn't even look like anyone's been butchered here." Darren, who was opening up more to Miles now that he seemed different, grinned with gentleness, then said, "Yeah, that's what happens when you've been spending your whole life covering up crimes. You tend to get good at it." Miles smiled, then asked "Soo... what's next? You're the one who seems to know his direction out of this mess." "Of course, I do, I've always considered this as a possible outcome. We need to eliminate Tommy, then get the hell out of this town. Our welcome has been long overstayed. If the cops haven't caught on now, then they will eventually." Miles suddenly seemed overtaken with concern. "We can't just kill him in broad daylight, that would be absurd!" "Who said anything about doing that? No, you misunderstand my motives. I... intend to win. If I know anything about my brother it is that he will come back. We will be here when he does so. He did not kill our parents for no reason, I killed his best friend in front of him then he almost beat me bloody with my own baseball bat. I am aware enough to see that this ends with me or him gone. Like the Wild West, this world isn't big enough for the two of us." "Well okay then, good plan. What do you say we go kill some people. Since, you know, we have some time to kill."

Darren remained unphased by what Miles had said. However, he did appreciate his idea. He said "Miles, I kill people to relieve myself from the burden of existing. Like a crack addict under a bridge waiting for his next hit. In other words, seeking peace is my reason. What is your reason?" Miles responded by saying "I-I have wasted all my life trying to fix myself and my family from who we were. But to see that no matter how hard I worked, my efforts were futile, I finally realize there is no point in finding morality. I want to indulge in what I am, the chaotic, barbaric monster I was born to be." "Hmph. Perhaps I've misguided you, brother. Maybe I will take you up as my next protegee." "Really? That would be sweet!" "No, you imbecile. I'm like Batman, I work best alone." "What about Dick Grayson? Jason Todd? Tim Drake? Damian Wayne? The Justice League? Why can't we be like them? Why does Batman not have Robin?" "What happened to all of them again? Oh yeah, that's right. They either moved on, died or turned on him! Batman works best alone, so do I," Darren responded. Miles said back "So, does that mean we can't kill anybody before we deal with Tommy?" Darren gazed at the ground, then back at Miles, replying, "What's the procedure for breaking into a house? Do you even understand how efficient you must be to never be seen like a shadow at sundown? It is a feat deserving an award to flee from the police for decades. Hell, add our parents' time killing and you would be in for a generation of dispensing degenerates with elegance." Miles looked away, uncertain for what to say. He said "I don't know Darren, I spent most of my childhood ignoring your guy's torment upon my soul. I don't remember much of the bad stuff, I remember how they made me feel. But the memories fade as they all do. Fine. If you don't want to, then I will. Join me if you must, yet I won't count on it." Darren appeared annoyed that Miles thought he could just go killing willy-nilly without using efficiency. Darren said "Killing another person isn't a game... it's art. An art I've worked hard to display correctly. Do not soften my judgment. We may be twins, but I've been killing insects before you could even speak!" "So is that a yes?...." "Hmph. I suppose I could use the meditation before we embrace our journey forward. Let's go. I will teach you a thing or two about how to properly execute a murder in real time." Miles smiled, excited to experience the true essence of murdering someone. He thought about the randomness of their plan, and said "Wouldn't it make more sense to go get his girlfriend or trash his work? We can kill two birds with one stone". Darren did not consider this, however, he did not believe Miles was ready yet. He wanted him to show his skills before considering him worthy of helping him destroy Tommy. Darren replied "That is not necessary, what we need is Tommy. Nothing more. I will not allow my temptations to get the best of me again. We get rid of this mistake, then we move forward. Okay?" Miles nodded, ready to partake in pure, premeditated chaos for the very first time. Well.... besides the girlfriend he butchered earlier, but that was nowhere near premeditated. In fact, it was leaning heavily on the opposite end of the spectrum.

They walked out of the door together, one with glee to be finally included, the other with a whimsical serendipity traveling briskly along his face. The pair were a match made from heaven, the kings of Anguish and Despair had united under one umbrella. These tortured souls knew no bounds beforehand, but now, to be connected by something as intimate as murder, the connection was more prominent. They shared a bloody resolution for each of their issues separately. Together though, who knows what sort of damage could be done. Tommy needed to not just run, but hide as well. He needed to hope the both of them would not find him. Otherwise, who's to say how far their conquest for vengeance would take them?

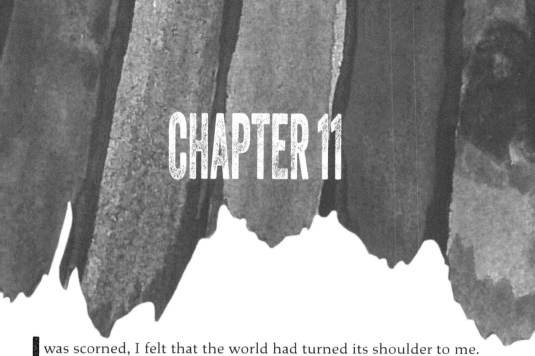

CHAPTER 11

I was scorned, I felt that the world had turned its shoulder to me. Why did I believe I did the right thing, but feel inside that my mind shattered in that moment I decided to indulge in my family's way of living? Courtney walked me up to her room while holding my hand extra tightly. I was certain my situation was starting to seep into her thoughts. I can never tell what anyone is thinking, some smiles deceive me. Emotions and me do not sync regularly. I generally misread people's feelings, considering I did not grow up like other kids, I did not consider this difference until now. Now, to have been a Hansen momentarily, I see how profound the damage done to my mind has become. The greatest evil is not done by those who do it, but by those who allow its existence to continue in this world. I laid in Courtney's bed, unmoved by the events coursing in my head. My brain was playing the moments that led up to this in a linear sequence like a machine reeling back a VHS tape. I held onto Courtney's fluffy pink pillow with momentary idleness as I was taken back to clutching my dying best friend one last time. The survivor's guilt infested into my inner terminal, shutting down all the thoughts arguing otherwise.

As I remained frozen under my own skin, clutching her pillow, weeping until the wilting feeling was done, Courtney sat down and brushed my arm with her little violet fingernails. Her tender touch relieved me of my immeasurable pain, of all the guilt and shame

I'd repressed for ages. The repression only led my emotions to be expressed in such a vibrant way. The exuberance of the emotions I was feeling currently were incomprehensible, like Lovecraft's color from out of space. The emotions seemed to be the insanity itself, not the root from which it grew from or the seeds which it sprouted from. I wondered once again why God would send me here, why he would let me make one best friend just for me to send them to the guillotine. There is no fairness in this dark lair, down in this domain where the sun doesn't shine, there is only deep despair and wails of anguish that never quite reach the walls they're aimed at. I remained sitting still as a sprouting vegetable for some time, otherwise disso-ciating so far from myself I was dissolving entirely.

Once I regained enough focus to see the situation in its entirety, I rose from the bed like a seed eager to sprout out of the ground. I jolted towards the door before Courtney said, "Wait a second! Tommy! Where are you going?!" I turned around, struggling to face her for fear she would not agree with me, then said "Courtney, you need to stay here. I will be back." "Fine! If you want to get yourself killed the so be it! I'm so sick of giving a shit about your safety!" I felt my eyes burn bright like they were thrown inside a furnace. I did not know what to do with this burning sensation sweeping through me like a terrible scourge. I withheld this surge of electricity in hopes to not hurt my queen any more than I already have today. I said "You... are the reason I must go. I let one person get too close, and now I'll never see them again. Courtney I can't have that be your fate too. You deserve so much better, even if it's without me. I cannot let any-thing bad happen to you, life would not be worth living if my own torment caused the only girl gentle enough to ever love me succumb to its insidious consequences. I can't, Courtney. I can't live in a world where people like my brother are still out there. He deserves to die for his crimes." "Then do as you must. I will not tell you how to live your life, Thomas."

Courtney pulled me close then hugged me, switching sides with me so she could stand in between me from leaving. She was like a nine-year-old piling boxes in front of the door trying to block it. I stopped my resistance against her wishes. Maybe my masculinity was pulsating more energy than before, nonetheless, I figured out how I could satisfy both worlds. I told Courtney, "Okay... okay. I won't go now. Why don't we... just...." before kissing her with the same amount of magnificence as sharing halves of a passion-fruit with your spouse-to-be. The shade she casted was like sitting under a fully grown apple tree, one that grows from seeds that are sweet like fresh peaches. Even in peril, my girlfriend's tenderness rose above all other indiscretions. I put on some music to alleviate the tension, my goal was to get my queen to sleep comfortably so I could leave without disturbing her peace. The song of choice was "All I Ask" by Adele. There was something about her voice, and how she pushes it to the threshold of its limits that remained blissful to me and my love. Courtney was very fond of Adele, especially since she's the only other female artist besides her to make me cry. I knew this love-making would be different, and difficult. Because in my soul I did not know if this truly would be the last time.

In showing courtesy to my sweet Courtney, I will not touch on our time together. I will instead use this ledger to express the part of the song that caused bells to ring in my empty, candlelit hallways. Art was the expression of life, so did that make life an expression of something else? I did not know, what I did know was that art is a masquerade reality wore when she wanted to feel pretty. When Adele sang as I made my queen feel happy for what could be the last time, it reached parts of my heart never once touched by the light: "I will leave my heart at the door, I won't say a word. They've all been said before, you know. So why don't we just play pretend. Like we're not scared of what's coming next. Or scared of having nothing left. Look, don't get me wrong. I know there is no tomorrow. All I ask is, if this is my last night with you. Hold me like I'm more than just a friend, give me a memory I can use. Take me by the hand while we do what lovers do. It matters how this ends, cause what if I never love again." When the song reached its end, I felt abridged. We continued exploring each other until my "fire and ice" playlist was finished. My queen appeared gentle yet she required an insane amount of ferocity to subdue. Like a large lion whose appetite cannot be controlled by such mere slivers of scraps the packs of hyenas leave behind. They wanted the whole gazelle. The song we ended on was,

'Here Comes the Sun' by The Beatles. It's delightful symphony put Courtney straight to sleep.

Once I was at ease, I left through the window so I did not disturb her slumber. I felt bad betraying her judgment as I was, but I had misjudged the severity of my situation for too long already. I needed to cut the heads off the hydra before it had time to strike back. Like the Romans, my parents created a wasteland and called it peace. There is no happily ever after if Darren is still alive. Like Eddie Brock's Symbiotic Suit, the evil will always follow if not fully conquered. Even a sliver of its remnants are deadly. I ran for my house with belligerence entering my nervous system. I felt like a coo-coo clock ready to burst out a bird from its tiny house. My thoughts were so scattered, I fell down several times while running to my house. I started humming 'After the Love is Gone' by Earth, Wind, and Fire to keep my mind occupied. The houses I passed by gave me flashbacks of the time I went on that raid with my parents. When I peeked into those people's homes, I wished that I was in there instead of that van. The memories of the sitcoms I would watch in my room, hoping I'd be teleported into their dimension. The thoughts that I would fit right into the Tanner family or with the Cheers! cast at school reflected back inward. I wondered what a sitcom of my life would look like. It would probably be labeled a "Dramedy."

After arriving home, and tripping over my thoughts for half an hour, I entered in the door, alarmed that Darren's truck was not parked outside. Miles's car was here, but when I called for him I heard no one reply. My face flushed all sorts of colors, I was amazed to see my parents bodies gone! We're they really not dead??! I saw them die.. I said, uncertain of what to do if they were still alive. Like one of those Deadite's from Evil Dead. Yet, the horrendous odor exuding from the basement told a different story. I said before heading up the stairs, "Gee, I hope Miles didn't have to find them like that. I hope Darren took care of them personally." The sense of dread and decay overwhelmed me, a house that had some semblance of life was not entirely dead inside. There was no crackling sound coming from my mother's cooking, no television with highlights from a time my father wished he could return to, nothing but silence. The shower door was opened, so I went in and washed my face with some faucet water. On the floor I saw one of Miles's work shirts, I picked it up to discover there was a whole lot of blood on it!

The possibilities were endless, what could have happened in the span of me leaving? The thought of Darren getting his hands on him after what I did crossed my mind. But I chose to ignore that, what mattered was figuring out what the hell to do when my brother returned home. I stood no chance against a professional executioner, yet what I did have was intelligence. Physically, there was no competition, but mentally, I felt there was some sort of equal footing. We were both very smart people with too many problems. If things had turned out differently, perhaps we would have been the best of friends. Yet reality is often more disappointing than the movies make it seem. I fished in Darren's room for all possible weapons. The sword I left downstairs was not there anymore, so I needed to resort to other measures. My brother had everything: daggers, throwing blades, machete's, a prototype for the Jagdkommando Tri-Dagger, a blade capable of leaving a wound needing a team of surgeons to stitch up. I've seen him use that thing, but only on special occasions. He told me that he believes using a weapon of this caliber was "cheating," as if there was some sort of moral code regarding the art of murder. In his twisted world, there seemed to be one.

After grabbing as many items as I could hold, I hid in my room. I did not come here with a plan. I came here with a desire to reap vengeance for my best friend's death. Darren was dumb enough to take someone he knew I loved, better yet, evil enough. Hubris is consuming, he does not realize how insatiable the hatred inside of me had become. Madness really was like gravity, all you needed to do was be pushed to feel it's full ferocity. The Joker was onto something when he told Batman a similar statement while dangling above Gotham. I could feel it's inertia flooding through me like a river through a rocky barricade. Any other version of me would not dare pick up a weapon. Yet, in this universe, I am the one who lost my best friend due to my hubris. I would give anything to have him back. For that, I would equally give anything to ensure that he was avenged. It's not even a question if he would do the same for me, I witnessed for myself how far Andre would go to keep me from dying.

Why he felt my life was more important than his own fails to define itself for me, the shrouded mystery may never reveal its true nature.

I opened my notebook, the one scribbled with little poetry and my thoughts on my situation since I was old enough to grasp it. I couldn't believe Courtney read through these words earlier. How much of me she must of seen... I was afraid shedding my skin to show my bare face would scare her away. *Why didn't she treat me any differently?* I wondered. I was succumbing to the trap anxiety lays out for all those who wander in its field of desolation. I cried quietly among my own audience while reading through my diary. To approach my work from an outside perspective was surreal. How do I feel such torment yet choose to keep going? Was it arrogance, or an attempt to vanquish my anguish? The answer was not prevalent, neither were the other forty-seven questions I asked myself. I became uncomfortable with the thought of leaving Courtney by herself, yet I took a gamble that my brother wanted me more than her. Andre was at the wrong place at the wrong time, I hoped I wasn't wrong. The silence glided along the night sky, it filled my mind with swarming locusts. I could not control myself, the fissure in between the hemispheres of my brain was too wide. I tried remaining defiant. Andre's face before he died kept flashing in my mind like lightning strikes on the Fourth of July. I could not run into any of my empty hallways, even if they were now candlelit. I had to stand here, and face it. *He-he needs to die.... He killed my friend. I can't ever forgive him for that. Whatever it takes...* I whispered to myself, not even sure if I believed the words coming from my mouth. I entered into my abyss once already, I did not feel prepared to do so again.

Yet, within the peril, I felt my anguish angrily turn into pure hatred. My mind morphed into a wormhole, leaving behind brutality on the other-side of the portal. Andre should not have died... it should have been me. Because it wasn't me, the survivors guilt became too intense. The part of me that wanted to be better retreated into solace, all the way into the darkest vortex space has to offer. How do you run away from pain that is ingrained into your brain? How do you run away when the stains never wash away? How do you run away when your feet are stuck in the sand? I did not want to see any more of this monster than I already had. For once in my life, besides the brief moment where I fell down the madness like being pulled by gravity, I felt what it was like to be a Hansen. To be someone so completely engulfed by anguish you do not see anything above the horizon except depraved hatred. This change in nature was compelling, not enough to love it entirely, but enough to see where it would lead me. If beyond these badlands is where it takes me, then so be it. If it leaves me there to rot in them then perhaps that's what I needed. Either opportunity seemed golden to me, yet the sliver of sanity remaining in my charcoaled heart reminded me that Courtney was ultimately the goal. If I was a soul lost on a coast, next to jagged rocks and sunken boats, then she was the airplane that came to pick me up. When those thoughts washed away like the tide thrashing on the wooden pilings under a pier, I recollected my reasoning for being here. I sat on my bed, brandishing an array of weapons carved sharp enough to destroy even the toughest of soldiers. Professional or not, a blade has no name on it. You can drive ninety-nine times and die on the hundredth. As you can kill ninety-nine people and suffer the consequences of the one hundredth. I swung my legs off the ledge of my bed, steadily prepared to bring terror to someone whose spent their whole life disposing it onto everyone he encounters. Today... today though, would be the last time Darren ever took a life.

CHAPTER 12

Darren said "I didn't ask for Dijon, did I? What-What is this? I specifically said Dijon, not Honey Mustard." "Why does it matter? Do you really hate all things that taste sweet? You're like a walking comic book character. Be a real human for one minute please and eat the damn sandwich. I paid for it anyways, you could say thank you before bitching at me about which god damn mustard was put on there." Miles replied, already annoyed to be hanging out with his brother. Darren, who was irritated with his brother's sarcasm, said "Do not speak to me like I'm some nine year old, mad that his chocolate chip cookies were actually oatmeal raisin. I'm not being pestilent, it goes against my personal philosophy to not have something exactly the way I want it to be. Be not as you are, but as you should be. That is what I do with food, with murder, with the occasional woman in bed, and with life. I will eat the damn sandwich, but it's not as delicious as it could be." Miles laughed, and said "You're just a big burning ball of pessimism aren't you, Christ. Is this what working alongside each-other will be like? I sure hope not." Darren said "What makes you think we are some sort of superhero squad now? Miles, I said I would go kill with you, this will not be a regular occurrence. You're no killer. You don't have it in you. Now let's eat these mediocre sandwiches before adding a couple bodies onto your lackluster kill count, so you can be done playing dress up." "When will you accept I am no longer the same! That previous person is gone, he died when he found his life's work dead on the floor. I am what is left of him. I am the discarded parts of my consciousness, the parts I worked so hard to hide from the world." Darren chewed his food slowly, not enjoying his food as much as he could be. He said "You don't think I can't notice a manic person when I see one...? You're just like our mother... that doesn't change anything though. To kill someone is so much more than just spilling blood. For me, it is transcendence into the blinking iris. It is what relieves me from the burden of existing. Murder is something I revere deeply, it is my expression of art. I've never been able to connect to other people with success, with this intuition, I don't have to. It is my way of dealing with the obscene world I live in, whether that is warranted of worthiness or not, I cannot decide." "Hmm, maybe it is mine, too. I believed I could connect with people by fixing their god-given ailments. Also the ones provided by them. But I've given up on helping, the people I wished to help the most are now dead. There is no reason for me to be kind to this world anymore. I am all yours to learn if you'll let me, Darren. I've observed your patterns my whole life, no one knows your style as well as I do. Not even Tommy." "Perhaps you're not as useless as you appear, I will work with you just this once. The moment you deter me, or turn on me, is the second your death will linger on my hands. Are we clear?" "Loudly, I will not let you down," Miles responded solemnly. "Of course you won't, because I don't particularly care if you excel. Yet if you fail, you already know what awaits ahead. I will torment your soul for so long that you will wish you were dead when I'm finished." "Okay Dr. Morbid, the message is transparent. I will learn from the best to ever do it." "Don't kiss my dick, I don't deserve to be belittled by having my balls fondled. Let's get this over with so we can be home for our brother. He's the only soul I want to reap right this instant."

They drove around town with the windows down, Darren showed Miles some of the spots he has already slaughtered people at. Miles enjoyed bonding with his brother, he never felt at home when he was with The Hansens. Mom and dad were always arguing about something. Usually about Tommy using explosive language when she only made dinner for two months at a time. Darren did not care for social interaction unless the discussion was of a higher level and Tommy was too emotionally distant to interact with anyone most of the time. Miles has spent so much time alone in his room, he now saw the virtue of being with his brother. Not in an autopilot, 'ought to say hi while I pass by' way, but in a profound, catching a glimpse of a rainbow floating over an ocean or a rain-ridden-road type of manor. The serendipity was illuminating, so much so that it remained. Not fleeting into the breeze like every time he'd tried to find human connection previously. Miles asked Darren "Can I put on some music?" "You do have human hands capable of doing so, don't you?" "Well, of course. But I figured I should ask first before touching your stuff". Darren did not appreciate the sudden shift into kindness, he said "Why do you insist on being polite? I have beaten the light out of your eyes several times for saying things half as stupid, and you wish to repay me with politeness? It becomes harder and harder every day that passes to accept the fact that you and Tommy are my siblings.... Fix your posture while you're at it! You weeping willow, what are you supposed to do with anything life throws at you if you look like a tree with no leaves...." Miles smiled, then said "Okay then. Fine. Darren, I'm putting on some music." "Better, but keep it to the classics. I will smash this dashboard again like I did with Tommy if you play any of that 'modern day' shit. It is a travesty, and to call it music is a crime against the artist who created actual art. Recycled garbage isn't my cup of tea, so please, no songs made in our era of existence." Miles pulled out his phone then said "I'm way ahead of you, I only listen to classics in the car. It's my retreat from the modern day travesty people call music. I want to punch my radio whenever I hear a new artist on their who sounds like they scraped a cheese-grater along their brain before recording. The music nowadays is too mind numbing for me to even consider enjoying it." "I'm glad we can agree on that, what do you have in mind?" "Led Zeppelin, Stairway to Heaven." "Who? I think we have different views on what classics are. I thought you would mention Vivaldi, or Mozart, someone of the higher arts." "C'mon, this is a recent classic. If Vivaldi had the ability to play guitar like Led Zeppelin then history would be written differently." "Perhaps, put it on then. We need to pick a neighbor-hood quick, we don't have all night." "Alright, then pick one. You're the only person who knows who's been antagonized or not. We're obviously not picking a spot you've already swept through." "You catch on quick little soldier, good job, it's harder than you think to pick a spot around here I haven't terrorized."

The neighborhoods all seemed the same. Besides the heart of Helen, everything in this town was relatively the same shape and size. The river intersecting through the town was always a delight, it produced wonderful tubing when the warm weather strikes. But everything on the outskirts of town was abundantly similar. Darren did not remember all of the places he's visited. He considered it a waste of information to remember the homes he'd invaded. Yet in this situation, it would have been helpful. Darren decided to drive until his gaslight came on, he figured fate would play a better hand than he could. Darren's unusual blood-lust for his brother made him irate and irrational. It made a usually calculated thinker struggle to think properly. His angst between making his brother suffer versus killing him outright battled for his concentration. Miles, however, was airy, in a totally opposite head space. He wanted Tommy to pay for what he had done, no doubt, but he became less worried about vindication the longer he gave into his temporary break from sanity. His mask of sanity was not peeling off like Darren's, his was melding into his skin. Miles became the melding of his slipping sanity and the unvanquished hatred he has for his situation. They were no longer separate entities, it's era of separation was gone. Miles sang to the music without a clue as to how dire the circumstances they entered in were. Maybe he was aware, just not very much concerned. "She's buyingggg a stairwayyyy..... to heavennnnn," Miles sang, while holding his head out of Darren's truck window. Reminiscent of the Dark Knight's Joker, they both exuded their freedom from within the madness they inhabited.

Darren's Red Ranger bellowed, the grumble coming from her engine was riveting. The blood stains remained of the old man and his dog Darren ran over to set an example for Tommy. Even splotches of fur were still stuck in the grill. Darren's Red Ranger had seen a lot of carnage, had even become a part of it in some instances. It was Darren's prized possession, his recklessness earlier caused him to castrate the truck's front bumper. It was worse than when he splattered that damn dog along with their owner all over his truck.

Miles continued allowing the air from outside the truck to flood his face, while Darren pulled into a neighborhood, feeling the night sky glimmer on his skin. This was his favorite time of day afterall. Like a werewolf or a vampire. The song changed from 'Stairway to Heaven' to 'We Are The People' by Empire of the Sun when Darren parked. He went to turn the volume down yet Miles insisted he keep the music on. Miles said "Bro, do you not want to work with tunes on?"' "The sounds of their screams are enough for me," Darren responded. "You depraved alien, I always work at the lab with music. Murder must not be much different than clocking in at the office, isn't that right Mr. Triple digits?" "The numbers are of no concern to me, the magic happens within each moment. Statistics are an after the fact matter." "Noted. So how are we going about this? One through the back door one in front? Or...?" "Do you really think I use my brain when I perform my art? Because if so, then you're wrong. I use the part of me that doesn't think, my heart. My advice to you... always go for the kill, do not play with your food."

Miles and Darren crept along the hedges of the house they intended to break into. They were unaware that the family was having dinner together. The house they picked was a pretty one, the Greek-themed pillars in front of her stood vigorously. Miles touched the pillar, hearing centuries of Greeks speak to him as he felt the finesse of the architecture. He whispered to Darren, "Do we go-go now?" "Shhhh...Follow me." They went around the back, right under the dining room window where the family was eating peacefully. An echo of their conversation escaped through the ajar window. The mother said, "How was your day at work today, honey? Did you do anything exciting?" The father passed his daughter some salt for her steak, then said "Ever since the market crash back in '08, we've been doing great. Every day is an adventure at work. I feel bad for the sad saps who never rebounded from that.... Anywho. How does your food taste, my sugar plum?" The mother smiled as her daughter stuck up ten fingers to show her father's food received a perfect score. Miles brushed with his past self while eavesdropping onto their conversation, his longing to make his family 'normal' again crept up on him like a shark ripping apart a lost marlin. He disregarded his thoughts about how wrong he was, how wrong all of this was. How he worked so hard to differ from his family yet became the very thing he fought against. Darren's influence made Miles roll back into the fog, far away from those thoughts that entered in when he eavesdropped on the family's conversation. Darren said "Alright, Miles, are you ready to collect your first check?" "What does that even mean? I-I guess so," Miles hesitantly responded. Darren put his hand over his face, then said "How do I share a single chromosome with you? I'll try again. Are you ready to kill your first person?... disregarding the girl I discovered earlier. That one was on the house." Miles appeared despondent, he said "Bro your analogies are not working for me, can we just get this going already?" Darren said back "For someone so scientifically smart, you're dumber than a box of rocks. Let's go."

Darren slithered under the porch while Miles aimlessly followed. Darren acted with precision, never allowing a single opportunity to go to waste. Each word he heard from upstairs was spared for him to crunch leaves over, and he ascended the porch staircase with elegance. He was treating each step as it was own mission to complete. Miles, however, was not as adept in stealth as Darren, like playing an off key piano, he stepped on every leaf at the wrong moment. No matter how hard he tried to keep his balance, he stumbled around like a pinball in motion. The steps did not help his case either; Miles was just too clunky to keep up with his brother. If being scary was a superpower, then Darren would be going against the Avengers all by himself. To witness Darren perform his craft with such meticulousness, never missing a single detail while inflicting precision with extreme attentiveness, made Miles bones shiver. Darren whispered "On my go, we're jumping in through the window. Brace for impact... and for glass."

Miles appeared alarmed, now uncertain of his brother's critical thinking abilities after making such an absurd suggestion. Before they jumped into their window like a barracuda leaping out of the sea, shattering the surface of the barricade in between them; Darren reached into his jacket to grab his newly repaired mask, which was neatly folded like a handkerchief. Like dawning on the armor of Achilles in Homer's 'The Iliad', the moment Darren put on his third prized possession he felt as if he was touched by a god. That all of the greatest warriors who ever have lived now have access to him. Darren's usual cold blood boiled at an immensely high temperature. Perhaps Darren and the Devil were holding hands while dancing under the moonlight. Whatever the case, Darren inhaled deeply, keeping his piercing stare directed at Miles. The interlock of souls was torment for Miles. He saw for himself how far his brother had gone to become...the most ferocious killer to ever exist. There are most certainly ones who've killed more souls than him, but in Miles's mind, after looking deep into Darren's darkness, the darkness looked like a thunderstorm on a coast inside of his dilated pupils. He believed his brother could hold his water to any of them in terms of pure ambivalence. Miles gazed back at his brother, nodding ever so slightly. After watching Darren slip his mask on, slipping into the darkness like a shadow after sunset, Miles realized Darren was performing calculated chaos. Miles always believed his brother was dumber than everyone gave him credit for, yet after his display of supreme experience sneaking up the stairs and sinking into complete somberness on command proved him wrong. Darren tapped into total despondence, perhaps to prove a point. Not only for Miles, but for himself. Within Darren's radiating aura, the fog continued to roll on ominously through Miles's blank-as-a-clean-slate brain. His inhibition to murder returned, he still remained scared of the consequences, yet he did not differ any longer. Miles nodded once more, then said "ready."

Miles crashed into the window like a mad man, splaying his hands and feet out in a star shape on the family's dining room floor. Darren calmly stepped over the glass, exercising extreme caution. Miles laid on the ground like a dumb-ass, glass-ridden hedgehog. Darren's plan was pure poetry, all he needed was a way in. Sharon, the daughter of the family, started to cry, unaware of who these goblins in front of her were. Her wailing made Darren's anguish quickly turn into anger. The father leaped from his chair, with too many cares in the world to just pick one. He said, "Wha-?! Who in the hell are you two?! Get the hell out of my house!! You... you just smashed my freaking window?! What for?! Oh, mi amor, are you okay? It's okay, Daddy's here to hold you." Darren did not hesitate to point his dagger at the little girl, he told the father "Put the girl down, she doesn't deserve to see this. I will allow you to let her leave." The father appeared horrified, he said "Wha? No....What about my other one? He's just a child!" Darren replied "He seems old enough to me. How old are you there... kid. Old enough to get tackled by the big kids in school huh?" The father jolted in his chair, he exclaimed "Don't you dare hurt my son! Take me! Let my family go... what do you want from us? Our money? We can give you money if that's what-" Darren smacked the father so hard he flew out of his chair when one of the legs broke. The kids cried, "Daddy!!!" While the mother screamed, "Honey!!" Miles writhed on the floor, still incapacitated from the leap while Darren told the father to stay down. Darren said "I'm not interested in your bullshit capitalism, I consider myself more of an anarchist anyhow. Your negotiation holds no weight against me, I want what I came here for." The father pleaded amid all signs leading to no, "There has to be another way! Please! Spare my family, take me instead! Isn't that enough?" Darren leaned in close to the father's bruised face, then said "You could not possibly provide me a fraction of what I'm after."

Darren placed the concussed father's face on the ledge of the fallen chair's leg, then stomped his mouth into the splintering wood. Teeth sprung out like springs fleeing from a mattress. Several molars hit Miles on the forehead, he was too disoriented to even notice it. The mother grabbed her kids and fled, Miles grabbed her leg while still writhing on the floor, causing her to trip down in front of him. The kids continued running without their mother as she instructed them to. Miles climbed on top of her and smashed a handful of glass into her face. He attacked her with freakish intensity, allowing his hatred to take over until her bones were broken. Darren stared at his brother with immense satisfaction. For once in his life, he felt he could consider killing with someone else. The wife gurgled on her own blood and spit as Miles hissed venom from within his bellowing grimace. Jagged shards of glass were scattered across the ground, some in the woman's face while the others remained embedded in Miles's hand. Pictures hanging on the wall had fallen off among the commotion. Darren picked the father's carcass up to remove his souvenir. Miles fell upon a spout of laughter, the mania was taking a toll on his psyche. The deranged individual wiggling in this woman's blood was once just a thought that infiltrated his mind. Like a parasite, it had now finally come to life, taking the hosts soul with it.

Darren picked Miles up from the ground, brushing glass off of his jacket before saying "You wanna hit another one? After we handle these children?" Miles exclaimed "Holy shit! That was.... amazing. But Darren, we can't hurt the kids.." "Didn't you just shove glass into their mother? Why do you care? Let's get rid of them before they cause us any issues." "I'm afraid I can't do that Darren, they're kids. They don't deserve any more damage than we have done already. Let's let them go, and kill some more people." "Your consideration demeans me, we are Hansens! We are killers! This is what we do! I've tried convincing you and Thomas since the day you've been alive! We don't condone anyone, we don't take prisoners... Do you see what that cost me with Tommy? ......We will spare them this one time, but next time, they're mine". "You're a depraved person Darren, you really do view all people the same, huh?" "Not you.. not Thomas. People as people can be exceptional, yet as a whole they're a joke. Humans should be herded and slaughtered like the miserable sheep that they are. There are zero exceptions." Darren and Miles hopped out of the window they broke into then headed towards the Red Ranger.

Darren grabbed his baseball bat out of the cab of the truck, in return handing Miles his snake- skin dagger with a blade in the shape of a viper fang. Darren said "You are now a Hansen, Miles, let's get going. We can't invade two homes in the same neighborhood. It'll be too suspicious. Let's hit a house further up near town, then we make our way back home. It's fine to have some fun, but we have a job that needs to be done." Miles sat enraged, feeling the frenzy of his first murder spree. Miles said "That rat bastard, Tommy promised me he wouldn't kill them or turn them in.... He betrayed me." Darren slightly smiled, something unusual for him. He said "You're a simple individual Miles, you wanted so badly to change our family because you believed that was better for them. Yet, that wasn't what they wanted, nor do I. No one needs to save me, I have chosen this life. Did you ever consider they didn't either? Not everyone wants what you want, that's why your plan sucked. You're a genius who is too stupid to see that, it amazes me how crippling your lack of intuition is. You're too dreamy sometimes, wake the hell up!" Miles replied "I didn't ask to be born in this family! Okay?! Is that what you want from me? I worked my ass off trying to fix the situation but it was for nothing. I thought I could make them happy, non-sociopathic, but I couldn't. Family feels like the crossroad in all of our stories". Darren leaned in close to Miles face then said "We are the people who derive pleasure from pain, why can't you accept that?" "I didn't before, but I have now". "Then let's end this discussion and go fuck someone up! We're here". "Can I take the lead on this one?" "I don't take in orders from anyone, but I will follow your lead. The moment I feel the need to act according to my own instincts then I will do so as I please. Sound reasonable?" Miles laughed, then said "Considering I know everything about you, we are biologically as close as two people can get. I would say yes, this might be the most I've ever heard you use reason before. You have some level of indiscretion the Devil himself would be impressed with, Darren. Let's make this worthwhile, why don't we?" "If you want to listen to music so badly then put it on, let go of my hand you little kid. I didn't bring you out here to teach you the ways of the 'force', this situation right here is like what Yoda did for Luke. I don't have any desire to be your teacher. Yet if you manage to learn something from me then all the better. The only question that matters is, are you a killer...or not? Cause if so, put that damn music on and let's go!" Miles put on 'Barracuda' by Heart, then put his phone back into his pocket. Darren looked at him with disdain, he reached into his truck and tossed Miles his pair of earbuds he kept in the recently destroyed center console. Darren said "I don't wanna listen to that shit, it'll interrupt my process." Miles smiled as he plugged the headphones in, flicking the switch like his brother so easily did. He may not have been equipped yet to tap into the darkness without music to help him slip into it, but this latter rung was a step in the right direction.

Darren stared at the house of choice's window, standing still as a scarecrow, though-roughly enjoying the opportunity to use his favorite tool: fear. His planned this plot around entailed more creativity than curb stomping someone's father on their own table chair. Which by his standards, was considered a mediocre performance. He began tapping on their window, hoping to alarm someone within to his presence. Yet no one came to the window. He chose to keep standing there without a care for how long it would take to be noticed. Miles, on the other hand, hummed 'Barracuda' by Heart to himself, basking in the vivid moonlight while taking a different approach than Darren. If Darren is the Great White Shark, then this part of the story when the Barracuda feels brave enough to swim in the big leagues all on its own. Miles had twenty years less experience than his brother, but what he had in fate was also exchanged in equity. Miles could stand tall on his brothers shoulders, and on all the giants before him. Knowledge is power.

Once again, this family was eating dinner together. Darren peered in through the window on a large group of people eating pork-chops and lobster bisque. The problem was that all of these man-children looked immensely bigger than anticipated. Eight big ol' boys sat at the dinner table surrounding their parents. Miles assumed they played football together, given that they were wearing numbered shirts at the dinner table, circled around their parents. Those kids looked like they were grown in an incubator, not from the gentleness of their mother's womb. Even among the size difference, and the amount of kids; Darren's frown withered into a wide, eye-creasing grin. The challenge presented before him was too exciting not to try, what was the limit of his ability? Considering Tommy was the first person to test that resolve, Darren himself wasn't sure of what reaching his ceiling really was. He could kill a person in under two seconds, yet to take on ten all at once was a different story. Darren measured his capabilities very carefully. The liveliness of the family inside did not phase Darren's decision to take some steps back and charge at their window with little indiscretion. Miles questioned his brothers bashfulness, why did he not plan anything with him beforehand? he wondered. Like a backhand to the jaw however, as the music soothed deeper into his soul, he realized Darren acted on his intuition. No matter how much he enjoyed planning, he relied on his instincts just as equally. As cold and calculated as he was, his ability to improvise was next to none. Miles assumed the element of surprise was his best bet against these giant teenagers. Maybe that was Darren's thought process as well. These testosterone injected teenagers did not hesitate to take action like the previous victims.

As the shattered glass on the ground and the bat Darren held firmly in his hand indicated he meant business with these people. He did not kick through their window for an opportunity to sit down then talk over cookies and coffee. He came to experience the bliss murder gave him.

The freakishly tall children converged on Darren, leaving the parents to panic in their chairs. Two of them dropped dead before even having the chance to charge at them. Miles dispensed those soon-to-be men as swiftly as when he ended his girlfriend's existence earlier. Darren smacked the blonde-headed boy mad enough to attempt tackling him like a quarterback in practice. Two of the brothers grabbed Darren and began beating the shit out of him. Miles managed to drive his knife into the side of one of their spines before being thrown back by one of the brothers like a sixty-yard pass. Miles and Darren surely regretted picking such an intimidating house to attack. Darren exerted his inertia back onto the brothers bombarding him with hammering blows. Once he was free long enough to flee, he leaped across the dining room table, sending the families Lobster Bisque onto the ground. Darren picked up the table and began pushing it against the boys who nearly beat a hole into him. They resisted as he expected, so, he improvised. Darren gave some resistance to slip one hand into his pants and retrieve his father's knife. The knife had been gifted to him when he performed his first kill, it was the one his father had received in Vietnam. He stabbed the brunette brother on the left in the neck, causing him to spew blood all over the right guy's face. The blood slowly seeped into his eyes like a sinking sweat bead. With this change of strength, Darren easily turned the table onto the disoriented linebacker. When he was completely covered by the table, Darren began stomping on the table to crush the poor individual. It was similar to how the Mongols would sit on top of their victims and have dinner to the sounds of their screams while they eat a feast.

Darren picked up his bat with slowness, the handle sloshed around in his hands from all the blood on it. The handle slipped so much that there was no formidable way of handling the slippery grip. Even among the crippling agony Darren was experiencing, he was happy. The thrill was too exuberant not to pursue, like a drug addict chasing the dragon only to be burned by the raging torrent of flames exhuming from its scaly serpent-esque face. No matter how much his craft tore him down brick by brick, he performed with elegance as if the very thing he loves isn't the thing hurting him. Miles understood through these few interactions that Darren was not a godless monster, he was an obsessed artist. He was willing to enter into any abyss no matter how deep to receive the tidings his muse supplied him. That is what the expression on Darren's slightly purple face said. His mask had been completely tattered, hanging by a thread along his cheeks and chin. Strands of skin belonging to Darren's mask dangled off of his face, then plopped onto the floor. Darren emitted rotten intention, he displayed the weathered gaze of a man who just entered into the sixth dimension, who then returned and was asked about their experience. Words were in short supply for Darren, he was too battered from Andre, Tommy, and these overfed football players to rise above the anguish. His mind was on fire, while his body was with water. As long as he had charcoal to shove inside of his mind's burning furnace then he could fuel his fire forever. Yet, like a glass of water, there was only so much source to drink from before the glass was empty. His mind burned with the might of a million solar systems, but his body was a droplet away from being a glass half empty. The parents, who were too scared to move during the ruckus, collapsed onto the floor and mourned for their children. The father begged for them both to be spared, while the mother asked for her children to come back. They would never return, not even to kiss their mother goodbye. Darren decided that Miles should take this situation in his hands before collapsing onto the hardwood to catch a breather. Miles tossed the dead bodies on him aside, noting how large these boys were. "The thrill of the kill.... I see how addictive it is. These guys are three times our size, yet that only seemed to entice Darren more. Now, so am I," Miles said to himself. He was still slightly spaced out from their interaction with half of the Milner High School varsity football team.

While Darren laid there on the floor recovering from exertion, Miles grabbed the jagged knife out of the back of the son he stabbed it in, then said to the parents "You know, it would've been someone else we did this to if your house wasn't so fucking wonderful. All I ever wanted was a family who'd love me, who'd eat a damn dinner with me…. Yet people like you have it and don't even appreciate it." The father moaned on the floor, wailing like a banshee who just lost her baby. He said "You don't know what you're talking about, you… you monster! How dare you take my kids away from me!" Miles replied "Your kids, did this to themselves. They should have stayed seated and not tried to be heroes. Perhaps it is you who is confused, I see right through your veil of disbelief. Allow me to shed some light on the situation, you both are like every other deficient parent clouding their child's judgment with money and self-righteousness, who fills the void for dozens of lost opportunities by spewing those insidious ideologies into your own children. I see a Christmas tree peeking outside the window when it's October! I see pictures of a father who played football but relatively few of those of your kids playing. Did they share the same passion you had, or did they bring you hatred instead? Did they not care about the sport you sold your soul to as much as you did? You miserable people make me sick, I wish your children the best of luck where they're headed. It will be hot, and filled with fire that yearns to burn forever. Every child deserves a parent, but not all parents deserve children."

Miles handled the scared parents with care, he picked up Darren's baseball bat to try it out. Darren didn't resist nor budge, he was too exerted to do anything about it but wince to the sound of his own audience. If it had been thirty years earlier when 'Pops' was in Polo's taking pictures at the Georgia Tech Stadium when he played football for them, perhaps he would've had a chance against them. Reality is often more cold than you can imagine, he was far from that person. The person he was and is currently weren't even recognizable anymore. So he could do no more but watch a batch of screws nailed into the top of his wife's cranium. Then into his own face. The melancholy subsided when Miles turned off their stereo. He couldn't hear it because he had his headphones in. Yet the violence behind the bat caused one of his earbuds to become unplugged from his ear. The music he heard was somber, borderline distasteful. Not because it was bad music, on the contrary. Miles just didn't appreciate such sad music playing during such an amazing sequence him and his brother just performed. The song of choice was called "Static" by

Steve Lacy, Miles was familiar of his work, given the song him and Meghan first had intercourse to was 'Bad Habit' by him. Ironically, a bad habit is what led Miles to lose more than his marbles with the one woman who was there for him. Among a family who didn't understand him, she did. And he killed her for it. As 'Static' continued playing in Miles's mind, even when the stereo was shut off, the paralysis soon kicked in.

Darren rose to his feet once he felt good enough to use his bruised legs. He looked around at the carnage, wondering what cost his addiction would demand of him. First Andre, then Tommy, now this family have put him to shame. His slate of a perfect record hung on a thin wooden raft floating out in the vast ocean. "Miles... we need to go home. Now. I-I don't know how much more I can take tonight. That little shit is in my head..." Darren said, wondering why he hesitated so many times in the previous encounters with Tommy, Andre, and the family they just butchered. In any other instance, two decades experience of being evil would topple any form of resistance they put up. Good does not win when the evil it stands against is much more formidable. Miles's fragmented mind separated even further, creating a fissure between his brain's left and right hemisphere. His mania lashed out of control, phasing in and out like lighting a match then blowing it out. Darren noticed his brother's indifference to his statement, as if he was speaking to a knight's hollow armor inside of a castle. Miles looked like he had seen several people eaten by a giant crocodile. The blood dripping down his face was not his own, the damage he sustained was more internal.

Darren started snapping at Miles, hoping to regain his fleeting attention. To his dismay, no one answered. Darren pondered on what he had caused, yet remained stoic and unapologetic. In a moment, he could've chosen compassion, he chose indifference instead. He shook his brother, hoping to shake the static out of his head. Yet, Miles chose to ignore him further. Diving further into the void was the only choice that seemed important to him at the moment. Darren grabbed his brother then ran out through the window he barreled into minutes before. He figured Miles was finally experiencing the full force of the guilt trailing behind him this entire time. Would this burst his bubble? Or would he emerge out of the abyss like a caterpillar exiting a cocoon? Darren didn't know, he was too wounded to do any complex calculation. His time driving home was spent thinking slow, then fast. His heartbeat followed the same rhythm, along with his breathing. Slowly but surely, Darren became in sync with the situation again. Miles remained in his brain, tripping down a velvet staircase with no bottom step in sight. Darren tried snapping again but to no avail, he wondered if he had broken his brother. There was timidity developing in Darren, he had never cared for anyone in his entire existence. Not even his own parents death moved him to feel anything, but his brother was different. Darren did not want him to be in despair, in his mind, he was his other half. They have shared the same energy since birth, their essence is intertwined by the fibers of their shared DNA.

Darren directed his attention back towards the road. He hoped his brother would return, because for the first time in forever, he felt everything except hatred for Miles's situation. Even Tommy's suffering didn't bother Darren, Tommy was just too different to even consider his pain. They shared parents, but not ideologies. Miles was his twin brother, no matter how badly Darren wanted to separate himself from his brothers anguish, he felt every bit of it, so much so, he considered how his actions led him here. This feeling was something foreign to Darren, who usually moved forward from feeling things faster than a photon traveling at warp speed. Once they arrived at home, Darren nudged Miles several times, to no avail. Darren smacked his dashboard, shattering the glass between himself and his speedometer. He yelled "Damn it! Why won't you wake up! I should have never brought you with me. What was I thinking?!" Miles shook his head several times, blinking about a million times before saying "I-I was just exploring, that's all. I seem to have broken through the wall. I feel.... Awesome. I could hear you speaking, yet this tethering force kept me compelled to dig further into this abyss. This crevasse is filled with such wonderful things. I see the beauty you must see, Darren." Darren's eyebrows lifted, his expression emitted happiness even though it rarely performs this action. Perhaps instincts are indicative to someone's true nature. Darren exclaimed "Miles!! Thank God you're alright! Did you just have a coma? I thought I lost you there for a second..... We're home though.... are you ready?" Miles was still dazed and confused, but not enough to be unable to perform his duty. Miles said "I wouldn't call it that, a coma is a state of prolonged unconciousness. That was different. I was still concious, just unable to respond. That... was different." Darren said "Can you save the lecture for when I care? Don't try to teach me science after I just carried your unresponsive ass to my truck. What the hell was that??" Miles said "I-I don't know. It's like my mind was fighting against this descent. Like it has been my whole life. I've always felt this inner evil, but my innate goodness kept me away from making irrational decisions. Now that the darkness reigns control, it's like the light wants to shine again." Darren replied "Well shut that shit off, you've made your choice. Accept it, don't sit and wallow in it. Your indiscretion will kill you before anyone else could. Are you aligned? Or do you need more time?" Miles said "I feel fine, Tommy needs to pay for betraying me. We could've fixed our family." Darren presumed his brother was okay, enough to carry out the mission at least. Darren said "Simplicity is the drug of all mankind, isn't it? If you realized earlier that life was taking place in fifty shades of grey instead of black and white like the movies make you believe, then you wouldn't have wasted your life trying to change human nature! Our parents were horrible people, and in return, created more horrible people. You spent your life trying to change that! While I spent mine accepting that fact. Learn your lesson, Miles. Life isn't so simple as to think a miracle drug will cure the ailments of a crazy person. Especially when their environment and society has molded them into that person. You think rewiring brain chemistry like a motherboard will fix all the viruses still inside the system? You can't just software update someone back into docility, especially when they <u>want</u> to be that person."

Miles turned away towards the window, understandably upset that his brother was right. Darren patted Miles on the shoulder. He said ,"We can make this right, then live a new way of life. You and I. We can fill the void our dumb brother has created." Miles, newly devoid of all emotion, agreed to Darren's sentiment for something new. Whatever was behind him was burning in a large fire, a fire strong enough to rip apart the sound of the static still lurking in the back of Miles mind. The static was replaced by crackling, ashes, and the sound of flowing magma. His enraged hatred for his wasted existence engulfed the static that was holding him back. Miles asked Darren a question he wasn't expecting, Miles said "Can I borrow your mask? I want to tap into whatever darkness that thing brings." Darren stared at the ground before repairing his mask. He added the new piece of skin he plucked from Andre's face near the forhead area. It wasn't pretty, but he sewn it back together as best as he could. Darren unhooked the straps to his mask before passing it off to Miles. Darren said "Take care of it, will you? It will be a heirloom. Besides, I want Thomas to see my face as I rip his throat out of his neck."

They walked towards the door of their home with similarity in their stride and footsteps, prepared to take out the final semblance of their past life. The house stood menacingly, perhaps absorbing the death and destruction lingering inside her. Darren looked up at the house, counting down the houses from his past life. They had to be in double digits now, their murder spree had taken them across the country, into many motels and a few houses. The house standing before Darren made him reflect on all those memories. Miles clicked the shuffle button on his playlist and stayed on 'Burning Down The House" by Talking Heads. He believed it best emulated how he felt about the current situation. Darren remained stoic as ever, with only one thing cultivating inside of his thought process: how much blood needed to be spilled before he could relinquish his essence from this anguish he brought upon himself. Like a person dependent on crack-cocaine, Darren's addiction was no longer subservient to his whims and commands. It demanded everything in return to be fulfilled. A victim is tasty, yet a runaway is succulent. Darren's rationality dissolved in a bottle of acid, it started the process when he killed Andre. Now, it had fully submerged under the rippling current of acidity.

CHAPTER 13

Ten minutes before

While I waited in my room for Darren to return, I read Plato's 'The Republic' on the edge of my bed frame. Andre recommended me this book along with 'Meditations' by Marcus Aurelius when I told him about my bouts with depression a while back. I felt an intense amount of anger holding that book, sometimes the smell of certain items or touching an object brings back distant memories. I skimmed through the beginning as my tears began falling onto the pages like a rainy day. The droplets caused some of the words to bleed, yet I could still read without interruption. I was locked in, I was not adding up one plus one equals two. I surpassed that, I was operating at five plus five equals ten. The connections within the dim lit hallways that have never been traveled through provided my mind vibrancy. I could concentrate on reading Plato, mourn over my friend, wonder if Courtney was safe, listen for the door to open, and wonder how I would stop my brother all at once.

I stood up and turned on my stereo to full volume. No one was in the house anyhow, so I figured it was time to indulge in art before my brother arrived home. Stevie Nicks angelic voice infiltrated the silence that was quiet enough to infect the entire house. I wasn't quite sure what I would do when Darren came in through that door. I leaned over the banister to see if Darren's truck was out front while singing among my own company. "When the rain washes you clean, you'll know" I said, aware that this road ahead was a death trap awaiting to spring on me. I kept my composure, assured to seek closure and see this horror story finally come to its conclusion. At any cost, any measures necessary. The emptiness of the house seemed more of a natural state than my serial killing family doing god knows what inside her walls. I wanted to turn the lights on, but a part of me desired this house to wither within the wind. Once my business with Darren was finished, this house needed to burn down with all of my family's mementos still in her. If not burn and wither away like it should have when we first stepped foot into it, being toppled down to the ground like Rome when it lost its profoundness would suffice.

I sharpened Darren's sword on the edge of my door-frame, making sure that each swing would bring evil tidings. All of my life I spent running away from my family, but on this day, it all came full circle. My running, had led me back to them. The path had forks and pivot points pointing me away from this insanity, even then, it lead be back to them. I thought about 'no country for old men', "Of what use was the rule" if it ended up leading me into the same direction my family were headed. Nonetheless of my indiscretions for how I got here, I heard Darren's truck pull into the driveway as Stevie's voice faded into obsolescence. The sound of that damn key jangle sent seismic shocks all around me, my feet were pulsating. They quaked as the tremors from within exerted themselves to the surface. I ran into my room then shut the door quickly so Darren didn't see me.

The chandelier swung side to side when Darren slammed open the door, then again when he closed the door with the same amount of force. His vigor was palpable, even that woman who ran around the house like a headless chicken all those years back didn't cause him to react like this. I felt Darren's ambiance all the way upstairs in my bedroom, the Devil's son had left hell where he was born and raised to bring torment to my domain. I heard voices downstairs, yet I found it odd because it was unlike Darren to have conversations with himself. He was an avid self-talker, but not full-blown conversations. My mind was warping towards that reality, because I heard two voices! One sounded muffled however, I could only pick up my brother's voice. I wondered who else was with him. Darren did not care for apprentices, so it seemed unlikely he'd bring anyone other than my parents. Yet they're gone. So the plausibility of that being the case was next to nonsense. I grabbed Darren's sword then prepared for whoever was to come through that door.

Darren continued talking to whoever was downstairs. I could hardly hear what they were saying since my stereo was turned up so loud. I debated on whether to turn the music down and alert the intruders of my whereabouts; or if the music remained my ally. Footsteps the size of boulders came crashing down onto the staircase, shaking the very foundation of the house as if she was shivering from freezing degrees. I bargained whether killing whoever entered immediately was needed or if more humanitarian measures were necessary. Nevertheless, when I saw my doorknob jingle, I was not prepared for what to do next. Passivity vs reactivity were two different concepts, they differed greatly. They did not dance among each other in a butterfly filled field or walk along a thin tightrope together. To choose one would be to discern the other entirely. So I chose indecision among all options, with the belief that choosing neither was a better option than choosing the wrong one. I chose to stand there and accept my fate. Whether death was knocking on my door to lead me toward a Grimm fairytale or in a direction with less hellish intention, was hard to tell. Yet, the door opened ever so slowly, revealing for me the answer to my question in bold red crayon. Darren's mask peered into me, it appeared as hollow as an onion ring. As if there wasn't a person on the other end of its rotten flesh. A robust, robotic coldness emitted off of him like an overcharged electronic, yet there was a certain softness to his demeanor. The smell of the mask entered into the room before he did. It was mangled, moldy, seemingly molded into his skull.

This deformed oddity standing before me was no longer my brother, not anymore at least. Within the death of silence, my brother broke it by saying "Tommy, why-why would you do the one thing I told you not to do? You are the reason we are here…. Why we are entangled within this predicament in the first place. So save what you have to say, let's dance…..friend." I took a step back, then replied "It doesn't have to end this way… we're even now. Why can't you just

187

turn yourself in, and we be done with this madness once and for all? Do you really wanna run forever?" I said in return. My brother rebutted, "Why won't you just give up already? You've filed this family down to the last remaining atom. I have had it with you, stop talking like words will bring anything back. You had your chance to fix this situation.... Now dance under the pale moonlight with me why don't you?! The opportunity for paradise was lost when you killed my mother and father." I tripped over some scattered books lingering beside my bed frame, my brother continued to move towards me like a wood chipper even when the tree it's slicing is whining, "Please! Don't take me!" I pointed the sword at my brother, in regard to remind him that he has turned me into a monster. A modern Hansen. We locked eyes, battling between each other's fierce gazes. He looked into me, through me, then entirely past me. My room looked like a tornado had rained in on it after my brother and I tussled for control of the sword. Books were falling, curtains were dropping, blood was dripping out of the side of my right eye. The chase of this chaos led us both down the road of battering each-other like a one-man battalion. Like god's blooding each-other up to see who succumbs first. I gave him everything I had: each individual day of being placed in this horror story was taken out with each swing. As if the Allied and Axis powers were in the helms of two separate pairs of hands. The soldiers they deployed were inside of our individual souls, not dropped on the battlefield for war to take them swiftly. The soldiers were inside of my mind, within this horizon, I could see my brother's army stampeding over towards mine. I felt outnumbered, even though it was only us two in the room.

The paintings and drawings I keep on my wall began to fall like picture frames when bumping the staircase they sit next to. As we fought for dominance, I did not understand why my brother felt very different than when we last battled. I just fought him not too long ago when he battered my friend Andre's face into the train tracks, nevertheless of having grown up with him since I was born. His strength before was much more ferocious, this enraged attempt of disgracing me seemed so emotionally intertwined. So much so, it was like fighting another person entirely. Our tussle for the sword reached its high water mark when my brother hacked at me in a hatchet-slashing fashion. I crouched into my bed frame to restrain the hit, which it did precisely. The sword was stuck into the wooden board on the foot of my mattress. My brother grabbed my shirt then lifted me up from the floor, the stench of that mask attacked my nostrils. My nose hair was burning, it singed then sank to the floor where I once was. The feature I never realized existed until being within inches of it was that the mouth of Darren's mask moved as he spoke. The forehead area appeared newly added, like a slapping on a slab of fresh deli meat to replace the rotten block already there.

The scar in the far right corner was eerily similar to Andre's forehead scar, the scar caused by one of his classmates throwing a whiteboard at his head. Within the sickness of this realization, within the breathlessness of my brother choking the life out of me, continuously telling me how this is "my fault," I decided to dig a little deeper. I grabbed the handle of the sword and shimmied it rapidly. When the blade snapped off at the halfway point, metal shards flung off like tin colored fireworks. One piece of the blade was still embedded into my bed frame, it stuck out like a satellite dish embedded onto a roof. I stabbed the side of my brothers body with the blade I pulled out of my bed frame, he winced without hesitation. His whine was separated into similarly-sized segments. He plopped onto the floor with little resistance, he grabbed onto me as he fell down. Like the Leaning Tower of Pisa finally reached its peak in forward momentum, he leaned on me with all of his weight. I was cascading, I twirled him onto my bed so I could uncover his mask myself. I needed to see that he was dead, conjunction didn't mean much when I required the real thing. "You will never kill another person again, Darren," I said. "The Hansens bloodline is finally finished. Miles and I will start over again. We will be the reason this family's name means anything other than death... and destruction."

In the bellows of my brain, the part where the gallows sing and the guillotines ring, I heard a voice behind me say "I'm not too sure about that. Seems to me I have a few good years left. Why don't you unmask your true fate for me... Thomas." Goosebumps slid down my spine, the night sky lit up with overwhelming vibrancy. A tinge of red overtook the dead-by-dawn atmosphere. I did not want to turn around, nor did I want to investigate who in the hell I just stabbed if it wasn't Darren. My insides twisted and split down the middle, I was utterly disgusted with myself. As I slid the mask off, it became clear to me within those fleeting seconds that my brother Miles was under there. Like unraveling a curtain for a show not ready to perform, I was stunned to see Miles under the rotten flesh. His face was stained with blood. I could not tell whether he was dead or not, my immediate redirection was towards Darren. My brain did not contain enough processing power at the moment to comprehend the gravity of this situation. I stared at my brother, uncertain if this was truly the end of the Hansens. I ran and tackled him, and he hit his back on the staircase guardrails. We fought for what felt like hours, yet realistically couldn't have been more than minutes. He gave me every ounce of himself possible, the absolute full run for my money. This moment was everything my eighteen years of living was building towards.

We were punching, slashing, grabbing, and smashing each-other all the way out into the hallway. I held my own for the sole reason that I refused to quit or submit. Each time he smacked me down I was right back up, the bonfire burning within the embers of my black ash-ridden heart pushed me forward even when I did not want to keep going. Darren spun around me and thrusted me into my parents' bedroom door. The daze and confusion stunned me long enough for him to kick me down the stairs. I heard words from every person I've encountered as I fell down each staircase step. Words from Andre, My girlfriend, Darnell, my father, Darren, all sounded the same when they spoke in unison. I thought of my mother's words before dying bellowed in my mind, "This is all your fault! It should've been you!" Once I descended down the final step, I laid there in anguish, in a pool of my own blood. I was certain I had already died. Yet the ambiance trailing my brother's enraged hatred for my existence was palpable. It was no doubt reality I was experiencing. Even if I didn't want to believe it so.

"Is this what you wanted? You stupid fuck?! I gave you everything! I gave you amnesty! But now, my thirst for blood knows no bounds!" Darren said, savoring each step he took to continue talking. "I will make you bleed until you scream about it! I will stretch your skull, you mindless buffoon! How dare you think you are anything more!

You are a Hansen! A child created by two parents who loved nothing more than to murder! This. Is who you are! You freakish little monster! How can you possibly think you are capable of defeating me!? Embarrassing! I am a killer, you are a worthless insult to our family. To our legacy. The name Hansen will ring forever in the ears of all who hear it because of me! Me!" Darren proceeded to snap a railing off of the wooden staircase banister and jam it into the area below my belly button. I grabbed at the jagged wood as he shoved it further into my body, my hands began to bleed from attempting to stop the splintering wood from entering further into me. Yet it was futile.

I winced like a little girl, the air was taken out of my lungs. I tried to speak, but nothing would leave past my teeth, the words only resided in my throat awaiting to be spoken. Darren dropped to the final staircase step, sitting and seemingly to be reflecting on every decision that led him to this very moment. Like Thanos when his hunt for the infinity stones reached its conclusion, once the snap had done its magic, he was at peace. Darren seemed to exhibit this same sentiment. He was so mediocre as he watched me fade from existence. I really was too far gone to see what went wrong. Within a burst of hindsight, it all seemed so clear. Clear as a roughly cleaned crystal. No matter how far I dug, I could never dig deeper than Darren.

There were a million opportunities to stop my family dead in their tracks. Yet, deep down, in the darkest waters of the pond I call my consciousness, I loved them. I wanted them to quit while still being alive to be my family. I see how my desire for a family had taken me too far away from reality. I was unable to see that beating them required me to enter into the abyss. Not ascend from it. My innate nature to choose good over evil, the mushrooms my brother Miles fed me, the psychedelic transcendence of meeting my favorite people, none of these things could lift me further than the wasteland I was created in. My only measure of resistance in this entire miserable existence has been fighting fire with fire. Even my own brother who I believed to be fighting evil with me, was actually fighting it from himself. If we had used fire earlier, we would not have to extinguish such a shitty, ember-ridden situation.

I phased in and out of consciousness, unaware that Darren was still speaking to me. He kicked down the peeling staircase banister with ease, then proceeded to pivot back and forth while thinking out loud. The house appeared to be molding, all the damage my family and I had caused within the span of several hours was abhorrent to behold. I was trapped in paralysis by the magic Darren had casted onto me. I remained immobilized, unable to move much without wincing immensely. Family portraits of my parents, and of my brothers and I as little boys fallen on the floor during the commotion. Maybe I had imagined that part, I could not differ what was happening in my head and what was happening in the land of reality. Staring at one of my picture frames that had fallen made me ponder about the people who meant the most to me while on my journey of life. I thought about Darnell, how he was a part time father figure for me. Then came Andre, a rush of emotions flooded when he entered into my thoughts. He was too good for his own nature, too good to be involved in my exceptionally evil existence. After Andre, came Miles. I wondered why he did what he did, and I apologized among my own audience to have failed him the way I did. When Courtney came into my mind, it was then the wooden piling sticking out of my lower abdomen hurt a little less. Enough so, to touch the wood with my hands, I tapped it with my fingers then began to wiggle it free.

The aimless nature in Darren's demeanor and walking patterns was like drawing outside of the lines in a coloring book. Everything he did seemed to engage against the knowledge that has been ingrained into him since adolescence. He paced around under the chandelier like a lost dog, all while continuing his conversation with himself. "I really did it... they're all dead. I have manifested this gift into existence. I can now kill without limits. Playing the game with rules is bullshit, I—I think California will be a lovely state to live in. Killing surfers and Starbucks baristas has always been a dream of mine. I can now finally travel the world and kill people all over without anyone holding me back. I am much more efficient when I work alone," Darren said. "It sucks that Miles had to die, yet it was a well worth sacrifice for my happiness. I wonder whose blood I will bathe in first? I would say Tommy since he has caused me the most problems, however his is delicate to the touch because of what he's done to me. I want to thoroughly enjoy what I am going to do to him." Darren continued pacing back and forth, completely oblivious that I was still struggling to stay alive. His voice overrode the sound of my uncontrollable wincing. I pulled the wood out of my lower abdomen like pulling a candle out of a birthday cake. The blood stains did look an awful lot like cherry colored icing on a birthday candle. I was in shambles, physically but more-so mentally. The sickening sound the wood created while exiting my body haunted my worst nightmares. I twirled the wood in my hands, ensuring the sharp end was directed towards Darren.

While he walked in circles, so arrogant as to not even look in my direction and consider that I could still be breathing. Without hesitation or any dramatic moment to tap his shoulder and risk him deflecting my stab like they often did in the movies; I impaled my brother into his back with the makeshift dagger. His stream of thoughts was interrupted, instead of more words. A sole exhale left his chest. I trembled all over. Being halfway present and the other half already one foot in the grave, I could not articulate well. I whispered in my brother's ears back his sentiment towards me. I wish I had forty years to profess my hatred for him, even then I did not feel that would be nearly long enough. Instead, I said "You may have unmasked my fate, yet this.. this is your fate. It always was.... Darren, if I didn't do this... then surely someone else would have. You may rest in peace now, even if I believe you don't deserve such gratitude. To me, you dying with as ample suffering possible is considered justice to all the lives you've ruined. You're so ignorant to what death can cause! Now feel for yourself how powerful it is."

Darren tried to push the wood back out through the hole it entered like I did. But to no avail, he dropped to the floor with a thud similar to smashing piano keys together. A bonfire was reduced to a simple flame, then belittled even more so into a heap of charcoal not strong enough to keep even a single flame from burning out. He withered, then writhed on the ground like the Wicked Witch of the West. I didn't suspect so necessarily because I actually stabbed him, not just punched his teeth down his throat, but because he never expected it at all. The way my brother presented himself minutes before I found the courage, and ability to stand up was telling of this. The hardest hits are the ones you never see coming, the ones that creep indiscreetly in the ashes of shadows awaiting to reap spirits without discrimination. Darren laid there on the floor, piecing the picture together, staring at the stars that were sailing across his mind. Perhaps the emotion I should have exhibited was evangelical, yet I did not. I smiled softly, not enough for anyone to notice other than myself, but just enough so I could feel the warmth of enlightenment. My smile grew wider as I stood above my defeated brother, I felt like Beowulf after battling the giant dragon. The more heroic I felt, the more weary I felt as well. I looked down at my abdomen where I had been stabbed. I only remember touching my bloody shirt before slipping into a different dimension. Once I faded from my consciousness, I could not comprehend anything that happened until after I woke up again.

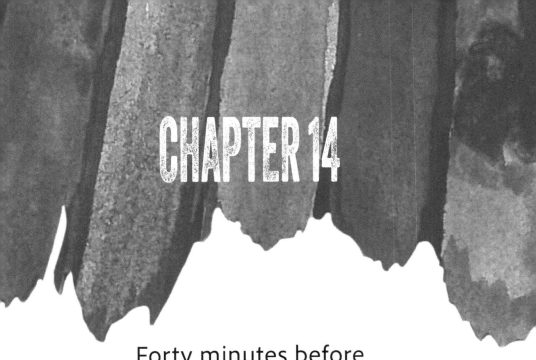

CHAPTER 14

Forty minutes before

"**C**ourtney, my love, are you awake?" Her mom, Natalie said, concerned to see her daughters window left wide open again. She knew Tommy had been over once more without knocking first. Her mother wondered why he was so worth causing a fuss over, any other boy she told Courtney to avoid was at least given consideration. But Tommy, was never on the table to abandon at any point during their relationship. Even when Natalie did not understand the origin of her obsession with him. She assumed her father abandoning them had something to do with it. Nonetheless, Natalie woke up Courtney and asked her if she was hungry. While Courtney's conscious was still loading in from being in sleep mode, she noticed Tommy was gone. "Mom! Is Tommy here?! Please tell me he's in the bathroom?!" "No my darling, I'm sorry, I assume he left through there," Natalie said as she pointed at the ajar window.

Courtney's beady eyes became clouds filled with thunderous sounds. Streaks of lightning slashed across her minds night sky. She was very upset that Tommy left without saying a word to her.. Even in peril, she treated her demon like a little angel. Natalie asked Courtney, "How much more can you put up with from him, my dear? If you keep giving him rope, he will hang you on it. Why do you let him walk on you like this? My baby deserves a man who stays the whole night, not one who just leaves when his needs are met." Courtney seemed frustrated at her mother's inability to understand her feelings. Courtney knew deep down why Tommy left, it wasn't for any other girl. It was for vengeance against the family whose oppressed him since the birth of his existence. Courtney responded by saying "He didn't do anything wrong, mom. You have no idea what he's going through right now. Maybe you'd understand if you had an ounce of compassion for him instead of toss him into the gutter like you do with every single man you've come across with who can't attain your freakish standards!" Courtney continued talking while putting her shoes on, then she stopped talking to stare at her mom. She proceeded towards her bedroom door before Natalie asked "Where do you think you're going? Don't tell me you're actually chasing after him? Shouldn't you accept my advice, my pride and joy? I don't want you to end up lonely like me because you chose the wrong man too early on."

Courtney blew steam out of her nostrils, then said, "I don't want to end up lonely never choosing one at all, mom! I don't know why I love Tommy, but I do. I'm going to go check on my man. He needs me, and I will help him. Even if he told me not to. I have a bad feeling about Tommy's well-being at his house. I'm going to call the police and meet them there. If something happens to me while I'm gone, mom, just know that I did everything I could for him."

Natalie appeared distraught, something about her daughter seemed off these past few years since she started dating Tommy. Why was she so adamant about going after a guy who seemed less interested in dating rather than saving himself from the torment of loneliness? Her mother pondered this sentiment for a second, then asked, "When will it be too much? My darling. Do not fall into the same snares as I did for your father. I know you love this boy with all of your heart and soul, just be sure he does the same. I loved you before him, I want nothing more than your happiness. Do not walk out that door if you're not sure he wants that for you too..." Courtney had to dance on fire and ice, she withheld important information that could have saved Tommy's reputation. Yet, she understood the repercussions of saying said information to her mother. If Tommy feared what would become of his life once he shared his story, then surely Courtney would feel a similar anguish knocking on her soul's doorstep. She decided to keep her secret to herself, and to let Tommy prove his own innocence. Natalie would be utterly surprised to find out the guy she despises her daughter dating was in fact risking his life to ensure she kept hers. Other reasons intertwined of course, yet the spiderweb connects to the same center of origin as before: freedom from his predicament. To Tommy, Courtney was the Mayflower. He was the pilgrim anxiously awaiting to set sail to a better land, to a wonder-filled place that accepts him for just the way he is.

Courtney told Natalie "I will be okay mother, Tommy may not be. I will not let anything happen to him. You may have different opinions about Tommy than I do, but I love him. I will not let him die!" Her mom responded "What is going on Courtney? Why are you keeping me hidden in the dark?! Why is Tommy going to die? You haven't explained anything about his situation to me?!" "You wouldn't understand mom... parents never seem to. I will explain when Tommy is safely back here. It's not my place to spout his information all willie-nillie anyways. He has the right to tell his story." "Courtney, you're starting to scare me. What has your boyfriend done this time?" "What has been done to him is the better question... but that's not important now. Mom, I need to leave, I have an incredibly bad feeling about this." They ended their conversation rather abruptly. Natalie gazed at her daughter with a look in her eyes that indicated she had been this girl before. How much of herself would she sacrifice to make another man happy? Courtney's mother did not want to discover what lurked under the surface of her daughter's thoughts and intentions.

Courtney called the police before entering her car, hoping that they would arrive by the time she got to Tommy's house. She wondered why no one had thought of this previously, yet she recognized how much she loved her mother even if she was overbearing some days. It's not in the same ballpark but she could still swing at it. Besides, she knew all too well cops here were more useless than pig shit. She should know, her father was one. "Shit! Why did I fall asleep! I'm screwed, I knew he was going to leave once I passed out! Damn him! Does he want to die?! What the actual fuck is happening right now!..... oh shit. I'm having an anxiety attack. Just breathe you dumb, doe-eyed woman, this is my punishment for not knowing beforehand. I mean, he hides it well, but holy hell! I cannot believe he has been living two lives this whole time....for me? That's... that's r-really sweet. And stupid as fuck! I could've helped him get their asses in jail before the sun rises....... I understand loving your family until the bitter end but god damn. How long did he allow his family to kill before finally turning on them? I guess that's not important now.. his safety means more to me than him explaining this insanity properly..." Courtney confirmed to console herself in her car, as she was much accustomed to doing. She took great pride in her ability of needing no one to make her feel better when in distress. Since Natalie and Courtney's relationship was finicky from the absence of a father figure, she did her best to internalize life's information alone. Not to say a single parent can't raise an amazing, self-fulfilling person. Yet a major theme in living life is every child deserves parents, but not every parent deserves a child. Courtney deserved to have her father, just as Tommy deserved to have parents who cared for him deeper than the shallow surface allowed.

Courtney drove with intention. Even though she wanted to get there as quickly as possible; her mind was thinking slow and fast at the same time. The trees around her seemed to be artificial, as if she was fading away from a Matrix she never knew was present. The aura of her golden boyfriend fizzling into the nether regions of existence finally concluded its sequence. She felt so stupid to not have seen any of this before. Young, semi-unrequited love has a tendency to blind us of our rationality, doesn't it? Not that Tommy didn't share the same sentiment for her feelings as she did, yet, Courtney gave herself fully to Tommy. A conscious part of Courtney did not know how to move forward correctly. Like as a guy when a girl tells you she's insecure about something so fond about herself that you have no idea where to begin expressing how virtuous this quality really is. Courtney knew she loved Tommy, there was no difference of opinion with this information presented to her. But to say moving forward appeared as a linear path in her scrambled mind was doing a disservice to how she truly felt.

The flashing lights paraded around Tommy's house, like an LED firework display featuring only red and blue colors. Courtney quickly got an uneasy feeling climbing in her throat, and squealing noises emerged from the very back of her brain. Sounds of mud-covered pigs and others of rabid raccoons ran through her thoughts. As Courtney got closer to the door, she heard the sound of an ambulance approaching. The gravity of the situation seemed too heavy to ever be lifted. A police officer by the name of Isabelle Marshall intervened in between Courtney and the door. She interviewed Courtney on why she was here, adding that no one should be here right now. "This is a live crime scene, you need to leave for your own safety." Courtney said, "I am the one who called you guys, my boyfriend is inside. I need to see him, it's a matter of life and death." "Considering his condition in this instant, that's a poor choice of words." Isabelle replied, ".....I understand your concern ma'am, I lost my fiancé to an automobile accident a while back before I joined the force. He was a police officer too, it's not losing someone that sucks. It's living every day without them trying to find your footing again, in the end, it just feels like a continuous sequence of tripping over your two feet..... You can ride in the ambulance with your man if you'd like, just in case he doesn't pull through, you deserve to be with him for every second he's got left."

"At 0800 hours, we have found one wounded victim in the premises, after searching extensively there seems to be no other people inside. I believe the victim may have inflicted this wound himself. However, there are signs of a struggle. The evidence is inconclusive to determine causality. We will move forward when we know more information." Officer Dansby radioed in to his sheriff. He walked around the puddles of blood and came across the living room. He got an uneasy feeling being there, as if he felt every insatiable interaction that happened here within the time the Hansens arrived until the very present. The presence of evil mortified his mind, a mind that has seen countless acts of depravity on the job. Besides the filth, uncleaned sink, and trash built up for what seemed like generations, the officer could find no other people inside except Tommy. No bodies, no parents, no anything. Whoever was here, they left behind tracks that were wiped up the moment they were left behind.

Officer Dansby returned to his squad car, and awaited Tommy to be taken to the hospital. He had questions that needed to be answered before being able to proceed piecing this story together.

After Tommy was picked up to be carted off towards the ambulance, Courtney held his hand the whole way through. She did not know what would become of her sweet angel, but she was so certain about so many things with him. She held Tommy's hand softly, trying hard not to hurt her man any more than he already had been. The blood stains painted a mosaic across his clothes. Courtney could see where Darren stabbed him, she gasped in horror then began to sob morbidly. A EMT named Nicole Soriano comforted the crying Courtney while her coworker Samuel Chace tended to Tommy. Their level of accommodation was outstanding. Since Helen was such a small town, the paramedics took extra care of their patients here.

"I will give it to you straight.... He's got a high chance to live. That's the good news. The bad is that I can't guarantee a hundred percent. He got stabbed pretty badly. But it was below the belly button which is a notoriously gracious spot to be stabbed in if your ever in any situation that requires you to be so.... Sorry. I realize how inconsiderate that sounds... I'll shut up." Courtney turned her frown upside down, then looked at the paramedic with watery eyes. She said "You're okay.. this conversation is keeping me at bay anyways. I'm internally fissuring, so thank you for keeping me at peace for the time being. What made you become into an EMT?" Nicole froze for a moment, as if loading in her memories preceding this very moment. She said "I believe we should save lives instead of take them. I used to work for a pharmaceutical manufacturer, a big one at that, for a while. Up until I began to understand how many lives we harmed, and how many lies we were armed with to protect our interests. I realized I could not stop systemic corruption all by myself, so I quit. Once I came to the conclusion I wanted to save lives instead of take them, I decided being an EMT would allow me to fulfill that purpose. I didn't want work somewhere "hands off" like my last job, I aspired to connect with every individual I worked with. Getting my certification took forever and then some since I was never much good at anatomy. All the different names of body parts confused me in school. Yet I excelled when I went to get certified, inspiration is a hell of a thing."

The cream colored hospital sat on the outskirts of Helen. Courtney sat among her own presence with a monotone, drone-like haze infiltrating her brain's operating system. She drove down her river of thoughts, then was stricken by a sizable slice of lightning when one ominous thought crept on her. 'No one Tommy knew would be coming to visit him while he was in the hospital'. Everyone he loved was either dead or disappeared into the desolate darkness seemingly always present when existing. Except her. She was all he had left. Normally such a thought would send someone down the deep end of their dark abyss. Yet Courtney remained stoic as ever, readjusting her angst to the situation with a more compassionate approach. Not only to the people around her during this difficult time, but more importantly, to herself. She was very gifted in shifting her emotions when needed, being nice to herself midst all she had done is a different dimension of self-love she had not obtained yet.

Once they arrived at the Isabella Ragsdale Medical Center, Tommy was immediately rushed into the emergency sector of the hospital. Courtney felt an abscess forming in the slits of her lips, traveling to the outskirts of her mouth. She felt sick that God was not here to help her, he left a bunch of stupid servants to serve for him. Courtney and Officer Dansby, the cop who escorted Tommy to the ambulance, awaited many hours for Tommy to awake. Courtney stayed because she loved him, Dansby stayed so he could question him about his situation. Courtney sat by, shivering and filled with intense guilt. She wondered if perhaps she was more present during her interactions with him then this could have been avoided. She had been so high in the clouds when with him that she never considered such an awful, Lochness-sized monster lived inside his mind. There are always thoughts, and ideas, yet to be standing on something so concrete. All for it to fall in front of you too quickly to follow where it leads to is detrimental. Courtney placed her palms on Tommy's cheeks, feeling the warmth after a car ride of coldness cheered her freezing heart up. Officer Dansby asked Courtney, "So you're the girlfriend huh? I have a daughter that looks just like you, I am terribly sorry that this happened. I'm sure he means a lot to you, do you happen to know what happened?" Courtney sighed, then said "He means..... the world to me. He doesn't even understand how much he makes me happy. How do you explain something you can't even begin to comprehend…. You should talk to Tommy when he wakes up. He will be able to provide you more information than I can on his predicament". She put her face onto Tommy's resting chest, his stillness was magnified by Courtney's seismic crying. His body rippled as she continued to cry. The officer took his hat off, and paid his condolences to her fallen warrior. He fought so hard to keep her away from his life, so much so that he paid for it severely.

As all hope seemed to be lost, Tommy finally opened his eyes. He regained his consciousness, and the ability to move again. The doctors did a wonderful job stitching him back up, as monotonous and soulless as the medical profession can be, it worked wonders when it came to saving lives. Courtney nearly jumped with joy, her animation of excitement filled the officer's eyes with contentment. Even he grew worried of his return, he imagined the grief his own daughter would feel if put in the same pretense. Tommy refrained from saying much, other than "Am I dead?" Courtney reminded him thoroughly that he was still alive and that he won. Tommy lied down, wondering at what cost did this siege for defeat bring. Would this be considered a pyrrhic victory, or possibly something darker? Like killing the venom symbiote only to discover it left behind a nickel-sized drop that attaches onto your ankles. Nonetheless, Tommy tried to not think of these things. He instead appreciated Courtney's warm presence, then immediately was filled with grief when seeing the police officer. He questioned how much damage his family had done, how much he himself had done.

"Thomas, I know this isn't a good time for you, but can we discuss a few things?" Officer Dansby asked with a tinge of politeness, "We just need a few answers so we can conduct a proper investigation. Can you tell me anything about what happened? Do you know who were the people who did this to you?" Tommy was dumbfounded, in his mind, the people that did this had died in the house along with where he should have. Identifying them should not have been difficult. Tommy could not bring himself to speak, so he used his body language instead. His expression of genuine confusion, lack of eye contact, and overall inability to exhibit emotion showed the cop all he needed to know. Tommy clenched Courtney's hand tight like wrapping rubber bands into a ball, indicating he wanted her to speak for him since he was unable to. She remembered Tommy's monologue about his family's involvement in everything going wrong in his life. However, she was oblivious to the reality Miles had broken bad.

"His family did this to him," Courtney said. "His father, his brother, his own mother..... everyone except his brother Miles are monsters. His parents should not be allowed to operate a water faucet, let alone raise a family. But his brother, Darren, seems to be the worse of the bunch. According to Tommy at least." Tommy nodded along with what Courtney was saying as if listening to one of his favorite vinyls. He appreciated hearing her voice, even amongst these extreme circumstances. Officer Dansby scooted back in his chair, then stood up with vigor. He walked over to Tommy, patted him on the back, and hugged Courtney. He said, "You both are very brave. You're one hell of a girlfriend to stick with him during all this. You should count yourself lucky, young man. For being alive after everything you've been through mostly, but also, for having a woman wonderful enough to stick with you through these trying times. I can assure you that we will take this matter seriously, once you get some rest I need to ask you a few follow up questions on who these people who stabbed you looked like."

Tommy was lost in translation; Courtney noticed the frustration on his face. She asked Officer Dansby "Was the person, or people who attacked Tommy not there? From how Tommy looked it seemed like someone mauled him. Wouldn't they leave behind blood, or something?" "Our forensics crew will be able to determine whose blood is whose, but until then, we did not find any bodies besides Thomas's. So I need any relevant information on who we will be looking for. From the looks of it, this may need to be a FBI related investigation. We need to announce that there is a dangerous band of serial killers on the loose." "No, no. That can't be. Tommy told me his parents died, if there were two blood splotches other than Tommy's. Then that must mean.....Miles..... I-I... don't know what to say. They got away??" "Unfortunately. Still, we did not recover any bodies. If I'd put two and two together, those brothers of his disposed of it before we could get to them." Tommy clenched Courtney's hand, visibly in dismay. The thought of his brothers still being out there, awaiting to run into each other again frightened him farther than Lord Voldemort did to Harry Potter.

The conversation carried on for a little longer, Tommy chose to dissociate from the situation. He thought he really won, that he really beat him. At least the possibility of them running off into the sunset provided him some relief. Maybe they would not come knocking on every doorstep until they reached his. A spade is a spade. They took so much from him, he took some from them in return. In his eyes, they were even. The blood debt had been paid. Even if Tommy had to live the rest of his existence in anguish for every ounce of pain he had to experience, he felt relieved to sever half of the Hansens connection to the world. The hospital bed felt a little more comfortable for Tommy, as he fell back asleep, he dreamed more peacefully than ever before. Not because the job was done, it wasn't, but because he felt a great deal of evil release from him. While he knew darkness still lurked out around every corner and alleyway, his breath felt a little lighter each time he breathed. The action of getting rid of his parents finally settled in his system, he could comprehend what he did with full clarity. As the nightmare of Darren one day tracking him down lingered like a bad cold, all Tommy cared about in this moment was that his soul felt a fragment more free than it has ever. Like St. George laying his life down for the Dragon, Tommy gave everything to vanquish the fire breathing demons seeking to reap his spirit. In his peril, and amongst his losses, he came out on top. For now.

Two weeks later

I can hear birds chirping, so loudly and profoundly it almost sounds like singing. The piano keys on Courtney's piano gleamed vibrantly. A week removed from the hospital, I could safely say I felt okay. Processing everything that has happened to me is arduous. Arguably harder than experiencing it in the first place. The tides would probably crash on my pilings once again, but for the time being, the seas were calms on all ends. Courtney's mother decided to take me into her home after Courtney filled her in on my situation. I felt relieved not returning to that damn house, that home was a part of my life I hoped would decay then wither away in the wasteland it created for itself. Natalie did her best not to ask me too many questions, yet the thought of my serial killer heritage interested her fondly. She said "It's like something you'd read out of a Stephen King novel!" when I told her the first time. I tried my best to explain my situation while being respectful to the departed. Not for my family, but for Andre.

I laid in bed with Courtney, feeling whimsical as ever. There was an insidious dragon lurking in the back of my head that needed to be quelled. Other than that, I was lost in the paradise inside my girlfriend's eyes. I fell back asleep for what seemed like a moment, but when I woke, Courtney was not beside me anymore. She had moved over to her piano, possibly thinking I went back to sleep. I tried not to shuffle too loudly so I could hear her play in peace. Like any great

artist, she was at her best when she was alone. The few glimpses I've snuck in while she is occupied are like hearing thunder for the first time. Perhaps like seeing lightning for the first time worked better, better yet, it was both. Courtney was humming, touching the keys as if she loved them passionately. Each note she strummed was played with grace, not for perfection as she did when I watched her. Her rendition of "La Vie En Rose" is still one of the most magical things I had ever heard. Her music was uplifting, as if I was smoking on one of Andre's well rolled joints.

I drifted off when she began to sing, my heart was following her symphony. Yet I tuned in towards the end. What I did hear was, "And when you speak, angels sing from above. Everyday words seem to turn into love songs. Give your heart and soul to me, and life will always be, La vie en rose." Courtney continued humming, while she hummed I could hear birds outside following her harmony. When she was done, she started sniffling and wiping away her face with her shirt sleeve. "Courtney? Are you okay?? I do not mean to intrude on your musical session, but.. that... was incredible." Courtney jolted as she heard my voice, she pivoted in her chair and turned over towards me to say "I'm sorry for disturbing your peaceful sleep my dear, but yes, I am okay." "Then why are you crying, my sweet pea?" "Because, la vie en rose translates to 'life seen through rose-colored glasses.' I know with a mountainous amount of pride that you have passionately provided me that. These few weeks since you've told me about your situation have been hard on my psyche. It makes me question myself if I did enough.... When I sing this song, I cry because I wonder whether I have provided you that amongst everything you've been through... you deserve to see life in rosy hues as well my love. More than anyone I know." She left me speechless, maybe because I my brain was still loading in, but mostly because I couldn't fathom how I could have come this far without her. Perhaps I did not see life in rose tinted glasses as she had, yet, Courtney made my life infinitely more vibrant. And brighter. Almost like being a character inside the novel 'The Giver', I've spent many days withering away in shades of black and grey before being given an array of colors for the first time. Courtney was the vibrancy inside Pandora's box, so much so it would burden her to know how much she truly meant to me. It's best she not be concerned with such things. She fears something she could never hope to understand, nor could I for that matter. The complexity of the cosmos is not designed for us ape-brained primates to comprehend.

We ate breakfast in bed, well, more specifically, I ate breakfast while she cleaned up her room around me. Keeping everything around her tidy was her way of managing her stressful environment. Everyone has their way of coping I suppose. I just wish mine hadn't cost me the greatest soul I've ever encountered thus far in my journey of life. We truly are the sum of our choices. Courtney touched my hand, then said, "Tommy, I know this will be hard, but would you like to go to your spot one last time? It would be best to say goodbye to Andre before we left for good." I sat and thought about her question, unsure if this would be the correct antic for me to take given my current mental situation. I feel like one loose twig will send me off the edge, where the abyss lies awaiting for my return into its shivering darkness. I felt exiled out of my own mind, especially after finding out my brothers had not died in that house that night. Yet, Andre was one loose end I wanted to end on 'good' terms with. The mountain of grief stood before me, awaiting to be climbed. The traverse appears to be extremely lethal, as I imagine it to be so. The jagged rocks and pitfalls make it seem impossible to climb, but like finding my way out of an abusive family; I will walk and crawl until my wrists and hip falls off. I owe Andre that much, because if he were still here, he would have already been over the mountain. Probably painting a mural of me on the ledge with all the spare time he had left over. Once we put our "leaving the house" clothes on, we made our way to the trail where I last walked with my friend. It's crazy how all the pathways in these woods connected. In one extended leg, was the trails I'd take Courtney when we first started dating, In another, Andre and I would walk across the train tracks with a blunt in our hands. The funny thing about memories is that they don't seem to leave you, even the bad ones. But with enough time and patience, I hope to embrace everything coming towards my way. Courtney asked me "if you feel uncomfortable at all, just let me know. We don't have to walk all the way there. I'm sure you're still sore physically and mentally, so if being here enhances any neg-ative feelings please tell me. Hold my hand, let's walk together. I'm sorry I could not stop this Tommy... but I promise from here on out, you will never have to fight a single battle alone again. You ready?" I smiled, certain that she would be, and said "I will be okay, I'm ready to say goodbye to my friend. He will always be with me, I feel him everywhere I go. I know that wherever he is, he knows we won. I will spend my lifetime trying to pay that debt back." "Forgiveness is about yourself, Tommy. Andre chose to do what he did, if I know my friend, he can live with his decision to do good when evil rears its hideous features. It's who he was, his nature would not have willed against him to act any differently in regards to letting his best friend suffer any longer. The question is, can you live with it?" "We will have to see, won't we?....I see the train tracks up ahead, let's go sit for a second then get out of here. I'm getting a lot of anxiety."

The train tracks appeared somber, they shouldn't have, they were regular old train tracks. Yet....They looked like winter had hit them hard, their luster and shine were lost, tarnished even. My mind was an armada trying to stop thousands of fleeing feelings from exerting out of me. I remained strong however, remaining present during this hellish feeling was the best thing for me. I needed to remember how much it hurt losing him, so that I did not have to pay the price again with Courtney if the time ever came. I do not know my fate, I wish it were inscribed on the giant tree of life so that I could under-stand where my choices would lead me. Yet, it never is that easy. I walked along the train tracks, unabridged by the tension cresting in between my chin. Both of my jaw sockets were popping profusely, like needing to get a tooth pulled from each side. It was unbearable until it wasn't. It was almost as if Andre had given me an inch of his clarity so that I could take upon this moment with more sincerity. I sat down and took it all in. Watching the memories fly by that have lead me to here. I looked over at Courtney, who was playing with some pine straw with her feet, and thought to myself, *I will protect her, for the both of us*. I hate that Andre died so that I could live my life with my hope-to-be wife someday. With his limitless potential, it seems miserable that I must live with this indiscretion. Yet, since fate spins the tables, the least I can do is make sure he didn't die for nothing.

Courtney hugged me when I returned over from the train tracks, she kissed me while pulling on my curls. She said, "You did it, Tommy! You did a brave thing! Gold star for you, my big strong man!" I held her for what seemed like forever. If my family were the demons outside of the garden of Eden, then Courtney was the peach they were seeking. I noticed a Ziploc bag tucked in the branches of a shrub nearby the path we walked on. To my dismay, my name was on it. Courtney shrieked as I picked up the baggie, I however, was frozen. As if Medusa's skull was inside the baggie, I stood there mortified. Andre's face laid inside that sandwich bag, staring right at me. The message was all too clear to me. This "game" we were playing was not yet finished. And if I know my opponent well enough, it is that he will never relent until he gets what he wishes. Courtney's cries of horror seemed to show me she feared the same thing. I felt like one of the Joker's victims when he shot them with the 'KABLAM' gun, but mine was filled with roses, butterflies, and pixie dust. My brother had managed to stab my heart without even needing to touching me. Yet, I welcomed it. Not with anger, or anguish, but out of endearment to receive vindication for all that my anguish attains to. I gazed at the plastic bag; with my mind still in fragments, then smiled back at my best friend's 'frozen in amber' face. The last thing I thought about in that moment was humming to the tune of a Bruce Springsteen song, and how I too was born to run.

The Hansens...what's left of them, will be back.

From the author...

"Writing is the only true form of immortality" -Cicero.

I start with this quote to orient why I chose to tell this story. For me, writing is the bridge between the sane part of myself and well...the other half of the pie. I grew up in Georgia with my wonderful mother, Farrah, and my two amazing siblings, Kali and Kyler. I wrote this specific idea after losing a woman who I invested my entire heart into, a girl named Courtney who had (and still has) such a sweet smile. A smile that captivated me the moment I gazed upon it. I knew she would be the one who got away. I have a very twisted sense of humor. The night I lost her, I took a couple of Xanax to forget about my heartache and said to myself, "I don't know what could be worse than losing her. Even if my family were a bunch of freaking murderers, I would still be happier." That very moment (I wish I was kidding), it hit me like a two-ton brick. I felt the surreality of the situation this said person would be put in and how original the idea was.

I'm a horror story fanatic. I've scoured bookshelves and movies, enjoying everything from stories of emotional distress to straight-up slasher flicks. Yet I had never seen or heard of anything like what I had in mind. It excited me like nothing else has. I felt compelled to tell the story of a boy, from his own perspective, who had to hide the world from the truth that his family is a bunch of psychopathic monsters—balancing the morality between allowing evil to exist if the cost is too great of an expense to pay. Especially from his best friend and girlfriend, who he hides his world from the most. With the undercurrent theme of how wicked love is, we are all willing to sacrifice our own happiness to satisfy the people we care for.

Mac

Printed in the USA
CPSIA information can be obtained
at www.ICGtesting.com
CBHW061155241024
16330CB00048B/994

9 798218 360290